Buffy
the vampire slayer™

Wicked Willow I
The Darkening

Yvonne Navarro

An original novel based on the hit television series
by Joss Whedon

SIMON SPOTLIGHT™

NEW YORK LONDON TORONTO SYDNEY

Buffy the Vampire Slayer™

Buffy the Vampire Slayer
(movie tie-in)
The Harvest
Halloween Rain
Coyote Moon
Night of the Living Rerun
Blooded
Visitors
Unnatural Selection
The Power of Persuasion
Deep Water
Here Be Monsters
Ghoul Trouble
Doomsday Deck
Sweet Sixteen
Crossings
Little Things

The Angel Chronicles, Vol. 1
The Angel Chronicles, Vol. 2
The Angel Chronicles, Vol. 3
The Xander Years, Vol. 1
The Xander Years, Vol. 2
The Willow Files, Vol. 1
The Willow Files, Vol. 2
How I Survived My Summer Vacation,
Vol. 1
The Cordelia Collection, Vol. 1
The Faith Trials, Vol. 1
The Journals of Rupert Giles, Vol. 1
Tales of the Slayer, Vol. 1
Tales of the Slayer, Vol. 2
Tales of the Slayer, Vol. 3

The Lost Slayer serial novel
Part 1: Prophecies
Part 2: Dark Times
Part 3: King of the Dead
Part 4: Original Sins
Omnibus Edition

Child of the Hunt
Return to Chaos
The Gatekeeper Trilogy
Book 1: Out of the Madhouse
Book 2: Ghost Roads
Book 3: Sons of Entropy
Obsidian Fate
Immortal
Sins of the Father
Resurrecting Ravana
Prime Evil
The Evil That Men Do
Paleo
Spike and Dru: Pretty Maids
All in a Row

Revenant
The Book of Fours
Tempted Champions
Oz: Into the Wild
The Wisdom of War
These Our Actors
Blood and Fog
Chosen
Chaos Bleeds
Mortal Fear
Apocalypse Memories
Wicked Willow Trilogy
The Darkening

The Watcher's Guide, Vol. 1: The Official Companion to the Hit Show
The Watcher's Guide, Vol. 2: The Official Companion to the Hit Show
The Postcards
The Essential Angel Posterbook
The Sunnydale High Yearbook
Pop Quiz: Buffy the Vampire Slayer
The Monster Book
The Script Book, Season One, Vol. 1
The Script Book, Season One, Vol. 2
The Script Book, Season Two, Vol. 1
The Script Book, Season Two, Vol. 2
The Script Book, Season Two, Vol. 3
The Script Book, Season Two, Vol. 4
The Script Book, Season Three, Vol. 1
The Script Book, Season Three, Vol. 2
The Musical Script Book: Once More, With Feeling

Available from SIMON PULSE

For:
Weston,
whose laughter lights up my life
like a brilliant Arizona sunrise.
Viva la chili peppers
and purple flames!

Acknowledgments:

Thank you to Lisa Clancy,
and to my husband, Weston Ochse.
Without their encouragement and support, this
would have just been another wild idea.
A little language help came from
Stephen Clarke and Alda L. W. Smith
of the DIA/DSDC.

Simon Spotlight
An imprint of Simon & Schuster Children's Publishing Division
1230 Avenue of the Americas, New York, New York 10020

SIMON SPOTLIGHT and colophon are trademarks of Simon & Schuster, Inc.
Printed in the United States of America
First Edition 10 9 8 7 6 5 4 3 2 1
Library of Congress Control Number 2003114493
ISBN 0-7434-2774-2

Prologue

They say that there are millions of alternate life pathways, that each and every one of us generates a new path and alternate persona with every choice we make. Turn left instead of right, and the number thirty-four bus ends one path because of a brake failure; pause to admire a butterfly and yet another path forms—the original continues to its fateful meeting with the faulty bus, while the new one arrives, luckily, too late at the intersection and the malfunctioning vehicle speeds past without incident . . . only to crash into the old Cadillac Seville idling on the corner, the one with the couple in it who drove over from Tuscaloosa to visit friends. Existence is an unseen spiderweb glittering with endless possibilities. And while we seldom break through the veil of alternate universes, and most of us will forever insist such things cannot be, all these things, all these secondary personas, do, indeed, exist. . . .

There was a lot of blood, but Willow had expected that. The sight of it didn't shock her, but she really hadn't expected it to—she'd certainly seen enough of the scarlet goo since Buffy's arrival in Sunnydale and their becoming friends. But Willow had thought she would feel something . . . *better,* something like vindication. Instead, seeing Warren hanging there like a combination of some kind of biology book cross-section and a freshly prepared side of beef only angered her more. Was he still alive, even without his skin? Probably not, and that was a good thing. Where was it written that this pathetic excuse for a human, this sorry *worm,* should live when it was by his hand that her beloved Tara was dead? On the other hand, why should Warren's death be so quick—painful, but relatively easy compared to her own blackly empty future yawning in front of her?

Warren had been saying something, blathering on about absolutely nothing that could change either his dirty deed or her mind, before she'd gotten bored and skinned him. And the undoability of that was what it was all about, the fact that he couldn't *fix* what he'd done, that he couldn't bring Tara *back*. Just like she couldn't restick his skin to his ugly body.

An eye for an eye.

A death for a death.

The limp thing that used to be Warren made a little moaning sound, so soft that only Willow heard it. Even so, she wasn't sure if it was a groan or just some odd noise wind made when it slid across surfaces not naturally exposed to its touch—like bare, glistening muscle and the rounded tops of blue-red veins. Surely he wasn't going to open his mouth and start yelling again, was he? Best to make sure that didn't happen, not because she was worried about anything—it was far, far too late for anyone to come to his rescue—but because she simply didn't want to hear the racket.

A twist of her finger made sure Warren went the rest of the way into the arms of oblivion, this time riding on the flames of Willow's fury.

As the night breeze took the smell of blackened flesh and wrapped it around her senses, Willow heard a noise behind her. She turned automatically and, again, wasn't surprised as she saw Buffy, Xander, and Anya gawking at her from a few yards away. Beneath her dark knit cap, Buffy's eyes were wide with shock and disbelief. "Willow, no . . . what did you *do*?" Beside her, Xander and Anya looked just as stunned, like poor little kids who'd just seen the neighbor run over the family dog.

For a moment the only thing that wanted to come out of her mouth was *"One down, two to go."* She opened her mouth to say it as she reached inside herself and started to build up the power to shimmer away, but then she hesitated. There was a split second of . . . *weirdness,* in which everything around her that she could see, feel, or hear just sort of went still, yet trembled at the same time, as if some strange chill had gone up the spine of the universe. Had she caused that?

Maybe. Because things were going to be different from now on—

Very different.

Oh, yes.

She was going to cause a lot of things to happen. A lot of really *monumental* things. Willow turned her head and stared at the young woman who had for so long been her best friend.

Things would never be the same for them again.

"Maybe you should get your eyes checked." The sarcastic words sounded like they were coming from a stranger, with none of the familiar we're-all-friends-here tone so often present in the past. "I thought it was pretty obvious."

"You killed him!" For a second Buffy sounded like she was going to choke. "Willow, he's not a demon or a vampire or a big beastie of the night—"

"Matter of opinion," Willow interrupted coldly. She felt odd, as if something about her had changed, almost been *freed*. In fact, *everything* felt slightly strange—the night, herself, Sunnydale—as if all of it was a little off-kilter. Like the whole world had tilted a little on its axis and sent everything and everyone off in a new direction.

How . . . exciting.

"He's a *human being*!" Buffy was saying, plowing on as if Willow hadn't spoken. "Flesh and blood, a soul—"

"First of all," Willow cut in, "Warren had no soul." This time there was such fury in her tone that Buffy shied away from breaking in. "Or if he did, it was so shriveled and twisted that he was a lot *worse* than any

of the vamps you so happily dusted. Secondly"—
Willow's mouth spread into a wide, dark smile—"you
keep talking about him in the present tense. In case you
didn't get the memo, Warren has now gone on to the
big slime pile in the sky, where he can spend the rest of
eternity with all the bad and unwanted little cockroaches just like himself."

"Somehow I don't think his destination is in the
overhead direction," Xander muttered.

Willow's gaze passed over him, and she acted like
he wasn't even there. She still felt like she had to say
those words, and she didn't fight the urge. "That's one
down," she continued, "with two to go. You can't be so
dense you don't realize I'm going to send along a certain duo of Warren's scuzzy friends to make sure he
doesn't get all lonely-like."

"Will," Buffy said, stepping toward her. "Don't
you think you've done enough? You've had your
revenge—"

Willow's eyes suddenly flared red. "Enough?
Enough?" Her teeth ground together and her fists
clenched. "There is no *enough,* Buffy. Don't you
understand that? There isn't anything on the face of
this earth that's *enough.* Enough would take me back
to yesterday morning, and it would let me take Tara's
hand and pull her away from that damned window."
She laughed, and the sound was harsh and sharp, like
black, broken glass floating on the night wind. "I'd
even say it was enough if I could trade places with her,
if it could have been *me* lying on the floor with a bullet
in my back!"

She lapsed into silence and stood there, swaying slightly. For a long moment no one said anything at all. Then Buffy decided to try again.

"I know this hurts," she offered. "But you've already killed one man, and that won't bring Tara back. Nothing you do tonight, or tomorrow, or the day or week or year after that *will*. When you face off with something like this, all you can do is accept it and try to move on—"

"I WILL NOT!"

The force of Willow's scream, the actual, physical consequence of it, made them all stagger back. Anya went down on one knee and Xander quickly hauled her upright again.

A few feet away Willow stamped her foot against the ground. Such a little movement, but with a big backlash—spreading outward from her foot and toward them, the grass dried out and withered, then blackened and cracked, hardening in a hellish replica of a volcano's aftermath. "I won't accept any of it," she hissed. "I won't rest until Jonathan and Andrew are as bloody and dead as their gun-toting partner. And I certainly won't accept Tara's death!"

"I don't think you have a choice," Anya spoke up. Xander elbowed her in the ribs, but she waved him away and took a tentative step toward Willow. "I mean, the universe has very clearly defined rules about that. You were able to bring Buffy back because she died due to mystical forces, but Tara was killed by man-made circumstances. They aren't going to allow—"

"Catgut or silk?"

Anya blinked. "I beg your pardon?"

"I'm going to sew your mouth shut," Willow said blandly. "Like I did Warren's for a little while before he died. But since it's you, I'm giving you a choice of threads."

Xander pushed Anya to the side, hoping to distract Willow. "Listen," he said, "killing the other two might give you a temporary high score on the Venge-Ometer, but in the long run it's just going to eat away at your conscience. Do you really want to live with that?"

"Conscience?" Willow laughed before he could continue. The sound of it made them all wince. "Don't you guys get it? I don't *care*."

Buffy started to say something, then lost her words as Willow's statement triggered a nasty memory, giving her an ugly flashback to when Faith had wrongly assumed Mayor Wilkins's assistant was a vampire and rammed a stake into his chest. Hadn't her companion slayer said those very same words?

I don't care . . .

That statement has triggered enough big and bad to rival any of the biggest and baddest that had happened in Buffy's life. If history was running a repeat show, that meant a whole lot of crash and bang was coming down the Wiccan pipeline.

"But—" Xander began.

Willow held up her hand, then put a finger to one cheek and tilted her head coquettishly. "Hmmmm. What was it I said just a few minutes ago when Warren was begging for his life? Bored now. *Again*."

She raised her hand and started to form a Wiccan

symbol in the air. Before she could finish it, Buffy tackled her.

Willow shrieked as she went down under Buffy, but the cry ended in a drawn out *whooooof* as the air was forced out of her by the Slayer's weight. When Buffy tried to wrap her in a sort of bear hug, something she obviously thought would keep Willow harmless and not hurt her, Willow almost giggled at the absurdity of it.

Almost.

But still, there was that rage thing inside her.

That huge, dark, *hungry* rage thing.

Dragging herself backward like a crab, Willow kicked out instinctively and was rewarded when her knee caught Buffy's chin. Buffy's surprised "Ow!" gave Willow enough time to twist sideways and get one arm free and upraised. That was really all Willow needed, and one ever-so-slight twist of her hand, painting an ancient Wiccan symbol in the air, sent Buffy slamming backward against the thick trunk of a nearby tree.

For a long, long moment, everything seemed to stop.

While everyone around her seemed to freeze, Willow used this time for a little bit of self-examination, kind of like a lawyer cross-examining someone in a courtroom.

Was she really out for revenge for Tara's murder?

Absolutely.

Was she worried about the consequences?

Nope.

Was she going to let herself be bogged down by the whole weight-of-the-world-on-her-shoulders conscience thing?

Be serious.

Would she let anything, or anyone, get in the way of her having that revenge?

NO!

She blinked, and everything in the world started moving again—the breeze wiggled through the leaves in the trees, and the bushes rustled as Xander barreled toward her in a second-wave attempt to subdue her. Willow pressed her lips together in irritation. Surely he knew better, surely they *all* knew better. They always went for brawn over brains; she had the brains to squash their brawn right off the bat, but she also had *more* than brains going for her. They should have figured that out long ago.

Xander grabbed her by the wrist, but the instant he touched her, Willow could sense that he would never be able to bring himself to do more. So then what? Did he really think he could just drag her along like a dog would tug an oversized bone? And to where? Most likely the Magic Box, where someone would come up with some miracle cure that would salve her heartbroken soul and send her back on the path to forgiveness and redemption. Blah blah blah.

Not in *this* universe.

Willow glanced at him, then frowned slightly at his hand. One itsy-bitsy mind flutter, and then—

Xander yelped and yanked his fingers away from her skin, then did a frantic little pain dance around the clearing in front of where Warren's body had hung just a short while ago. The skin on his palm and fingers was red as a lobster and covered with small, oozing blisters. "Jesus, Willow—what'd you do to me?"

"What's the matter, big boy?" A corner of her mouth lifted in a contemptuous smile. "Am I too hot for you to handle?"

"Willow, think about what you're doing," Anya implored. Willow studied the young woman as she spoke, noting that in spite of her pleading tone, Anya held her head confidently as she came forward, with none of the frailty that had occasionally surfaced since D'Hoffryn had busted her from vengeance demon down to human a few years ago.

An oh-so-tiny hint of concentration in Anya's stare and . . . ah, yes—the vengeance demon in her had finally resurfaced, as Willow had long suspected it would. It wasn't as though Xander hadn't given her reason enough—Willow still recalled the sight of Anya walking alone up the aisle on her wedding day as tears streamed down her cheeks. On the one hand, Willow knew the agony of finding yourself alone after everything you'd planned for and counted on was unexpectedly yanked away; on the other, she felt strangely detached from Anya and any empathy for her. Maybe that was because Xander was still there for Anya, standing only a few feet away with his heart still beating strongly, blood still pumping through his healthy body. No matter what Anya thought, Xander would be at her side as long as he or she had breath in their human or otherwise lungs.

Willow scowled at the thought, feeling a surge in the darkness already bubbling within her heart. Her beloved Tara had not been so lucky, and now here was Anya, thinking that becoming the answer to every jilted woman's prayer put her on equal footing with Willow.

So foolish.

She held up one hand and Anya ground to a halt about three yards away, unable to come any closer. Confusion flitted across the slender young woman's face as she struggled against the invisible bonds, and then she relaxed and stopped fighting. Apparently the memories from her earlier freeze session at the Magic Box were still fresh enough to make her realize how futile it was. Buffy and Xander stood on each side of Anya's paralyzed form like wary sentries waiting to see what the enemy would do next.

"What are you?" Willow asked Anya, even though she already knew the technical answer. She walked a slow circle around the vengeance demon, but there wasn't any visual indication of the answer. "Are you human? Or demon?" She tilted her head. "Good? Or evil? Or is it that you just can't make up your own mind?" Willow frowned when Anya didn't answer, and then she realized what was wrong. "Speak," she said absently.

Anya's breath came out in a *whoosh* as if she'd been trying desperately to get the words out the entire time. "What *I* am isn't under the big hot light here," she said. "Why don't you ask yourself that question? The mote in thine own eye and all that."

Another humorless laugh came from Willow, and it was an absolutely dreadful thing to hear. "Now *this* is entertaining," she mused, crossing her arms. "A vengeance demon tossing quotes from the Bible at me." She rolled her eyes and tried to look frightened. "Ooooh, stop! It burns, it burns!" Her mouth twisted into a sneer, making an angry black-lipped slash against skin that seemed whiter because of the unnatural darkness of her hair. "Really, Anya, is that the best you can do?"

Anya looked like she wanted to shrug, but she still couldn't move. "Sorry. I thought it was okay in a pinch."

Buffy had rallied herself and gathered her courage. Now she was advancing, trying to let Willow distract herself with Anya's prattling. The Slayer froze instinctively as Willow's head swiveled in her direction. "I could hurt you," she said matter-of-factly, "but I have two other fish to fillet. Or should I say *flay*."

Willow raised her left hand in the air and made a swirling motion, and before any of the others could speak, she disappeared in a spiral of hellish red lights.

Chapter One

When she shimmered—moved from place to place using mystical energy—Willow got what she thought might be a brief taste of eternity.

It was difficult to describe, that sense of having yourself pulled apart and just sort of . . . swept away. For the briefest of instants, everything got left behind—her problems, her responsibilities, everyone she knew. Even the massive pain of losing Tara was blasted from her mind, leaving nothing but a clean, white slate that had been emptied of everything that might give it color. Just . . . *white*. There was no sense of good or evil, right or wrong, love or hate. This, Willow thought, might have been what Buffy had talked about when she'd finally spilled the celestial beans about the Buffy version of death and the after-nothing. The problem, of course, was that Willow didn't have the luxury of *staying* all shimmered apart and sensation-free.

Snap—

—and she was leaving one place. Then—

Snap—

—there she was, in whatever other place on this earth she'd been aiming for.

With all that wasted peace in between, and all her devastation and agony waiting for her on the other side.

But she could deal. She *would* deal.

Oh, would she ever.

Willow came out of her shimmer in the alley in front of the nebulous doorway to Rack's scuzzy little drug haven. She stood there for a good forty seconds or so, disoriented and wobbly in the knees, coming down from that unique little rush gained from her zippy sub-reality journey. Then Willow felt the hard concrete beneath her shoes, smelled the ripeness of something in a Dumpster a couple of yards away that had gone bad sometime around yesterday afternoon. Somewhere at the alley's far end, a girl and a guy were screaming at each other, the tone of their argument carrying to where Willow stood even if she couldn't quite make out the words. She and Tara had never gone the vocal and vicious route. It had taken a while—seemingly forever—but they had finally worked out their differences, had gotten past the fighting and mistrust and had started to rebuild. . . .

Only to have their relationship violently torn apart.

The pain of Tara's death spilled over Willow again,

burning as though the universe had loosed a cloudburst of hot acid upon her.

Setting her jaw, Willow slipped through the liquid doorway and into Rack's domain.

She supposed if he just cleaned it up a little—nixed the three or four zonked-out junkies sprawled in the corners, along with the wanna-be buyers huddled on the chairs against one wall (and, oh yeah, replaced the ratty, infested-looking furniture)—it might have been a cool place. Add a few black lights and some of those hippyish posters that glow in the dark and it would be kind of like a sixties-seventies crash pad. Of course, what Rack was peddling here was a whole lot more explosive than the weed and pills of a quarter century ago. In fact, Rack's brand of buzz made even the nasties on the street, like crack and X and ice, look like candy by comparison.

Ah, well. The world was full of pitfalls.

Actually, right now? As far as Willow was concerned, it *was* one big pit. And this was just one of the entrances.

She walked toward the door unhurriedly, neither knowing nor caring that there were others in the room who'd been waiting for a long time, anticipating their turn at visiting the drug-master himself. One guy, a skinny little dude with a shriveled-up monkey's face and the long arms to go with it, got up and tried to stand between her and the sealed door to Rack's personal domain in the back room. He opened his mouth and hissed at her—"Not your turn yet, girlie!"—revealing bad teeth and worse breath. Willow paid him about as much attention as a troublesome gnat; one little swat—a mystical one, in the air—and he went tumbling away. He landed in a pile of bruised and tangled limbs next to a coffee table laden with the remainder of a dozen or more fast-food meals, and there he stayed, staring numbly at the leftovers while Willow boldly pushed open the door and walked into the back room.

In here, of course, things were a whole lot different. It could have been a room made for a king, something out of a Persian palace or an ancient opium den. There was lots of red and gold all through the room, from the overstuffed couch and floor pillows to the soft and luxurious draperies hung in folds to cover windows that might or might not have been there. There was an air of opulence about the place . . . no, of *decadence,* and Willow drank it in without saying anything. She didn't see him right away, but Rack was there, all right. All this richness was just camouflage. She could feel him skulking in the deepest shadows like a hungry predator. Which, of course, was exactly what he was.

"Hey, babe. I've been waiting for you."

Rack's voice came from the darkness at the farthest corner of the room. She turned her head and watched him stand, noting with detached interest that he moved a lot like the predator she already knew he was, a great and powerful cat slipping through her life and wanting to feed off her. But would he be powerful enough?

"Guess the rehab didn't take, huh?" He shrugged. "That's the way it goes sometimes. But I gotta say . . ."

He began to walk around her, a vulture spiraling down from the sky toward the hapless rabbit. "I could feel you coming a mile away. That power you've got." He smiled almost sleepily. "And you know something, sweetness? I liked it."

Willow kept her silence, letting the sensations from his nearness pulse through her. That same old hunger—he would take from her at the same time that he gave. But for him it was a sexual thing too; just like a junkie, he couldn't separate desire from a drug-induced high. She closed her eyes briefly and let a little smile of her own play across her lips. Let him think about that smile. Let him misinterpret it.

Rack moved around her again, getting closer. His lips were almost brushing her skin now, and Willow could feel his breath against her neck. "When you first came to me, you were just a little slip of a girl." He chuckled. "But look at you now—all growed up. Full of dark juice. And you still taste like strawberries. Only now . . . you're ripe."

Back in front of her, Rack was swaying now. Willow let her own body start moving with his rhythm, drifting slowly back and forth, perfect synchronization.

His voice dropped. Now it was husky and full of forbidden promise. "You came because you want something, don't you?"

Still not saying anything, Willow nodded slowly. She was quite happy to let Rack follow his own fantasy and foolish assumptions, his own addictions.

"Thought so." Rack sounded so smug and sure of

himself. "So tell me, Strawberry," he said, reaching out and touching her cheek with one hand. Out of the corner of her eye Willow noted dispassionately that his fingernails were dirty. How typical.

Rack was almost kissing her now, and she could smell a dark sweetness on his breath, the scent of a thousand taboo pledges. She parted her lips slightly, invitingly, and now he was whispering directly into her mouth, filling it with that intoxicating scent. "What on this earth do you want?"

Willow reached up and returned his gesture, placing a hand on each side of his face. Finally she let herself smile fully, felt her grip tighten brutally of its own accord.

"I'm just gonna take a little tour."

Rack's eyes widened and he tried to pull back, but it was way too late for escape. Willow's mouth crashed against his and the room exploded in multicolored tendrils of light as she ripped his energy and his life force free, pulled it into her own center and soaked it up. Even with his mouth frozen against hers, Rack was screaming, or maybe that was just in her head, the echo of everything he had once been wailing for help that would never come.

But there would be no more help for Rack. In fact, there would be very little Rack at all.

Willow was so suffused with power that she was twitching with it, fingers and toes jumping as though someone were poking each of them with pins. What was left of Rack's body—not much—floated limply near the ceiling, not so much a dead man as the empty husk of something, an abandoned cocoon or maybe one of those three-thousand-year-old mummies they kept in the Sunnydale museum. Hey, maybe she could make him walk around, like a jerky, papery puppet. Those were always fun—

"Willow?"

She pulled her gaze from Rack's dead form and saw Dawn standing in the open doorway a few feet away. "Hi, cutie," she said softly.

Dawn swallowed and took a few tentative steps toward her. At about step three she registered Rack's body above her head. To her credit she shuddered but didn't scream or question. At least not yet. "Will . . . are you okay? I mean, you look . . ." Her voice faded away.

Willow tilted her head, considering the question, then raised her hands to eye level and studied them. She knew she was filled with dark magick. What had Rack called it? *Dark juice.* Oh yeah, she could feel it, coursing through her like a hundred thousand volts of electricity, but she hadn't realized how much it would affect her physical form. But affect her it had—her fingernails had gone as black as Spike's, and black-tinged veins spider-walked just below the skin of her wrists and hands. Was the rest of her body like this? Her face?

Willow let her mind reach out and feather-touch Dawn's thoughts, just enough to see herself—beyond that, she had no desire to be inside this bubble-headed teenager's brain. Her efforts gained her a freeze-frame image of herself: blacker-than-black hair framed her face, her eyebrows matched her hair, and her eyes were dark pits of hellishly shining oil against china white skin. Black lips, too. And the veins . . . oh yes, they were there.

Nice.

She looked just like she felt.

Dangerous.

"What are you doing here, Dawn? If you're looking to party or do the shopping thing, your timing truly sucks rocks."

"No, I wasn't. I was looking for you. I mean—"

"Run along home, little girl. I hear your Buffy calling you."

Dawn scowled. "Willow, this is wrong. Look at that guy. I think you killed him—"

"It's an improvement, believe me. Just think of it as my good deed for humanity this evening."

"You can't just go around killing people!"

Willow laughed. "He wasn't people, Dawnie. He was a parasite, spreading his dirty little disease wherever and whenever. I just became the cure for that ugly problem, and besides," she said, grinning darkly. "I can kill anyone I want to."

"No—"

"In about three minutes those druggies out there are gonna wonder where their papa is, and why he hasn't fed them dinner." Willow concentrated for a second, then giggled. "They're already looking at your pig-eared demon pal in the waiting room and wondering if he tastes like pork . . . or chicken. I'd suggest you run back home to your psuedo-sister before they decide to have him for the main course, and you for dessert."

"Willow—"

Willow held up a hand to stop her. "Sorry, Little Miss Key. My days of baby-sitting mystic balls of energy masquerading as modern-day brats are over. Find your own way home."

She snapped her fingers and left a scared, shocked Dawn standing with her mouth open below Rack's slowly revolving shell of a body.

Chapter Two

"**W**e have to find her," Buffy said grimly. "I'm extremely open to any educated guesses, supernatural vibrations, or wild-ass hunches right now. If she catches up with Jonathan and Andrew before we do, they'll be lucky to end up as leather trophies hung on her wall. *Headless* leather trophies."

"I think I'm going to be sick," Xander said in a low voice. "I mean, I can't believe what I just saw. I can't believe she would do that and—"

"Get over it," Buffy said. Her tone was sharp. "She did it. It's done. It can't be undone, and everything is different now."

"She's probably gone to the jail," Anya said in a matter-of-fact voice. "Thanks to the police, that's where Jonathan and Andrew are, all wrapped up and waiting to be—"

"I think we've got the idea, Anya," said Xander. He sounded like he was gasping. He stopped and grabbed the side of a tree. "Ugh. The possible details—that was a mental image I didn't need."

"We don't have time for this, Xander," Buffy told him. She was so hot to get going she was practically quivering. "She might be there already."

Anya tapped her lips with one finger and considered this. "Actually, I doubt that. Not without more power, anyway. At this level she could go airborne, but she won't be teleporting." Suddenly she looked unsure. "At least . . . I don't think so." Then she brightened. "But we still might be okay, because even if she *could* teleport, she wouldn't have much oomph left to play ball afterward. She'd have to recharge on something first."

Xander grimaced. "Wait—recharge *on* something? Okay, I don't think I even want to go down the road to understanding what that could mean."

Buffy's gaze pinned Anya's. "But you—you've gone all vengeance demony again, right? So you can do the sci-fi flying through space and all that?"

"Well, I—"

"Right," Buffy said without waiting for Anya to finish. "Then it's settled. You'll just have to get to the jail and spring them before she gets there."

Anya's mouth dropped open. "*Spring* them? Do I look like I have a set of jail keys hanging off my belt?"

"No," Xander said. He gave her a wan smile that came out more like a sad grimace. "But you do look like someone with the speed and mojo to get the job done."

Anya chewed her lower lip. "Well, I *can* get there faster than you guys. . . ."

"The Magic Box," Buffy told her. "Bring them there after you get them out of the jail."

"Be careful!" Xander said, but Anya had already winked out of sight.

Had she ever been inside a jail before?

Anya couldn't recall. This one wasn't as bad as the ones she'd seen on television—those were filled with cockroaches, and the cells were tiny eight-by-six boxes surrounded by walls on which filthy words and pictures had been drawn with whatever tool was handy, including, possibly, certain bodily fluids. Sunnydale's jail was grim but reasonably clean, the walls plain and unadorned by the tales of those who had stayed there.

Anya zipped straight into the upper holding area, appearing right in front of the cell where the two wanna-be bad boys were stuck. As usual, they were squabbling like cranky children, and for a two- or three-second beat, Anya was tempted to leave their sorry butts right there, see how far their petty little arguments got them when Willow came in for their final visitation.

But no. She'd said she would do this, even if she was a vengeance demon. A true lady shouldn't go back on her word; after all, it was men going back on theirs that had made her a vengeance demon to begin with. How could she preach if she didn't practice? Tsk tsk.

"Shut up, you morons."

This time their bickering had escalated to where they were literally pummeling each other in the cell, and now they yelped and pulled apart, each scrambling backward on their hind ends until they recovered enough to talk.

"Wait," Jonathan said. "Why would *you* come to visit us?"

"We have to get you out of here," Anya said. Jonathan's wide-eyed little-boy look just made her want to smack him. "Willow is coming to kill you." She'd never been one to pull punches.

"What!" Andrew stared at her. *"Why?"*

"Because Warren shot Buffy and killed Tara. Buffy's all better, but she won't be able to get here in time to save your geekinesses."

"Well, if you could just loan us the money to make bail," Jonathan began.

"Did you replace your brain with one of those Star Trek thingamajiggies you're always spouting off about?" Anya demanded. *"Guard—help!"*

"Wait, what are you do—"

He jumped as Anya suddenly appeared in the cell with them. They heard footsteps hurrying down the hall, obviously drawn by the feminine voice. "Act like you're hurting me when he gets here," she instructed.

"What—"

Anya glared at the two of them. "Do you want to die today? No? Then just *do it*!"

As the guard rounded the corner, Jonathan grabbed her by one wrist at the same time Andrew grabbed the other. They began pulling at her like two dogs with a tug-of-war rope. "Hey—*ow*!" she protested, not faking it at all—the idiots were way too into the mine-no-mine thing.

"How did you two get that woman in there?" The guard's voice blared from the other side of the locked door.

That was her cue. "Help me!" Anya screeched in her best and totally fabricated I'm-so-helpless voice.

The door banged open as the guard twisted the key in the lock and barged inside. Andrew and Jonathan, true to their natures, squawked in fright and didn't so much release Anya as fling her toward the charging man. She toppled against him and grabbed his keys, then teleported to a handy spot behind him. He stumbled, confused, and Anya gave him a good, hard shove, sending him headfirst onto the cot against the back wall. "Go on!" she blared at Jonathan and Andrew. "Get out of here now!"

The guys darted past the guard, and Andrew instinctively slammed the door behind him. On the cot the guard scrambled around until he found his footing again, then grabbed for Anya. Before he could get a grip on her, she tossed the keys between the bar. They hit the far wall, then landed in a noisy pile, nicely out of reach.

"Stupid little girl!" the guard shouted. "We're stuck in here now!" His right hand went for his gun, but by the time it got there, the weapon was gone. His head jerked up, but Anya was no longer in the same spot; now she was several feet to the right, and in one hand was his service revolver. She gave it a fling, and it went sliding outside the cell to skid to a stop next to his ring of keys.

"First of all," she said calmly. "I'm not a little girl, you mouthy ape. I'm older than your family roots." He stared at her in amazement, but she continued before he could say anything. "And secondly, 'we' is not a word that applies to the me and you in this cell."

One heartbeat and she was standing outside the bars, looking in.

The guard staggered and stepped back, then recovered and threw himself against the locked door. "I'm not even gonna ask you how you did that. Just let me out of here right now!"

Andrew and Jonathan, wisely, had fled. If they had any true smarts, they'd definitely keep the "long" in "gone." Anya smiled at the policeman and calmly winked out of sight.

Already four blocks away—big fear could certainly make you move fast—Andrew and Jonathan crouched behind a hedge and watched as a middle-aged woman pulled into her driveway and got out of her car. Balancing her purse on one hip and a bag of groceries on the other, she pushed the door shut with a bump of her butt and then started up her walkway, purse swinging over her shoulder.

In the bushes the two fugitives looked at each other, then looked again at the big old boat of a car in the driveway. For once they actually worked together—Jonathan darting out and grabbing the woman's purse while Andrew yanked open the driver's door. She squealed in surprise, then tried to swing at him with the grocery bag, but all she succeeded in doing was spilling apples and canned vegetables all over the sidewalk. Andrew pulled on her purse, and when she wouldn't let go, he stomped his foot on hers as hard as he could. She cried out, and, just as he'd wanted, let go of the strap. Without her weight to balance his, Andrew lurched backward and fell, landing painfully amid the fruit and cans. A can of cream of tomato soup—*Ewwww*—rolled against his right knee and stopped.

The woman was hopping around on one foot and screeching, and it was only a matter of time before a neighbor or, God forbid, her husband showed up to see what all the screaming was about. Still clutching the handbag, Andrew scrambled up and headed for the car, digging into the purse as he ran until he came up with the keys. He threw himself onto the front seat, and Jonathan plucked the keys out of his hand.

"Dude, it's about time!" Jonathan hastily found the ignition key and shoved it home. The engine sputtered to life, but it was still a sweet sound. After all, it was the only getaway car they'd come up with. "What were you doing, teaching her how to two-step?"

"When did you get a degree in purse snatching?" Andrew demanded. "I didn't do so badly for a first timer!"

The woman had staggered toward her front door and was now pounding on it. Bad news, very indicative that there was a husband or son, or both, inside.

"Step on it, Bishop!" Andrew cried as the door started to open. "Or we're going to get pulverized into human pancakes!"

"Who's Bishop?" Jonathan asked as he yanked the gearshift into reverse. He hit the accelerator hard enough to send Andrew slamming against the dashboard.

"Careful, you idiot! I don't have my seat belt on yet!"

The car careered backward and bumped over the curb and into the street. Jonathan fought the wheel and tried to point it more or less in a direction—any direction—that would take them away from the house. At the house the front door opened and a man rushed out, his form burly and big enough to fill the entire doorway.

"Come on, don't you remember *Aliens*?" Andrew demanded incredulously. "Bishop was the android, played by Lance Hen—"

"I know *Aliens* better than you do!" Jonathan snapped. "I've watched it twenty-seven times!"

"Have not!"

"Have too!"

"Have no—"

A hand slammed against the rear passenger window, and they both jumped as Jonathan renewed his fight with the gearshift on the column. Finally it slid into drive, just as someone started yanking on the door handle. Jonathan floored the accelerator, and the car belched exhaust and lagged; for one breathless moment they thought the engine was going to die, but then the automobile leaped forward.

Twisting around, Andrew could see the woman and someone else shaking their fists in the air. "We'd better get out of town fast," he told his partner. "You know they're going to call the cops, and then every patrol car in town's going to be hunting us down like dogs."

"I think the cops are a piece of cake compared to Willow," Jonathan said darkly.

"Yeah," Andrew replied. "For once, I'd have to agree." Suddenly he brightened. "Hey, wouldn't it be neat to have a flamethrower like Ripley did? We could toast her!"

"Well, we don't have a flamethrower, dorkhead." Jonathan kept his foot heavy on the gas pedal, making a straight line for *out*. "And it's time to face reality instead of reruns. If we don't get out of Sunnydale, *we're* the ones who're gonna be burned. Big time."

Andrew was silent, but not for long. "Okay, road trip." He tried to sound cheerful, but the whole notion just wasn't very much fun without Warren, and he couldn't hold the expression. "Where to?"

"I'm thinking south," Jonathan replied. "Tacos. Burritos and siestas. Viva la Mexico."

And into the darkness they sped.

"I always thought cops were supposed to be bullies and badasses," Willow said. "You guys weren't so tough."

The policemen lying all around her on the ground didn't answer, although one, a few feet away, did let out a healthy-sounding snore.

Willow shook her head, but she didn't smile. "Sleepyheads," she muttered. "I hardly had to try."

Her entrance a minute or two ago amid a mass of swirling, otherworldly smoke and lights had caused quite the stir. Now tires squealed behind her, and she turned as a police car careened to the curb. Two officers jumped out and ran toward her, winding their way through the bodies of their fallen comrades. Someone must have gotten a call out on the radio before she'd put them down for their evening nap-nap. There was always someone who just didn't know when to stay quiet. Before these two could get within five feet of her, a wave of her hand sent them into dreamland with their buddies. Willow thought about blowing up the car just for the fun of it, just because she *could,* then changed her mind and turned away. She had better things to do with that energy.

Willow paused on the front steps, then raised her gaze to the upper floor. They would be up there, in one of the holding cells with the wire-reinforced windows. If she went in the front she'd have to deal with who knew how many more goody-two-shoes types, and it was all so tiresome. Better to skip the fanfare and just go straight to the top. She decided she would, however, like to see where she was going first.

She stared hard at the concrete building, concentrating. A few moments later cracks began to spider-web outward from the center of the second-floor wall. Her eyes narrowed as she focused, and the wall exploded outward.

She let herself go airborne and then she was there,

on the second floor and standing amid scattered chunks of concrete, wood, and plasterboard. She could hear the cops from the first floor already heading up the stairwell at the far end, their footsteps heavy and frantic. Heaven forbid they should actually try a little stealth. Before the first cop was even in sight, Willow bent and scooped up a handful of plaster dust and concrete bits, faced the open stairway, and blew it all in that direction. It fanned out in the air and flew toward the stairs, picking up big clots of material from the floor as it went. By the time the knot of police officers reached the second-floor landing, her makeshift wall was already chin high and growing; while they stood there shouting and trying to see over the top, it sealed itself up and she was looking at a crude new wall.

A corner of Willow's mouth turned up at the sight. "That's a little lumpy. Gotta work on my construction skills."

Someone was shouting behind her, and she sighed and turned, then stepped back in surprise as she saw the guard inside the cell. He had his hands wrapped around the bars and was yanking on them, just like a frantic monkey in a lab cage. In the cells on either side of him were a couple of men, unsavory types, watching her with wary and calculating eyes. But where the hell were Andrew and Jonathan?

She strode the length of the hallway just to make sure, but they weren't there. One of the prisoners got a little bold and grabbed at her sleeve as she passed, whining about getting out. She flicked his grip away, paying no attention as he howled in pain—that one little movement of hers had broken three of his fingers, but the fool deserved it for having the audacity to touch her. She was like a supreme being here, the high priestess among the acolytes, and even these brain-challenged lumps should know that.

Willow stopped in front of the cell where the guard was stranded, fixing her black gaze on him. When his eyes met hers, his motor-mouthing stopped and he let go of the bars and backed away. Studying him, Willow caught a whiff of something besides his puny fear. Could that be perfume?

Anya!

So Little Miss Vengeance had gone anti-Willow, had she? No doubt she'd been put up to it by the Slayer. Sheesh, Anya just couldn't make up her mind about whether she wanted to be good or evil, could she? Well, fine, but it wasn't going save Andrew's and Jonathan's adolescent little asses. "Where did they go?" she demanded of the guard. "The two men who were in here?"

The policeman held up his hand, as if doing so could fend her off. His back was against the far wall now, and he had nowhere left to go. "Look, lady, I don't know what's going on here, but if you'll just calm down—"

"Oh, I just hate that 'calm down the hysterical woman' crap," Willow snarled. She gripped the bars, feeling her anger mount. Beneath her touch the metal of the bars began to glow red. "You're supposed to be such a hot shot—big man with a badge and a billy club—and you can't even answer a simple question."

Now the bars were the color of iron pokers heated in a blacksmith's shop. The guard gaped at the sight, then began to stutter. "I don't know where they went, I swear it. They somehow got a girl in here and when I came in here to help her, they overpowered me and took my keys!"

"Liar," Willow said, but she was feeling a bit more mellow now that some of the heat had bled out of her and into the iron. "She set you up and you fell for it. Not exactly *NYPD Blue* material, are you?"

He flushed at the insult. "Look here—"

"Shut up!" she snapped. "Or I'll shut you up myself!"

He opened his mouth, then shut it again with an audible snap. Turning away from him, Willow hurried over to the gaping hole in the outer wall and reached out with her mind. . . .

No luck. She wasn't sure how, but Jonathan and Andrew had zipped out of her range, and even her power wasn't enough to locate them. Or maybe that meddlesome Anya had done something to them, given them a little cloaking spell to hide them from her sight. It was just so annoying how everyone wanted to be on the white side of the line.

No matter. That was nothing a little visit couldn't take care of.

Willow stepped out of the hole in the wall and into the air, then whirled away and into the night on blackened wings.

It was time to revisit the Magic Box.

In spades.

Chapter Three

"We have to go!" Anya spun through the door of the Magic Box, feeling absurdly breathless. She hadn't *run* anywhere, of course, but just figuratively running from a crazed, vengeful witch made her feel as though she had. Just in case, she'd teleported to the outside of the Magic Box before coming inside, wanting to make sure that Willow wasn't waiting outside or had sent someone or something else—who knew what was going to happen now that Willow had turned to the evil side of Sunnydale. "We have to get out of this town *now*!"

Buffy and Xander met her halfway across the room. "What happened?" Xander demanded. "Did you see her? Did you see Willow?"

"Thank you, but I like life, even after eight centuries. Our best bet is to get out of Dodge and just keep on dodging!"

Buffy shook her head. "Run? Not in my world."

"You don't understand!" Anya told her hotly. "This isn't *your* world anymore—now it belongs to Willow!"

Xander shook Anya's shoulder to get her attention. "What happened, Anya? Did Willow catch up with Jonathan and Andrew at the jail and turn them into human torches? Or did you get them out of there in time?"

Anya brushed his hand away. Even now, after all her anger and despair, she liked having him touch her more than she should. The darkest part of her vengeance self wished, at least in that respect, she could be more like Willow and just throw everything she had into hating him and making him pay. "Oh, I got them out, barely in time. Any brain cells they have left after watching all those B movies will point them far, far away from Sunnydale. In fact, space travel might be a good option for them right about now."

"What about Willow?" Buffy demanded. "Where is she? Can you sense her?"

Anya hesitated, and then her eyes got glazy for a second as she glanced around the room. "No," she finally said. "I can't. And that's a bad thing. It means she's gone beyond just wanting vengeance. She's *changed*."

"I'm guessing we're not talking self-improvement here," Xander said unhappily.

Buffy gave him a sidelong glance. "Well, we knew that."

"I guess I was hoping one would be enough."

"No," Anya said. "Not now. She's enjoying this way too much. And the safest place for us? Anywhere . . . *else*."

"I will not abandon Sunnydale and run like a whipped dog," Buffy said hotly. "We—"

"You guys, you're never going to believe what Willow did!"

The trio whirled as Dawn slammed into the Magic Box, towing an obviously reluctant Clem along by his sleeve.

"Dawn, I thought I told you to stay put down in Spike's cave," Buffy said angrily. "She could have killed you!"

Xander's jaw dropped. "You left your little sister with *Spike*?"

"She did the parasite mambo on that magick drug dealer guy!" Dawn continued.

"Spike would never hurt Dawn," Buffy said, then jerked as Dawn's words sunk in. "Wait—what?"

Xander frowned, obviously bewildered. "He took her dancing?"

"Would you just forget Spike already? He left town." Buffy was incredulous as she refocused on Dawn. "Not only did you not stay where I told you to, you went to a drug dealer's?" She whirled on Clem. "What kind of a bab—" She choked off the word before it could come out, but Dawn still glared at her. "—guardian are you?"

"Hey, wait a minute." Clem took a step back, his multifloppy face stretching into a distressed expression. "That's not usually in the job description, you know? I just like to eat and watch television. She wanted to leave, so I went with her. I thought that was pretty above and beyond the call as it was, but then she wanted to extend her range. I wasn't high on the idea, but she insisted."

"Did you hear what I said?" Dawn's nearly shrill voice cut off the budding argument. "Willow killed someone who wasn't Warren, Jonathan, or Andrew!"

"Which means she could kill anyone," Xander pointed out.

"I'm sorry," Anya said bitingly. "I thought I made that extremely clear much earlier in the evening."

Xander ran a hand through his hair. "And the tally rises."

Anya folded her arms. "I'm telling you guys, we *have* to get out of here. It's not safe!"

Buffy shook her head. "I'm not going anywhere."

"You never did take advice well." All of them spun as Willow glided through the front door of the Magic Box and stopped a few feet away.

"Willow?" Xander struggled to find words, but all he could manage was, "Oh, boy."

Anya's mouth dropped open. "Wow."

Willow's blackened lips stretched in a smile, showing startlingly bright and beautiful teeth. "Nice, huh?" Her skin was a fine shade of translucent white, a base for the fine black veins that crawled just below its surface. Her eyes and hair were the color of a tar pit, so dark they wouldn't even hold a shadow. There was a sparkle in her eyes, the only hint of life. Or perhaps it was the opposite: dead rage. "I'm all grown up now."

As quickly as it had appeared, Willow's smile was gone and her gaze returned to spear Buffy's. "But back to the matter at hand. Where are Jonathan and Andrew?"

Buffy lifted her chin. "No idea."

Willow nodded slowly. "And, of course, if you did—"

"I wouldn't tell you anyway."

Willow looked at her and disappointment flickered across her features. "I thought we were friends, Buffy. I thought that you would care about me losing the one light in my life. I thought you would understand."

Buffy's hard expression softened. "Oh, God, Willow—I *do*. I know you're devastated, and you feel like you're all alone in the world. But you're *not*." She gestured at herself and the others. "You still have us. No matter what's happened, we still care. But you can't keep on killing. Jonathan and Andrew, they didn't pull the trigger. You . . ." She hesitated, not wanting to say the word "murder." "You took care of Warren. He was the one who did it, who actually killed Tara. Isn't that enough?"

Willow shook her head. "No, no. Not by a long shot." Suddenly she laughed loudly, making them all wince. "Long shot—get it? That should be funny!"

Xander reached out a hand. "Will—"

"Don't touch me!"

He jerked his hand away, the nerves suddenly throbbing with the memory of the blistering he had taken earlier for trying the same tactic. "Okay, okay. Calm down—not going there."

"WHERE ARE THEY?"

Willow's scream was thunderous enough to make them all clap their hands over their ears—so powerful, in fact, that it blew everything on the counter right onto the floor along with nearly everything else around the shop that wasn't heavy enough to stay put. Paper and small glass doodads flew in every direction, trinkets shattered, and the lighter volumes tumbled off the shelves.

"We don't know!" Anya cried. "They left! Enough of the lung power, all right?"

Willow's eyes narrowed, and for a long, frightening moment she didn't say anything at all. The only sounds were the pieces of paper drifting to the floor around them, little fluttering sounds like the beatings of delicate bat wings. "They left," Willow finally said in a strangely calm voice. "They *left*." She glanced around the room, but she was obviously not seeing anything in it. "How far away do you think they'd have to go to be out of my sensing range?"

"Far enough to be safe, I hope," Buffy said. She lifted her chin stubbornly. "Will, you're out of control here. You've killed Warren and that creepo magick drug dealer—questionable as to whether that's a big loss or not, but that's enough. You've had your revenge already. It's time to *stop*."

Willow whirled with enough force to make Buffy back-step—Buffy couldn't help still being startled by those inky black eyes. Willow's eyes, coupled with her night-dark hair spinning around her head like a black halo, gave her quite an effect. "Let me fill you in,

Buffy. It's enough when I *say* it's enough, get it? I'm through taking orders from you, from Giles, or from anyone else. I'm on my own now."

But Buffy stood her ground when Willow started to stalk out, refusing to move or let her pass. "No. I'm not letting you leave like this. Not when you're so angry."

"Oh, I'm more than angry," Willow said. "And you're going to find out just how far into the hot zone I can go if you don't get the hell out of my way. You've got so much slayer on the brain that you think you're calling the shots over everyone, but I'm not one of your Slayerette flunkies anymore. Now *move*."

"*No.*"

Willow arched one eyebrow. "Abracadabra," she said in a deceptively quiet voice. At the same time she threw out one hand, palm first, toward Buffy. There was a huge sound, like a train roaring at full speed, and blue-black energy shot from the center of her palm toward Buffy, instantly enveloping her. But when Willow stopped the flow, she was shocked to see Buffy standing there, unfazed.

For a fraction of a second Buffy seemed just as surprised. Then she recovered—being a Slayer meant never having to second-guess your strength. "Ta da."

"Okay," Willow said. She studied Buffy thoughtfully. "I didn't see that coming."

Before she could try again, Buffy leaped on her. They tumbled to the ground and rolled, making Dawn and Xander move back in different directions. Clem had had more sense than anyone—he was long gone, having made a hasty and unobserved exit at Willow's first appearance.

"Xander!" Buffy yelled. "Get Dawn out of here—*now*!"

He didn't need to be told twice, and Willow paid him no mind as he hauled himself and the teenager out the front door. She hit Buffy hard enough to rock her world a bit, but Buffy punched her right back. All it did was make Willow's jaw sore and her temper hotter.

A good hard shove—the magicks made her physically Buffy's equal, or more—sent Buffy literally flying through the air. She landed back-first against the bookcases on the far wall and slid down to the floor with a groan.

"That had to hurt," Willow said with false sympathy. "Too bad I'm all out of Band-Aids." As Buffy tried to stand, Willow let loose another dark energy blast, this time doubling the strike by using both hands.

Nada.

"Damn," Willow said. There was admiration in her voice. "That's one effective counterspell. Who cast it? I'll have to remember to thank them personally."

Now Buffy was standing again, and this time there was no stopping her. She bowled over Willow like a truck with bad brakes, and the two of them toppled backward, end over end. Buffy held on, trying to avoid Willow's furious punching. "Will, I can help you stop!"

Willow twisted away, then gave Buffy a painful back-fist, trying to dislodge her. "Get *off,* superbitch! I don't *want* to stop!"

Buffy grabbed at her again, but Willow was on her feet now. Her well-timed side kick sent Buffy crashing into the front of the counter. Glass flew everywhere as Buffy flipped over it and got tangled in the curtain, pulling it free and revealing Anya, hunched over a book and frantically chanting a spell in a whispered voice.

"Shield around us, never broken, shield surrounds us, keep us from harm—"

"Well, hey." Willow's tone was calm. "That's interesting." Off to the side Buffy was fighting to get to her feet, but it was clear she'd lost the edge. "Anya's still here, chanting her little heart out. And I've been beating on the wrong girl!"

To her credit, Anya tried to keep going. But even her resolve ended when Willow, with incredible speed, reached out with one hand and plucked her off the floor. Dangling there, Anya's words ended in a frightened squeak, and the book fell from her hands. "Help me, Buffy!"

"Can't block my spells if you can't chant," Willow told her. There was no malice in her voice, just simple fact. "And you can't chant if you're sleeping."

And she threw Anya across the room as if she weighed no more than a child's rag doll.

Anya struck the far wall and fell amid a new shower of books. When she landed, she made a small, very quiet pile of pretty hair and brightly colored dress.

"There," Willow said with finality, "so much for that one. Now where was I?" She turned at the sound of Buffy standing up. "Oh yeah. You."

Buffy started toward her, but Willow held up a hand. Buffy paused almost hopefully.

"Buffy, I gotta tell you," Willow said. "I get it now. The slayer thing really *isn't* about the violence." From somewhere, from *no*where, a cold, violent wind came up. It began swirling around Willow, faster and faster, building in strength and power and sound. "It's about the *power*." And at the end Willow had to shout for Buffy to hear her.

"And there's no one in the world with the power to stop me now!"

Without Anya's protective spell to stop it, Buffy sucked in her lungs, realizing she was going to take the full force of Willow's rage-powered blast—but Willow got hit instead.

The unseen blast sent her flying in reverse, sliding painfully across the floor. When she finally stopped, Willow shook her head in stunned disbelief, even more incredulous when droplets of blood fell from her nose onto the floor. When she could finally focus again, she made out Giles's leather-jacket-clad figure standing in the doorway amid the plaster dust floating in the air. His glasses were gone, and he looked lean and mean. When he spoke, he was completely, utterly at ease.

"I'd like to test that theory."

It only took an instant for Willow to recover, and then she gave him an ugly grin. "Uh-oh. Daddy's home," she said nastily.

Giles just looked at her. "Do we really need to go into this?"

"Oh, I think we so do," Willow said.

She tried to stand, but Giles gestured at her carelessly. "Stay down." She sat back down, hard. Her expression darkened.

Giles hurried over to Buffy and dragged her upright. "Get Anya and get out of here," he told her urgently. "Hurry."

"Little late for that, Watcher," Willow said from behind him. She was almost to her feet.

Giles gestured at her again. "Stay dow—"

"No," Willow said and brushed at the air. Whatever magick Giles had thought to direct at her melted away and she rose easily.

Giles blinked, then eyed her cautiously. "Willow—"

"It's all right, Buffy," Willow said. Her gaze never left Giles. "I really don't have time to bother with you anyway. You just grab Anya back there and toodle on to some other happy place. I don't want to fight you." She gave Giles a black smile. "I want to fight *him*."

"Go, Buffy," Giles said.

Buffy coughed painfully. "No—"

"Think of Anya," he ordered. "She needs to be gotten to safety. Then you can come back."

Willow chuckled, watching Giles warily as Buffy reluctantly obeyed. "Like there'll be anything to come back *to*."

"Give me five minutes," Buffy ground out, but she was limping badly as she hauled the semiconscious Anya to her feet and steered her through the rubble to the front door. "Just hold out that long."

"Need a little help?" Willow asked innocently. Suddenly both Anya and Buffy were moving forward at three times their former speed, their feet stumbling to find the ground as it rushed past beneath them. They tumbled through the entry door, and it slammed shut behind them with a sound of undeniable finality.

And then it was just the two of them.

Willow.

And Giles.

"So," Willow said. She started circling Giles, noting offhandedly that he was doing the same. When the door to the training room was behind him, he slipped through it; she followed without hesitation. "You remember we had that little spat before you left? When you were under the delusion that you were still relevant here? That was when you called me a rank amateur."

She stopped and faced him squarely. Her eyes, already black, suddenly looked deep and liquid, like an ocean that might have been lapping at the shores of hell. Her aura took on a golden glow cut with shimmers of black, and the air in the Magic Box began to crackle dangerously.

"Well, buckle up, Rupert," she said. Her voice echoed around the room, and it seemed to be coming from everywhere at once. "'Cause I've turned pro. . . ."

Xander and Dawn were waiting only a block away, both pacing the sidewalk like a couple of overcaffeinated cats. When they saw Buffy turn the corner, dragging Anya along beside her, they almost tripped over each other trying to meet them.

"Anya!"

Xander reached for her, but even groggy, Anya managed to swat his hand away. "Hands off. I'll survive."

"What happened?" Dawn demanded. She helped steady Anya, then gripped Buffy's arm. "You looked like you got the tar knocked out of you. Did Willow do this?"

"Don't remind me," Buffy said shortly. She was amazed and embarrassed that Willow had actually roundly tromped her. "Now that Anya's safe with you guys, I have to go back," she said. "Giles is in there with Willow. It's dangerous."

"Giles?" Dawn's eyes widened. "But he's over in England. He—"

"Obviously he's here, or else Buffy saw a ghost," Xander interrupted. "The Ripper reappears to lend a helping hand."

"A nice thought, but if I don't get back there and give him some help," Buffy said grimly, "he's likely to *be* a ghost by tomorrow morning!"

Willow started toward him, but Giles held his ground. "Willow, stop. We can work this out. We can get you help, people who understand what you're going through and know how to deal with loss."

But even though she was staring right at him, Willow wasn't seeing him. "Willow doesn't live here anymore," she said hollowly.

Before he could react, she sent a bolt of energy at him, enough to knock him right off his feet. He grunted as he hit the floor, but when he sat up, he countered with his own. The harsh green light burst from the center of his palm and aimed for Willow's chest.

"Solutum," Willow said in a rather gentle voice, and the flash dissipated harmlessly in the air. Willow wagged her finger at him. "Fool me once——" She swept her hand at the assortment of weapons and daggers on one wall of the training room, and they floated forward, off their hooks.

Alarmed, Giles watched the floating knives. "Willow, you wouldn't."

"Shame on you," Willow said softly.

All the weapons whirled and arrowed toward Giles.

"Tego!" he shouted. To his right Buffy's practice dummy jerked into the air and flew into place in front of him, shielding him from the dose of flying death just in time. The lifeless object jerked and shuddered as the blades thunked into it, and Giles felt a little sick to his stomach when he realized that Willow wasn't just trying to hurt him. She could, and she *would,* kill him if he let her.

Enough of this playing around.

He shoved his palm forward. *"Excudo!"*

The bolt of power that hit Willow was as surprising to her as it was painful—she'd *never* been hit with anything like this. Pain exploded in every nerve of her body, and Giles's blast was enough to lift her off her feet and fling her not only backward, but right out of the training room and *up,* all the way up to the second-floor landing. She crashed into the railing and cracked it, then plummeted back down, face first, to the ground floor.

For a long, long moment, she just lay there, unmoving.

But she would not be beaten by this old man. And certainly not by a has-been watcher.

Her eyes narrowed to slits, and she pushed herself to her feet and faced him again. And then all hell in the Magic Box *really* broke loose.

Running up to the outside of the Magic Box, Buffy was stunned. Had it taken her that long to get back here? She would swear to anyone that she'd only been gone a few minutes, yet the place was nearly demolished, as though she'd been gone for hours. There was another crash from inside that sounded to her like dynamite. And when she forced her way through the front door, or what was left of it, she thought it might as well have been the big TNT, because that's sure what it looked like.

Inside, she saw Willow and Giles facing off at the far end of the shop, next to the rubble of what had once been the wall between the shop proper and the training room. They both looked like haggard and beaten street brawlers ready to go another round; Willow had oozing scrapes and bruises all over her, but Giles was in substantially worse shape. Not only did he look exhausted and shaky, but also there was a long, openly bleeding gash angling across one side of his forehead toward his temple.

"That all you got, Jeeves?" Willow taunted. "'Cuz

I could stand to go another ten rounds." She studied him with a smug half smile on her face. "Whereas you can barely stand, period."

Trying not to make any noise, Buffy began to pick her way through the ruins between her and the other two. Each footfall made her wince, certain that Willow would hear the crunch of glass, the grinding of a chunk of splintered wood under her heel.

Giles tried to draw himself up. "Your powers may be significantly greater than before, but I can still hurt you . . . if I have to."

Willow's mouth twisted into a sneer. "Hurt me? Boy, you just don't get it, do you? Nothing can hurt me anymore. This?" She passed her hand in front of her face and all her injuries simply vanished. "This is nothing. It's all . . . *nothing*."

Giles blinked. "I see. You lose someone you love and the other people in your life, the ones who care so much about you, become meaningless." He paused, then asked softly, "I wonder . . . what would Tara say about that?"

Willow's face hardened. "You can ask her yourself."

Faster than he could react, she jerked her hand toward the second-floor landing, then brought it down in a chopping motion. With the movement, the entire overhead structure gave way with a deafening crash. With nowhere to run, all Giles could do was gape upward.

Then Buffy hit him with a hard, running tackle that took the two of them almost out of range of the collapsing pieces of wood and mortar.

Almost.

Which, as everyone says, is really good in horse-shoes, but not so high on the happening charts when a person is standing below a collapsing building.

On the floor at Willow's feet, Buffy and Giles were pinned down by one of the support pillars. Even so, Buffy groaned and tried to get up. "Down, girl," Willow said, and placed one foot in the hollow of Buffy's back between her shoulder blades. It was only a fleeting thought, but in her mind her foot was a magnet, drawn to the earth's deepest core, and Buffy was trapped between the two like a flimsy piece of paper stuck to the fridge by one of those little plastic fruit shapes . . . but with supersized pull. Under Willow's Hulkanized version, Buffy wasn't going anywhere.

And there was Giles, considerably worse for wear, lying next to Buffy with a pillar conveniently resting across his hipbones. Caught like a mouse in a trap, wasn't he? She could walk away, go off in search of the Dorky Duo, but she had things to say to Giles, didn't she? And things to do, oh my.

His eyes were open and he was watching her. "You're such a hypocrite," she told him. "Waltzing back here with borrowed magicks, so you can tell me—what? Magick is bad? Behave? Be a good girl? I don't think you're in any position to tell me what to do anymore."

Giles tried to rise, but a finger gesture from Willow

cracked his head smartly back against the floor. Blood trickled from the corner of his mouth and he coughed.

"I used to think you had all the answers," Willow said pensively. "That I had so much to learn from you. But you were just a fraud—you were jealous and still are. You just couldn't bear that I was the one with the power, and that's why you ran."

"Willow," Giles began. "Please. You're expending far too much energy. Let me help you—"

"Desistre."

Whatever words he'd had planned died in his throat as his mouth snapped shut and stayed that way. All he could manage was a "Mmmuf!" of surprise.

"Don't interrupt, Giles. It's rude." Willow tapped her chin with one finger. When Giles tried to speak again, Willow just arched an eyebrow. "I'm really getting fond of the quiet audience thing. Now what was I saying?" She grinned darkly. "Oh yeah. You were saying how I was expending too much energy, blah blah blah. And then you offered to help me."

Looking up at her, Giles's eyes widened as he suddenly realized what was going through her mind. He shook his head violently, but he still couldn't make a sound.

"Oh, totally yes," Willow told him. "Very yes, indeed." With her foot still solidly in place on Buffy's back, she bent over him. "What do I need to fix that? A little pick-me-up."

Trapped, Giles could do nothing to defend himself as her hand shot out and bonded instantly to his chest. The space between them exploded into viciously bright tendrils of light, and Giles screamed as Willow's silence spell was forgotten and everything inside him suddenly felt like it was boiling. It took Willow five seconds to drain everything he had out of him, but to Giles, it felt twice as long as eternity.

Then Willow abruptly pulled away from him. She stumbled back until she hit the wall and slid down it. She landed in a half-sitting, half-crouching position. "God," she gasped. "Head rush!" She tried to stare at Giles, but the room was Weeble-Wobbling around her and she was finding it difficult to focus her eyes. "Whoa—who's your supplier? This stuff is . . . *wow*. I am so *juiced*!"

A few feet away, Giles said nothing. Her silencing spell had obviously disintegrated with her power assault, but now he was too weak to say or do anything other than make a low rasping sound. Willow didn't notice; she was still woozy from the forces coursing through her veins.

Buffy, however, was ready to start all over. The only problem was that while Willow's spell on her had also disappeared, the massive support post across her lower body hadn't. It was also still pinning Giles to the floor, trapping them both. Frustrated, Buffy tried to hammer at it with her fists, but all she succeeded in doing was getting a painful dose of splinters along the sides of each hand. Finally she felt her hips wriggle free just the slightest bit. "I'm . . . getting . . . there. . . ." she started to tell Giles. "Just a little bit more—"

"*No.*"

Buffy jerked and looked up. Willow was standing

above her, apparently fully recovered from her near overdose of power. Buffy had seen a lot of terrifying things in her life, but the view of her best friend looming over her like this was horrific. Dressed in black, with her hair and eyes unnaturally colored to match, Willow was like something out of a bad goth club cult fantasy, complete with makeup-whitened skin enhanced with black veins.

"You're not getting there, Buffy. Not anymore." Willow's voice was hollow and sounded far away, unpleasantly echoing. "You might have 'been there' once, but now it's my turn." She stared down at Buffy. "My turn," she repeated. "Forever and ever, amen."

And after all that, Willow simply walked out of the remains of the Magic Box and left Giles and Buffy lying in the dust.

Chapter Four

It was a beautiful night, cool and clear, with a light breeze and a painter's brush sweep of stars across the sky. Such loveliness . . . but it held no joy for Willow, no charm. It lacked something else, too, something more vital to her right now than anything geared for one of the six earthly senses: It lacked any feeling at all of Andrew and Jonathan, or where they might have gone. If they'd been anywhere in Sunnydale, or even a few miles beyond it, Willow could have gotten to them, could have sent a ball of flame that, like a heat-seeking missile, would have taken care of business for her.

But even as power-drenched as she was, she could pick up nothing.

And so she walked.

The houses passed unnoticed, the street names

unread, the people ignored. She walked through Sunnydale but existed only for Andrew and Jonathan, a walking container of anger that would be the means by which her lover would somehow be avenged.

Her lover.

After so long apart, they'd had hardly any time reunited at all. To regain something so precious only to lose it again so soon—

I should cry, Willow thought suddenly. *That's what people are supposed to do when they lose someone they love. They cry.* Yeah—crying was believed to be cathartic, purifying a person of pain and sorrow. But no, Willow couldn't do that. She wasn't ready to be rid of her pain and her sorrow; she would *never* be rid of it. Besides, to cry she needed to be alive, and she wasn't anymore, not really. Everything live about her had drained out in a big crimson puddle on the floor of the biggest of the upstairs bedrooms at Buffy's house.

It was amazing—she had all this power inside her, and yet she was still *nothing*. She could feel the impact of the soles of her boots hitting the concrete with each step she took, the rush of the crisp night air that filled her lungs with each inhalation, the sting of her own fingernails when she curled her fists and dug them into her palms. But none of that made her alive, it just made her functioning. Anyone, any*thing,* could function. It just needed fuel, and if fury could be harnessed as a source of energy, boy, Willow had plenty of that.

But now her fury could not find its target.

All that anger . . . Giles had been right; she had misdirected it, aimed it at those who had once been her friends and teachers. They weren't anymore, and who could blame them? The dark side of her soul wanted to blame Buffy. After all, Warren's big bull's-eye had been on Buffy, and it was his misplaced shot that had found its way through Tara's back. But Buffy had not pulled the trigger, and she had done everything she could to put a stop to those three scrambled-brains long before today. No, the fault was clearly with those three, and she had delivered the death blow to the one most responsible. But Buffy, Giles, and the others were wrong in thinking that Warren's henchmen should go unpunished, that she should consider the debt satisfied. No way; Warren's accomplices must pay as dearly as the evil person who drove them.

Giles.

Had she hurt him badly? Maybe. Probably. Well, too bad, so sad; he never should have stood in her way. And hadn't that just been the jolt of superjuju she'd pulled out of him? Very surprising—having that kind of power meant he was stronger inside than he looked. Besides, the old man had proved time and time again that he was damned near as indestructible as the Slayer herself. He'd be fine. They'd all be fine.

But not her.

Willow was a whole different person now. With a whole big list of things to do.

Buffy hated the sight of revolving white and red lights almost as much as she hated vampires. Too many times in her life she'd seen them, but the most notable, of course, had been the day her mother died. She vaguely remembered an ambulance after Warren had shot her, but Willow's appearance and healing magick at the hospital had blurred all that so much that the recollection was almost gone, like a carefully drawn Etch A Sketch picture that's gradually disappearing from the vibrations of a car ride. She could hardly believe that the same beloved Willow who had once literally brought her back from the dead, and stopped her from falling over its edge just hours ago, had done . . .

This.

Buffy could see the ruins of the Magic Box beyond the ambulance and the stretcher on which the paramedics had placed Giles. There would be no coming back to this, no rebuilding. How could there be? There was nothing left to rebuild. Willow might as well have picked up the building and tossed it into a mondo-size Shake 'n Bake bag. Anyone could see that what wasn't shaken had certainly been baked, and the leftovers were all broken pieces and smoking, cindery wood.

"Can we ride with him?" Anya was clutching the side of Giles's stretcher, and so far nothing the paramedics had said could convince her to release her grip. "He shouldn't be alone. He needs us."

"He's not alone, ma'am," the paramedic said, but Buffy could tell the man's patience was wearing thin. "If you'd just let go of the stretcher, we really need to get going and get him to the emergency room."

"But—"

"Anya," Xander said. "Come on, let them do their job. We'll follow in my car. Buffy?" He looked at her questioningly.

She nodded and glanced at Dawn. The teenager looked like a silent, white-faced ghost, and she hadn't said much since she and Xander had come back to the Magic Box and discovered the mess that Willow had left. "We're with you," Buffy replied.

But Anya still resisted. "Why can't I ride with him?"

Xander reached over and pried her fingers loose, then decided not to let go of her until she made him. The paramedics jumped at the chance to hustle the unnaturally quiet Giles into the ambulance. "Because they have all that medically inclined equipment in there," Xander told her. "And right now only Giles is medically inclined."

"I can get there faster," Anya said petulantly. "I can be waiting for them when they arrive."

"Not a good idea," Xander reminded her. "Not only will they wonder how the hell you got there so fast, you'll be wandering around the emergency room by yourself, getting more and more impatient by the minute. People could get hurt. Trust me, it's better for everyone involved if you just stick with the program. That would be the three of us part."

Anya's brow furrowed. "But everyone always says good things come to those who wait. So why can't I go and wait for Giles to get there?"

"Good things. Uh-huh." He looked at her out of the corner of his eye. "As if you have *ever* been good at the waiting game."

"We should stick together," Dawn said, before Anya could come back with something else. It was the first thing she'd said since the ambulance had arrived. "Just in case . . ." She didn't continue, but the unspoken implication was there: What if Willow came back to finish the job?

This, finally, seemed to get through to Anya. "Willow," she repeated. She still sounded a bit dazed. "That's right. She did all this. She hurt Giles. It's so hard to believe."

"This isn't the Willow we all know and love," Buffy said, and she meant it. "I've got a crawly feeling that Good Willow is gone bye-bye and Bad Willow's moved in."

"But to do the face-flip like this is just incredible." She looked at Xander and Buffy with wide eyes. "For a human, anyway. Demons do it all the time, of course; it's in their genetic makeup. They have to, so they can hide if necessary, or react to their environment—"

"Right," Xander said. "Demons and natural selection. Not routinely covered on the Discovery Channel, but we're with you."

"Xander, this is not the time for stand-up comedy," Anya said. Her voice was just a bit strident, betraying how scared she was. "I don't think you get it. Willow is now *the* most powerful Wiccan in the world, and we could be on her hit list!"

There were shadows under Buffy's eyes, and it was obvious by the way she kept glancing around them that she thought Willow might show up again at any time. "Anya's right. We have big reason to be big careful here, but we'll get into that later. Right now, let's get cracking." She pointed behind them. "Look—the ambulance is ready to leave."

The four of them piled hurriedly into Xander's car, but while the ambulance's siren screamed in front of them, inside the car the ride to the hospital was made in silence. Buffy was still a little loopy from the major sticky-tricky that Willow had done to her. She felt like at any second things—knives, swords, maybe the service revolvers of the policemen who'd shown up with the ambulance at the Magic Box—might fly through the air and stick to her, or worse, *into* her. Okay, so maybe that was a little far-fetched, but she could have sworn she'd seen a few of those metal gadgets hanging inside the open ambulance tremble on their hooks when she'd ventured too close. While Buffy the Human Magnet sounded interesting enough, it was more freak show material than superhero, and she wanted nothing to do with it.

Xander parked the car, and they all hustled into the hospital, following behind the paramedics rolling Giles inside. Xander hated hospitals almost as much as he hated cemeteries, and didn't one sometimes lead to the other? Sure it did, and too darned often. Plus, hospitals had that *smell* to them, that one-of-a-kind mixture of alcohol, cleaning liquid, blood, and latex, a scent that secretly always made him nauseous. Throw the odor of bad cafeteria food on top of that—tonight's greasy hamburger and fries and this morning's overcooked oatmeal—and there was a good chance he was talking yark city.

They got cut off from Giles when the paramedics

pushed his stretcher through a pair of double doors that said MEDICAL STAFF ONLY BEYOND THIS POINT, and left them all standing there, staring at nothing but an entrance painted obnoxiously red. For a moment none of them knew what to do. They turned first one way, then another, looked at the floor, and glanced down the hallway in the direction from which they'd just come. Finally Buffy spied a sign on the wall pointing toward a waiting area. "Let's go," she said.

So they waited, and watched, and listened to the echoes of pain and misery that always seemed to emanate from the walls of a dismal, death-filled place like this.

Anya was the first one to see the doctor striding purposefully toward them. She'd been slouching a little in her chair, listening to the far-off screams of some guy two rooms over. They were pleasant enough to her ears; the jerk had been two-timing his girlfriend, driving around town with another woman in his hopped-up black Camero Z28, when the front tire on the driver's side had blown and yanked the car across the street and into a mailbox. Now he had pieces of bright American blue deeply embedded in the arm he'd had hanging carelessly out the window, with a few thrown into his left cheekbone and shoulder just for giggles. He didn't know how lucky he was—had Anya run into his girlfriend, her current mood might have made her switch his arms for his legs. Maybe his new girlfriend would like it when he tossed his foot across her shoulder. Then again, maybe not.

"Guys," Anya said now, "here comes the purveyor of doom."

"Always Little Miss Sunshine," Xander said, but there was no true malice in his voice as he watched the surgeon approach.

When the doctor finally stopped in front of them, there was nothing warm or friendly about his face, no comfort in his eyes. Either he had a terrible bedside manner, or, as Anya thought for one truly panicked second, he was going to tell them that Giles was dead.

"How is he?" Buffy asked. "Is he going to be all right?" Beside her, Dawn looked absolutely terrified, and Buffy's heart ached for her. She hadn't forgotten her sister's experiences in this same hospital after their mother's death.

For once Anya decided to go for the positive thinking side of the coin. "When can we take him home?"

The doctor, who was wearing a name tag that said DR. BERELLI, looked as if he'd been about to answer Buffy, but Anya's anxious question made him turn his cold gaze toward her. "Take him home?" He sounded incredulous. "He's not going anywhere." He glared at each of them in turn. "I don't know what the hell happened here tonight, but that's a job for the police department, and I'm not involved in that. I also can't believe any of you would even think that Mr. Giles can leave here given what he's endured."

Xander swallowed visibly. "We just thought—"

"Well, you thought wrong," Dr. Berelli said. The doctor looked overworked and exhausted as he focused again on Buffy, then peered more closely at her. "It seems like you're the leader of this little group, young lady, and you look as if you took quite a beating yourself. Even so, you're in a lot better shape than Mr. Giles. As of right now, he's paralyzed from the waist down."

For a long moment no one spoke. Then Dawn managed to stutter, "P-p-paralyzed?"

"Yes," Berelli said briskly. "Paralyzed. We're hoping this is due to muscle swelling surrounding his spine, because we can't see anything specific on the X rays or CT scan. We'll know more in the morning, we hope, when he has an MRI and the results are evaluated. Until then he stays put—no movement *at all*—because we don't know that moving him wouldn't cause further damage."

"How long?" Xander asked. At the doctor's frosty expression he tried to explain. "I'm only asking because I know Giles wouldn't want to be in a hospital." He faltered. "Not that your hospital isn't a great place. I'm sure it's fine. Even the hospital food is probably the best in the world. I mean—"

"As long as it takes," the doctor interrupted.

Buffy found her voice and managed to speak with the utmost calm. "Can we see him?"

Berelli's chin lifted. "Are you family?"

"Yes," Buffy said quickly.

The doctor's eyebrows shot up. "All of you?"

"Oh, definitely," Anya said. "We're also the ones who'll be helping him."

The doctor took his time about deciding but finally acquiesced. "All right, but you'll do it one at a time or

I'll write orders prohibiting *all* visitors. If he's to heal, he must have rest, and lots of it. Understand?"

They nodded, and without another word, Dr. Berelli stalked away. "Well," Xander finally said. "Isn't he just the poster boy for patient relations."

"Who cares?" Anya sounded like she'd start wailing at any moment. "Didn't you hear him? Giles is *paralyzed,* for God's sake. He can't *walk!*"

"Oh, this is bad," Buffy said quietly. "Bad to the core."

"He could still have a good life," Xander said as they made their way toward the visitors' check-in window. False cheer made his expression ridiculously strained, but when Dawn punched him smartly in the arm, he winced and scowled at her. "What?" he demanded. "Giles could be like Professor X in the *X-Men* movies, motorizing around and giving directions on how to foil all the bad guys' attempts at world domination from the comfort of his custom wheelchair."

Buffy folded her arms. "Okay, now you're starting to sound way too much like geekables Jonathan and Andrew."

Xander looked insulted. "Hey, not funny!"

"Neither is this." Buffy turned away from him and signed her name on the visitor check-in sheet.

"I'm next." Anya reached for the pen.

"Don't bother," Buffy said. "We're all going in at once."

Xander jerked. "But you heard what the doctor said—"

Buffy shook her head. "On the tire-Giles-out scale

it's one short visit from all of us or four separate ones. Do the math."

"There is that," Xander agreed.

"Come on, let's go." Anya was pacing in a little circle, she was so impatient. "I don't understand why humans are so fond of standing around and waiting for everything, and all of you with such short-term, pathetic little lives. Don't you even realize you waste years just waiting at stoplights? Why don't I just teleport into his room and—"

"Scare the crap out of the charge nurse," Buffy finished for her. "Where screaming ensues and lots of people run to the rescue. I think not. Come on—follow me."

It was simple, really. In intensive care there were routines to be followed, scheduled medications to be given, and charts to be filled out. As with any hospital nowadays, there didn't seem to be enough nurses to cover everything, so it was just a matter of waiting— no matter how much Anya griped about it—until the IC nurse in charge of Giles finished her scheduled check of his vitals, then went on to the next patient. They didn't have much time, but then they didn't need it; the others followed Buffy as she slipped past two beds with occupants whose tubes and respirators kept them cooperatively quiet. Pulse and blood pressure monitors beeped around the large room, adding a sort of background music that was unpleasantly nerve-racking. Once they were at Giles's side, Buffy quietly pulled the curtain around his bed and motioned to the others to gather close inside so their feet wouldn't show beneath the hem.

They all stared, speechless, nearly breathless.

Buffy thought the former watcher looked like a pale shadow of himself. His face was swollen and bruised, and the skin between the heavy black and yellow-green bruises was the color of chalk. Even his hands were battered, although it was hard to tell if it was left over from his battle with Willow or from the numerous IVs jabbed into his veins. The man full of strength and magick who'd crossed an ocean to stand against Willow was, to all appearances, destroyed.

"Oh, man," Xander whispered. And then, because he was too stunned to think of anything else, he repeated himself. "Oh, *man*."

Somewhere along the line Buffy had taken Dawn's hand, and she could feel the vibrations along the teenager's arm, the warning tremors of coming tears. To keep her quiet, Buffy pulled her into a hug and held on, letting her younger sister sob soundlessly against her shoulder as she fought to find her own iron will. She had to be strong here, she *had* to. Not only for Dawn, but also for Xander and Anya. And for herself. Seeing Giles like this was almost more than any of them could bear, a shock past comprehension. There was no one but her to stand up to it and keep them together.

She *had* to. No matter how much Buffy wanted to cover her face with her hands, her own anguish over this would have to wait.

Anya made a little hiccuping sound, the prelude to her tears, that must have gotten through Giles's semi-sleep. Although heavily medicated, he still managed to force his eyes open and regard his visitors, and that was probably the only thing that kept Anya from going into full weeping mode. He tried to speak, but his words were thick and slow, floating on an industrial-size dose of morphine. "Wil . . . low," he managed. "Stop . . ."

"We know," Buffy said, keeping her voice almost at a whisper. Dawn reached out to pat his hand, then pulled back, afraid she'd dislodge one of the numerous IVs. "We'll look for her, I promise," Buffy continued. "We'll work it out."

Giles's eyelids fluttered. "Get . . . out," he mumbled.

Anya blinked. "Get out? You want us to leave? But we just got here."

"Nuh-no," Giles said. "Me . . . out."

"I get it," Xander said suddenly. "He wants us to get *him* out of here. Right?"

Giles nodded, the move nearly imperceptible. "Out," he said again, but that seemed to take the rest of his energy. Despite his efforts, his eyes kept closing. A few more seconds and he was asleep.

"Come on," Buffy told the others. "We've got to split before the nurse catches us."

"But you heard Giles," Anya protested. "He doesn't want to stay here."

"For now he has no choice." Buffy waved at the gadgets and geegaws around the bed, all of which were not only chirping heartily but were in some way attached to Giles. "We don't know what does what here. He needs to get a little further on the road to recovery before we take him home."

"And if the doctor's right," Dawn put in, "we'll need to figure out how to take care of him."

"I'll do it," Anya said. "He taught me everything about the world of retail and he did sell me the Magic Box. The least I can do is support him in his hour of need . . . at least until we figure something else out."

"Good deal," Buffy said. "But we still have to let him heal a little more. He's one of us genetically challenged humans, remember? No demon DNA to turbo him on the road to recovery."

"True," Anya said sadly. Then her mouth twisted. "You know, Willow did this, she ought to fix it. After all, a person has to stand up and take responsibility for what she's done."

Buffy pressed her lips together. "I'm not sure we ought to remind her of that right now," she said. "She's already taken that notion into overdrive in her belief that Jonathan and Andrew should pay for Tara's death even though they were in the slammer at the time." Buffy's eyes darkened. "I think the Willow who would have fixed Giles isn't even the one who healed me in the operating room. The true Willow is gone." She paused before finishing. "Maybe forever."

She let that sink in as she cautiously peered around the curtain to make sure no one was headed toward Giles's bed. When she saw the area was still clear, she quietly pulled the curtain open the way it had originally been. "Let's go," she said. The other three nodded, and like shadows they slipped through the hospital corridors and into the ominous Sunnydale night.

• • •

"I can rebuild it," Xander said.

"You sound like the opening of the *Six Million Dollar Man*." Buffy said it jokingly, but in a way she wasn't kidding. Rebuild the Magic Box? Xander must be insane, and she saw that opinion reflected on her sister's face.

"Now who's sounding like the tube-brained Trio?" he asked, but it was a halfhearted quip. Xander's gaze was flicking back and forth across the ruined front of the Magic Box, his mind ticking away measurements and materials and quantities, all those mysterious construction details that Buffy didn't understand. Nor did she want to. "It won't be easy, but it's possible, and I'll need to get my hands on some borrowed hydraulic equipment to reposition some of the support beams and the roof rafters. There ought to be some insurance money, provided the company doesn't just total it out and pay off." He frowned suddenly and glanced at Anya. "You *do* have insurance, right?"

"Of course." Anya paused for a moment, then brightened. "Hey, I'll help. You always liked me with a tool belt around my waist. Remember when I surprised you that night you came home from work, Xander? You said—"

"Not going there," Buffy cut in quickly. "Or in *there*." She pointed at the Magic Box's rubble. "My job is to find Willow and calm her down before she does any more damage to property or people. Specifically Jonathan and Andrew."

"Personally I think you should let her do the deep

fry on them," Anya said darkly. She shrugged. "I'd do it myself, but unfortunately I'm limited to mojoing the objects de affection of scorned women." She frowned thoughtfully. "Hmmmm. Perhaps I should look into their pasts, see if there are any old girlfriends—"

Xander cleared his throat. "Why don't we let Buffy handle that part, and you and I go over some plans to restore your place of business?"

Anya gave him a bright smile, her first genuine one since before Warren's shoot-out. "So we're back to the tool belt."

"Sure," Xander said obligingly. "If you want to do tool belts, I can handle it."

He glanced at Buffy, but she shook her head. "My thing seems to be to tear down, not build up. I don't think I'm wired that way. You two hammer yourself into builder's heaven—I'm off to find Willow before she finds trouble." She paused. "If I run across Spike, I'll send him over to add some muscle."

Xander rolled his eyes. "Color me joyful."

"Hey, like it or not, this is a little more than you two can deal with," Buffy said.

"Ignore Xander," Anya said. "A vampire's strength would definitely be handy right about now."

"And what about me?" Dawn demanded. "Third wheel again?"

"Oh no," Xander said. "We have a big project here. In case you don't have a career path set in your head yet, let me show you the inside job on being a carpenter."

"No—" Dawn began.

"Yes," Buffy said firmly. "Three is not a crowd, three is safety. You *will* stay with Xander and Anya."

"One of these days you're not going to be able to tell me what to do anymore," Dawn said, but all the fight had gone out of her voice. She sounded more tired than anything else.

"True," Buffy agreed. "But one of these days is not tonight." As she patted Dawn on the shoulder and left, Anya and Xander were already starting to dig through the rubble.

Chapter Five

Willow wasn't sure exactly how she found the very out-of-the-way place. She'd certainly never been there before; she was pretty well convinced that she would have remembered a place with a disgusting name like JuJu's Catbox. Obviously demon infested, it was in the basement of an old warehouse building, below storage for small metal parts and pieces. It was big on the dim and had lots of red—she liked that—although it was pretty grimy. The booths and chairs looked like they'd come out of a 1950s diner of the dead, and the metal-framed furniture—no wood, thank you very much—was tarnished with age, grease, and basementy damp.

There was a time when a place like this would have made her hair stand on end with paranoia, when she would have imagined that every hellbeast, bloodsucker, and skanky in-between human in it saw her as nothing more than tasty prey.

But not anymore.

She pushed open the door and everyone looked at her. All the chatter stalled, and the empty air just hung there, thick with unspoken comments and questions, ripe with speculation and delicious pre-rumor. She waited while everyone in the place looked her up and down, their gazes considering what she might do, evaluating her capabilities. She met each set of eyes without reservation or hesitation, and one by one, each creature turned away. When the last one was left staring into his cocktail—some disgusting-looking mix that obviously had aged blood as a base—she grinned at all of them and chose a stool on the other side of the cash register. That the stool was occupied at the time bothered her not at all.

"Go sit somewhere else," she told the spongy-faced demon sitting there. He could feel the aura of suppressed power oozing off her, and he wasn't foolish enough to protest.

She brushed the mind of the bartender and learned his name was Benny Speegle. He had a thin, narrow face with small eyes, and he reminded her of a weasel. He regarded her warily. "What'll it be, miss?" Willow knew he and the other patrons could sense her energy, because he was very careful to keep his tone respectful. She decided she could very easily get used to this Queen of the Realm thing. Oh, yeah.

Willow opened her mouth to order the first thing that came to mind—something cold and sweet and frozen like she always had—then she paused. Those things were in the past, and all of the sweet had gone out of her existence. "Wine," she said instead. Her voice was low and husky. "The darkest, driest red that you have. Something in . . . merlot."

He nodded, and when he brought her glass, Willow stopped him before he could move away. "I'm looking for something, Benny," she said. "A place."

For a moment, a very short one, the guy had looked like he wanted to mouth off. The foolish impulse died when she said his name, and he didn't bother to ask how she'd known. Right now he was thinking that someone had told her about him, or that she'd overheard someone saying it; let him believe whatever gave him comfort, but she knew the truth. The power she'd sapped out of Giles and blessed her with more effects than the fancy whizbangs of destruction and teleportation. She was . . . in *tune* with the things around her now—not truly telepathic, but *very* intuitive. Who he was—who *everyone* was— was more like an imprint on his existence than a true thought process; thus it was easy for her to pick up names, addresses, whether they'd liked their last meal. There were a lot of things easy for her to pick up now.

"Okay," Benny Speegle said. "What kind of place? To do what?"

Willow took a sip of the bitter wine and knew it was coating the inside of her mouth with dark, rich purple. She let her lips stretch in a horrific smile. "A place to call my own."

• • •

"It ain't so much," said the spongy-faced demon. Willow could hear the nervousness in his voice, could smell old blood and decayed flesh on his breath. There was a time when the smell of the blood would have disgusted her and brought to mind unpleasant memories, but tonight it didn't have any effect, and it certainly didn't frighten her. In fact, her relationship to the creatures of the world's underside had done an interesting about-face, and she rather liked the fact that this creature was afraid of *her* rather than she afraid of him. He was a big mutt of a beast, some supernatural concoction that was half zombie and half something else, and he fed on freshly dead corpses. She didn't know what the other half was—something with soft, wet-textured skin pocked with holes like a sea sponge—but the mix had a good dose of coward thrown in; for all his lumbering size, he was generally afraid to hunt his own food. So he scavenged at night and managed a solid middle-level income by renting out space in a few decrepit warehouses. Willow now stood in one of these spaces, on an abandoned second floor above an equally empty ground level.

Spongy Face—Willow had foregone the lesser demon's formal name for her own humorous label—spoke again. "'Specially for someone of your sort. The tales travel fast, ya know, and just overnight we all heard you's the big new mojorama witchy woman around."

Willow ignored the statement. She didn't have to explain herself to anyone, and she wasn't in the mood to listen to some low-level meat-muncher try to schmooze with her. He certainly wasn't anything that would either impress her or do her any good beyond this loft. "It might do," was all she said, and decided to let him simmer in his own anxiety for a little while longer. There would be prestige involved in being the one to give her a place to live, a standing protection in the underground community that couldn't be judged by dollar amount. And she had no intention of paying a dollar amount to begin with. She might grant a favor or two—*if* she felt like it—but that was all.

"It might do" was an understatement; in fact, it was perfect. Lots of great, wide-open space—how tired she'd grown of small bedrooms and the narrow spaces between crowded shelves of library books. The space before her was marvelous, filled with shadows from the support beams spaced throughout it, criss-crossed by streams of dust-filled light from the grime-covered, multipaned windows that lined the front wall. The floor was wood and deliciously creaky when they walked on it; she felt like it was talking to her with every step, whispering the secrets of those who had walked there before her, concocting premonitions of those who would come in the future.

Perfect.

"Yeah," Willow said aloud. "It'll do."

Spongy Face rubbed his hands together. "That's marvelous, just marvelous." Eons ago, in what felt like someone else's lifetime, she'd once caught a bit piece of a comedian on an old rerun of *Saturday Night Live,* Billy Crystal saying "You look mahvelous!" Spongy

Face said it the same way, and Willow wondered if he hadn't been watching a little too much late-night television in between dining out at the morgue buffet. "So," he continued, "let's talk rental. I can cut you quite the deal, you know, plus get you all kinds of amenities. I got good connections in this town. Special ones with the cleaning outfits. Say, you need furniture? Lamps? Dishes? I got it all lined up. . . ."

Willow tuned out his prattling and tilted her head to the side, considering the wide, dusty space stretching before her. After a few seconds she made a sweeping motion in the air with her left little finger and, voilà, all the dust and the grime was gone, and there it was, a beautiful warehouse apartment space just waiting to be filled with her own stuff. The windows sparkled and the floor shone and—

—and if only Tara were here to share it with her.

Willow felt her mood shift dangerously, and suddenly Spongy Face didn't seem so funny anymore, and his nonstop yammering was becoming seriously annoying.

"Oh, I see you can handle the clean-up just fine," he was saying, "but I got this friend who does decorating for a living, you know, and he's done some fine stuff for a few higher-class demons I've become acquainted with. Really jazzy stuff, lots of metal and industrial—"

"Shut up."

He must have recognized something in her voice that kicked him into an instinctive save-himself mode, because he didn't bother to finish his prattling about decorating. Instead he had the nerve—and in an off-hand way, Willow had to admire this—to again bring up the subject of rent.

"So anyway, it's a big space, but you're such the big bat's eyes around town now, that I'm thinking something low, like maybe four hundred a month or so. That ought to cover my expenses and taxes and stuff, and of course all your utilities would be included, even the trash and sewer. . . ." His voice faded away and he swallowed when he realized that she was looking intently at him. "Uh . . ."

Willow turned her gaze to the floor, all nice and golden-shiny now, leaned over, and passed her hand over a section of it. The air in front of their feet began to shimmer, and then it darkened and began to roll like a small gathering of storm clouds. The clouds turned in on themselves and finally began to show spots of color here and there, until they stretched out and formed a prone shape, a very recognizable prone shape, layered over with a startlingly large splotch of red.

Spongy Face swallowed again, this time quite audibly, as he stared at the apparition. "W-what's that?"

"Don't you recognize it?" Willow asked with acid-laced sweetness. "It's what the science fiction movies call a hologram. It's a custom one I made especially for you. It shows how you're going to look after I eviscerate you."

Spongy Face's mouth opened and closed several times, but nothing came out. Just for tickles Willow splayed her fingers and the slightly transparent image brightened and grew larger, then floated up to waist level. Willow let it hang there so the half-breed demon could study it in detail. "Now, how much did you say you wanted to rent this dump?" she asked with calculated blandness. She glanced at him, then grimaced. "Oh for heaven's sake, wipe your mouth. You're all slobbery."

Spongy Face shut his mouth with an audible snap of teeth, then scrubbed the lower half of his face across the back of one surprisingly well-pressed jacket sleeve. "S-sorry," he managed. "I was j-just a little, uh, surprised."

Willow said nothing . . . for now. But if this idiot started prattling again, she might just use a little ecto-plasmic superglue to quiet him down.

"I'm thinking that, uh, you know, since having you here might kind of class up the neighborhood, I really don't need any specific kind of monthly rent. Nothing, you know, set in stone, but hey, if you wanted to toss a few dollars my way now and then, 'cause I do have those greedy guys down at city hall wanting taxes and fees and all that kind of crap, whatever you felt you could spare, that would be terrific too."

Willow nodded. Much better. "What, your first smart decision all week?" she asked, a corner of her mouth turning up. "I'll be sure and do that."

He nodded, then pulled a couple of keys from his pocket and offered them to her. "Okay then, there you go. Two sets."

Willow looked at the keys for a long moment, and then her mouth curled into a smile. Keys—how quaint. She held out her hand and he dropped them into her palm, then watched as her fingers closed around the small pieces of cut metal. "I'll be changing the locks," she told him. Her fingers tightened into a fist and there was a brief burst of orange light from between the closed fingers; when she opened her hand, the keys were fused into a little lump of knubby metal. She tossed it to the creature and he caught it reflexively. "I won't be needing those."

Spongy Face nodded but made no move to leave. Instead he stood there, shuffling his feet, like a kid waiting for permission to go out and play.

"You can leave now."

Relief swept across the creature's face, and he turned to go so quickly that he nearly tripped over his own feet. Willow resisted the urge to help him along, deciding to save her energies for the more fruitful pursuits of furnishing her new abode. All that stuff she'd left at Buffy's house . . . it was irrelevant history, old memories of a now-discarded life. The clothes, most of the photographs, the stupid, childish memorabilia—all of it was unnecessary. At the very least, she might want a Wiccan trinket or two, a few of the rare herbs and spell ingredients; at the most, the things—very few— that had belonged to Tara. The rest of this place was brand spanking new decorating.

And oh, did she have plans for the decorating scheme.

Things would *never* be the same around Sunnydale again.

Chapter Six

"There," Xander said. "Finished and operational."

"It looks . . . awkward," Anya said. "Or commercial. Like it belongs in a department store." She, Dawn, and Buffy stood in the front hallway of Buffy's house, staring at the gadget Xander had just finished installing on the side of the staircase.

"I went to a Bed Bath & Beyond store in Los Angeles once where they had this lift thingy that would take your whole cart up to the second floor," Buffy offered. "This is like that, except with a wheelchair."

"I think it looks dangerous," Dawn said. She frowned at the small platform fastened to the steel rail that now ran up the outside bottom of the staircase. "There's no way that thing is going to support Giles's weight, much less him and a metal wheelchair. Not hanging in midair like that. He's going to fall on his head."

"And may I just say thank you for your vote of confidence," Xander said testily. "And let's not forget, 'Hey, Xander—thanks for all your hard work.'"

"Hey, Xander—thanks for all your hard work," the three of them said in unison.

Xander had to grin. "Women who follow orders. I like that."

Buffy ignored the crack and stared at the wheelchair lift. "I still can't believe we need this. It all seems so . . ."

"Unreal?" Xander pulled a handkerchief out of his tool belt and swiped at his forehead with it. It had been a full two weeks since the huge fight between Willow and Giles at the Magic Box, and his eyes still hadn't lost that vaguely shocked look. "No kidding. Somehow I had this idea that everything would magickally be okay in a couple of days, you know? Giles would wake up one sunny morning, have breakfast, then get out of bed and just start walking again like it was nothing special at all. I mean, everything's always worked out just fine in the past, so why wouldn't it be the same way now?"

"I wonder what Willow's doing," Dawn said. "Right now, while we're standing here." She backed up until she was in the living room, then sprawled on the couch. "She was so *different* the last time I saw her—"

"You can say that again," Buffy muttered. Everyone had been so preoccupied with Giles's injury that they hadn't noticed how she'd slipped out, night after night, and hunted for her former best friend. No luck so far, but now that Giles was headed home from the hospital, she was going to turn the heat on the hunt up to *high*.

"And now she's all alone, with no one to talk to or to comfort her." Dawn's eyes were wide. "I mean, think about what she went through, having Tara killed right in front of her, not being able to bring her back, and now she's lost all her friends. She has no one at all."

"Gee," Anya interjected as she came out of the kitchen and handed Xander his beer. "I wonder why *that* happened. Could it be that she suddenly turned psycho-killer witch? And that she tried to add the bodies of several longtime friends to her tally?" Her eyes flashed. "And let's not forget that she destroyed my way of making a living and left a building that's given us shelter for several years in complete ruin."

"Well, not *complete*," Xander said. He raised his bottle in a halfhearted toast. "Here's to a whole new look for the Magic Box."

"Might as well call it the Magic *Junk* Box," Anya grumbled.

"You know, that rustic, outbacky look is really the rave now," Dawn said. "You see it on the Discovery Channel all the time. And there's that whole Outback Steakhouse thing."

"I'm not interested in animal programs and medium-rare," Anya shot back. "I feel like I've moved my business to some backwoods Louisiana swamp where the local idea of a general store is to nail a bunch of boards together at the most haphazard angle possible."

"Wait a darned minute," Xander interrupted. "All my boards are nailed straight!"

Anya blinked. "Well, of course they are. I just meant that the used lumber look went out with the 1920s and Prohibition. I was there. I know. I much prefer sleek and modern."

"I'm doing what I can with the insurance money," Xander grumbled. "You didn't do much future-thinking when you chose your policy limits and—"

"I hate to interrupt your little argu-athon," Buffy broke in, "but it's time to go get Giles."

"I'm ready," Dawn said. Despite the brightness in her voice, they could all detect an undertone of fear. How was it going to be, with Giles living here with them and unable to function on his own? Speaking of insurance, his would pay for a caregiver to come in twice a day to help bathe, dress, and medicate him, and that was a whole new ball game. How were they going to deal with *that,* with a stranger or strangers hanging around and potentially being, as Giles himself would have termed it, quite meddlesome?

Xander unbuckled his tool belt and set it aside. "No time like the now time," he said. When all of them started to head for the door, he stopped them. "Whoa— we can't all go. We won't fit, not with bringing Giles and various medical paraphernalia back. So I drive and someone comes with me. That someone would be you, Buffy."

"But I want to go!" Anya cried. "Just because he

used to be her watcher doesn't give her dibs!"

Dawn was silent for a moment, then put a hand on Anya's shoulder. "It's not that," she said. "It's physical strength—being able to get Giles in and out of the car and into a wheelchair without too much trouble. Right, Xander?"

"I have plenty of strength in demon mode," Anya protested.

"Which would scare all the stethoscopes right off the unsuspecting doctors and nurses, remember?" Xander replied. He rubbed her arm but she snatched it away. "Sorry, Anya. Practicality unveils its spiky self yet again."

Buffy took a deep breath and glanced from Anya to Dawn. "Okay, then. The Giles Retrieval System is ready for pickup." Xander nodded at her and the two of them headed out the door.

Nothing about the hospital had changed, of course. It was still saturated with those same sounds, sights, and smells that Buffy so despised, although now she thought that Xander, Dawn, and Anya had grown to feel the same way. That there was no joy in coming here to get Giles just made it all the worse. If only he could've regained the use of his legs, no one would have cared about the grumpy charge nurse or the too-long wait while they hunted down the right checkout paperwork. At least they weren't in the emergency room this time, with people screaming in pain all around them and doctors who were too much business and not enough bedside manner.

Giles had called Buffy and told her he'd be ready, but the red tape added a good hour's wait to that. He'd told her on previous visits that he couldn't stand the daytime charge nurse, and seeing her in action now made Buffy understand why. She was loud, pushy, and completely overwhelming. With the circumstances what they were, Giles already wanted to get out of here; the nurse only served to horrify him more and want to speed up the process as much as possible.

The former watcher was mostly silent the whole time they had to wait, staring into space at some bleak and not-very-hopeful future that only he could imagine. Buffy had her own vision—as did Xander, no doubt—but she was sure hers was gloomy for a whole different set of reasons, none of which had to do with a sudden decrease in personal mobility. She and Xander tried the chitchat for a while, but they finally gave up and sat in silence with Giles. At least they could show their support by being there for him, and if he didn't walk to talk, then so be it.

"Here we go, all set." The nurse's pseudocheerful voice cut through their thoughts and made both Buffy and Xander jump. Giles just glowered at her, giving Buffy the distinct impression that over the past couple of weeks he'd dealt with as much of this overly chipper woman—her name tag read SHARON—as he could bear. Sharon dropped a pile of papers onto Giles's lap, and he stared down at them uncomprehendingly.

"Don't you worry your handsome little head about those, dearie," Sharon said with exaggerated sweetness. "I've taken care of everything. Are you all comfy as a bug in a rug? We'll get you right outside with your friends here."

As she stepped behind the wheelchair, Giles's face turned thunderous. It was, Buffy decided, probably the supremely stupid comparison to a comfortable bug that had done it. "I'll take him," she said quickly, and before Sharon could protest, Buffy bodily pushed her way in front of the stoutly built nurse.

"Oh, no," Sharon said firmly. "It's completely against hospital regulations for anyone but a trained professional to take a patient physically out of the hospital." She tried to move Buffy out of the way, then blinked when she discovered that even her hefty frame couldn't budge the much slighter young woman.

"He trusts *me*," Buffy said. There was a don't-screw-with-me tone to her voice that was impossible to miss.

"But I'm a trained professional," Sharon said again, this time more loudly. She looked ready to leap on top of Buffy, and her decibel level had risen to "discomfort." "How can he *not* trust *me*?"

"Maybe he, uh, just doesn't like your pin," Xander offered. He pointed to the piece of jewelry fastened to her collar; while he didn't say so out loud, he thought it looked like something a dead zombie grandmother would wear to her own funeral.

"This is a *fine* pin," Sharon snapped. "My grandmother gave me this—"

"Very nice," said Xander. "And I'm sure she was a lovely lady." Buffy was already wheeling Giles down the hall at a pace brisk enough that Xander had to trot to keep up.

Sharon was rapidly falling behind. "You come back here right *now!*" she called in a blaring voice. "You—"

But Buffy had already done a Mario Andretti around the corner with the wheelchair, and Xander was right on her heels. By the time the nurse managed to huff and puff her way in pursuit, the three of them were already safely in the elevator and headed down to the first floor.

It took two more days for Giles to snap out of it, but when he did, it was with all the painfulness of a suddenly broken rubber band.

"I refuse to be cowed by a physical disability," he announced on the third morning. "I may be confined to a wheelchair for the . . . for the rest of my life, but I will *not* be an invalid and I will *not* be useless."

Buffy and the others said nothing, merely watching him carefully. None of them had missed Giles's hesitation as he struggled to accept what the doctors had warned might be true—that he might never walk again. Inside, Buffy shuddered for him; what must it be like, to be confined for decades and decades to one small metal box? To be forced to endure the daily ministrations of a nurse you might or might not like, to have your blood checked constantly for infections you couldn't even feel you had? She might change her mind given some unforseen circumstance and terrifying monster, but right now, in this terrible moment of seeing Giles battle with his own reality, only becoming a vampire seemed more horrific.

But Giles wasn't going to give her any time to dwell on it.

"Buffy, what have you encountered on your nightly patrols?" he demanded. "Have any of the vampires talked before you staked them, tried to barter information for their lives? And what about demons? They always seem to have a handle on what's out and about before the general populace does."

Buffy blinked and forced her thoughts away from Giles's predicament. "Not much," she told him. "I haven't run into any demons at all, and to be honest, the general vampulace seems to be on a diet. I haven't had a good stake since maybe three days after you first went into the hospital."

Giles looked thoughtful, then turned his attention toward Anya. "What about you?" he asked. "Surely your vengeance demon friends have gossiped about the goings-on. Have you heard anything? Rumors? Fact? Anything?"

Anya frowned and looked down at him as if she were some kind of country club matron. "Maybe."

"Knock it off, Anya," Xander said. "This isn't some kind of boy-girl retribution board game. Monkey around here and everyone loses."

Anya nodded. "True," she finally said. "But you should count yourselves lucky I'm still in with you. People get paid big-time greenbacks for the kind of information I'm passing along here."

Dawn scowled at Anya from where she sat cross-legged on the couch. "Why is everything about you money related?" she demanded. "There are more important things in life, you know."

"Not many," Anya shot back, and then she purposely glanced away from Xander. "Though nothing really beats a good romp on the bed with—"

Xander cleared his throat. "Right. And we now bring you back to our special segment on the demon info-line."

Anya looked puzzled for a moment, and then her expression cleared. "Oh—right. Well, anyway, I heard the down and dirties are stepping very lightly these days because everyone's afraid of the new big bad in town."

Buffy raised one eyebrow. "The new big bad what?"

The look Anya shot Buffy made it clear she couldn't believe Buffy didn't already know. "The new big bad Willow, of course."

Giles tapped thoughtfully on the arm of his wheelchair. "So Willow's terrorizing everyone, is she?"

"Actually, no," Anya told him. "But they're afraid she *will,* I think. She rented a warehouse from a demon—sans rent—and has herself a permanent place of business all set up there."

Dawn tilted her head. "Sans rent? Can we do that?"

"Only if you can show your mortgage banker what he would look like if he were gutted like a fish. I understand that's the kind of slide show she gave the demon who owns the place."

Dawn made a face. "Bleh."

"So this warehouse," Buffy cut in. "It would be where, exactly?"

"That's the big secret!" Anya exclaimed. "Either no one knows for sure, or they're just not telling. I've heard zip about the actual coordinates."

"Find the demon who rented her the warehouse and we're set," Giles pointed out.

But Anya only shook her head. "Nice try, but no one's telling that, either. Apparently she terrorized him so thoroughly that he's dropped underground—maybe literally—and no one wants to take his place. That's it as far as the Anya Reporting Agency goes. From here on out, Buffy, you're on your own."

Good-bye, french fries and greasy burgers, Buffy thought as she walked out of the burger place for the last time. *I so will not miss you.*

She'd left her red- and white-striped uniform in the bathroom garbage can, and now, standing outside in clean clothes that *didn't* smell like frying oil, Buffy almost felt like there was a new world waiting for her. In a way there was: She hadn't told the others yet, but she had a whole new job lined up. This one was walking a little on the dark side, but sometimes dark times called for dark measures. Her patrols had been fruitless night after night, but that didn't mean the evil wasn't out there. Sure it was; she could *feel* it, the way a coming, unseen storm left a layer of nasty, cloying humidity on the surface of your skin. Now it was time for her to go out in the downpour. Besides, with tips she'd probably make more money, and with economics being what they were, that could only help.

She cut through two graveyards and three alleyways on the way to her first shift at the new job, but the vamps just weren't biting tonight. Without a fight or two to distract her, she was way early—too much so for the big fish to come out and play, and that was what she was aiming for. Rumor had it that her new place of employment, a nameless, grungy dive at the back end of one of the alleys along which Rack had once hidden his place, was pretty low on the scale of desirable—while it wasn't an outright demon hole, a good chunk of the clientele was less than human. This was okay by her; if she wanted the down and dirty, she didn't mind having to go down and gory to get it.

Still, at half an hour before true dark, the dead and not-quite hadn't come out to play, so there wasn't much happening. Instead of going inside, Buffy hung off to the side and stayed in the shadows, trying to see and hear what she could. Things around Sunnydale—and her home life—seemed to have settled into an uneasy quiet. Giles was quieter than before, but who could blame him? Personally she wasn't sure what to say to him anymore, couldn't find the words to comfort or encourage. Every time she started to try, her mental rehearsal told her the words were corny and sounded false, and to just keep it shut. For that, she felt about as bad as she ever had where her former watcher was concerned. How many times had he stepped up to the plate for her through the years, with not only words but deeds? Yet now there was nothing she could do to return the favor.

Dawn seemed to be okay with it, and while Buffy was relieved that her younger sister was handling things so well, she was also secretly . . . well, she wasn't sure *how* she felt about it. On the one hand, Dawn was adjusting quite well, sliding in to do perhaps even more than her share of the chores that having an invalid—and boy, didn't it hurt to apply *that* word to Giles—around the house required. On the other, Buffy couldn't help but wonder why Dawn wasn't more upset about this, why she wasn't more freaked out. The crying spells Buffy had anticipated had never materialized, and the bad behavior Buffy had dreaded —hanging out too late with friends in this so very dangerous town— had likewise not happened. Nothing, it seemed, was predictable around this place.

Well, except maybe for Anya and Xander. Sure, Buffy would never have guessed that they'd end up back together as an honest to God item, but anyone with a quarter of a brain could see they were headed toward the sack—if they weren't secretly there already. They practically exuded hormones as bad as, if not worse than, she and Riley had, once upon an eternity ago. But for them to be a *couple* again, after Xander left Anya to make her bridal trek a-la-lonely up the aisle? Even more incredible was Xander still wanting Anya even though she'd chosen to go back to being a vengeance demon.

Still, there they were, inseparable and nearly back playing house together at Xander's apartment, as if nothing had ever happened. Every day after Xander got off work, he headed to the Magic Box and pieced a little more of it back together, and then they traipsed over to Buffy's and lazed around there until around nine or so, watching the boob tube playing board games with Giles and Dawn, and keeping an eye on things while Buffy was at work. Buffy had a hard time believing it was all movie-level acting just for Giles's sake. Although only a couple of weeks had passed, the two seemed like they might be in love again. Maybe it was their proximity, the constantly being around each other at Buffy's while they all learned how to take care of Giles. Buffy didn't know what Xander had said to make Anya want to try again, but his convincing had been successful. If there was a downside, it was only that Anya had elected to stay a vengeance demon, albeit one who seemed to want to walk on the softer side of demondom and seemed more concerned with Xander and Giles than anything D'Hoffryn- or Anyanka-related. It was funny, the pathways that a person's life could sometimes take.

Buffy shuffled her feet and glanced around, but there wasn't a darned thing, alive or not, to see on the street. Speaking of strange pathways, she would have never expected to be standing around feeling vampire- and demon-deprived, yet that's exactly what was happening. Or more accurately, *not* happening. Where was the adrenaline of facing a bloodsucker who had that *Prepare to get your ass kicked* look on his face? The rush of seeing that expression snap into amazement as her trusty Mr. Pointy found a home dead center, pun *very* much intended? And speaking of bloodsuckers, where the hell was Spike, anyway? Fat lot of help he'd been, although really, he'd been pretty snappish with the attitude pre-Willow changeover.

Buffy frowned. Had he gone away for good? One part of her thought that was just as well, and good damned riddance. He'd started as a royal pain in the butt with the lovey-dovey stuff, then progressed to the I'll-prove-I-love-you-by-force crap. He'd done some damage there, and he knew it, but Buffy wasn't sure whether he regretted it or whether his failure to reach her, to *make* her return his love, had only made him angrier. Now he'd dropped completely out of sight and—

Oh . . .

Was he dead?

Buffy shook her head violently, not knowing or caring if anyone was around to see her. No, it couldn't be. She'd know, somehow, if that were so, if something that terrible had happened to him. After that scene in her bathroom, she half hated the vampire, and while she'd never had the connection to Spike that she'd had with Angel, she did feel . . . *something* for him. She *had* held a place for him in her heart, although right now she couldn't say if that still existed or if it was just habit born of his being around so much. She'd been shocked and hurt at the time, but now that she was past the shock of his attempted rape, she'd welcome the chance to give him a taste of just how furious she was over that. No, Spike was *not* dead. . . .

But Buffy couldn't shake the feeling that something equally as bad had happened to him.

"You comin' in, or are you gonna stand out here all night? It ain't even like you're standing out here taking a smoking break."

The grating voice cut into her thoughts like barbed wire, and Buffy had to stop herself from spinning around and shoving her fist down the throat of the man who'd come out of the bar's doorway. He was big, much bigger than she, and he probably had some demon blood in there somewhere that he was hiding, but she could still have done it.

But hey, it wasn't a good idea to go pounding your boss into the concrete on the first day of a new job.

She put on her best and brightest smile. "Headed right in. I was just getting some fresh air before my shift."

"Nice little girl like you'll run into trouble standing around out here," he retorted. "At least inside, folks know you're under my protection."

"Right," she said, and punctuated things with a nod as she stepped past him and into the smoke-filled darkness of the club.

Nice little girls like her.

If he only knew . . .

Chapter Seven

Not satisfied with the second floor, Willow took over the entire warehouse.

It was the security thing. Sooner or later, she knew Buffy was going to find out where she was. Then the Slayer would come looking for her, wanting to make everything right or fix everything or whatever. Buffy was always trying to do just that—fix things. Willow wasn't sure if Buffy realized it yet, but there wasn't a repair job in the world that was going to work this time around. Tara was dead—every time that ugly fact flashed through her mind, Willow winced—and so was Warren. Unless Buffy could find a way to unflay him, Warren was nothing but worm food and fertilizer, just the way Willow wanted him.

As for Tara . . . Willow had other plans for that.

Tara would have liked this place, Willow thought.

Well . . . maybe. There were lots of flowers and feminine things, but there were lots of darkly magickal things too, things that would never have been found in their lives before Tara's death, objects that Willow had agreed never to touch after her walk on the addictive side of magick. Jars of pieces and parts of things better left unnamed, spices and herbs generally forbidden to all but the most powerful, hard-to-find spell books and artifacts that could cause immeasurable damage and allow incredible wickedness in the wrong hands. And it was exactly that "incredible" part that Willow would, given enough time, find and bend to her will.

Because she would *not* be denied.

Why, Willow wondered as she walked from one end of the loft to the other, couldn't Buffy and Giles and the others understand that? They should be supporting her instead of condemning her. Wait, that wasn't really accurate. They hadn't actually *condemned* her at all, but they *were* continually scheming to find ways to stop her, to change her mind about Jonathan and Andrew. Giles probably thought he was the perfect example, him with his live-and-let-the-dead-live attitude about Angel, who had killed the lovely Jenny Calendar just when she and Giles were about to take their relationship into serious mode. Giles, Willow thought, was a fool, and there was no better example than Warren to show how Willow would have handled Angel had she been in Giles's English shoes.

Why could they not realize that what *they* could do on the forgive-and-forget scale didn't apply to her? Why couldn't they just accept what she needed to do to clear her heart? But no. They wanted to change her, to force her to forgive.

As Giles would no doubt say: Not bloody likely.

And so her place was finished, and here she was, standing in the middle of it. Everything around her gave off an air of soothing darkness—lots of black-red and burnt umber, the hues of fire and anger, yet still somehow calming to her soul, perhaps because of the results they promised she would someday achieve. The huge space was shot through with steel support beams at evenly spaced intervals, which she had wrapped in gauzy fabric to soften the sharpness of their metal edges. Odd-shaped jars of every size sparkled along a hundred shelves, their dust-free surfaces reflecting the light from an abundance of ornate shaded lamps and candelabrum. A decadently overstuffed couch faced the rough-hewn fireplace, and pictures of Tara sat side by side with Willow's most precious dark magick statuettes on the massive mantel. At the farthest end of the side space was her sleeping area, its centerpiece a king-size bed over which hung a draped canopy of the same delicate fabric entwined throughout the loft.

The sight of it—that massive, beautiful, and utterly empty bed—made Willow totally furious.

It wasn't so much *this* bed, but what it represented. A bed was supposed to be a place of love and laughter, the symbol of everything that comes together in a relationship. Lust was only a part of it, yet it was that part that could make or break the strongest of loves— witness her slight infidelity to Oz with Xander, and how it had ultimately strengthened her relationship with Oz but destroyed Cordelia's affection for Xander. Oh, and let's not forget how Oz had gone overboard in avenging himself, even unintentionally, with Veruca.

Willow swallowed and found herself fighting a stinging in her eyes. It was in just such a shared bed that she and Tara had traded their most tender and magickal moments. Sure, they'd made love, but they'd also laughed and talked for hours, trading childhood memories and stories of which no one else in the Scooby Gang had even the faintest notion. They had confessed fears and feelings and dreams that Willow was now supposed to accept were lost for eternity—a double lifetime built and then crushed by fate in a single devastating moment. It wasn't just the sex, but the love and the laughter, and the *forever* of it.

Or what should have been forever.

"Look at this place," Willow said aloud. Her voice echoed unpleasantly through the overly large space, bouncing from wall to wall the same way she sometimes felt her emotions did. "It's like a Wiccan dream palace. But it's an *empty* palace. There's no Tara, no love. I'm the queen of nothing and no one."

And never had something like that been more true. Willow had only to think of what she had done to the building, converting its oversized, empty downstairs space to one big maze of a security system and layering cloaking spells across the outside of the upstairs windows so that they couldn't be seen by passersby, human or otherwise.

Such drastic measures to protect herself when really, with all her power, why did she need to?

Her gaze focused once more on the bed, and her face twisted. She would *not* be alone in this place, would *not* see it be nothing but a warehouse for Wiccan supplies and an office in which she did little more than sit while she worked. Yes, she had a massive list of things to do in order to accomplish what she wanted, but where was it written that she must be alone while she did it?

Her red-tinted gaze swept the loft again, and the dark scowl on her lips melted into a darker smile. "Pets," she purred. "That's what I need. A couple of . . . *special* pets."

In the center of one wall was an antique worktable, eight feet long and made of hand-rubbed cherry that glowed in the soft light from one of the windows that stretched all the way to the ceiling. Willow went to it and cleared a large area in its center, then ran her hand across the five-foot space she'd left herself. Beneath her palm she could feel the grain of the wood change as she touched it, rising to form the peaks and valleys and structures of Sunnydale and the surrounding area. When she'd gone end to end, there was a low but three-dimensional map in front of her, and she couldn't help but be proud of her work. There was the high school, the police station and city hall, and all those lovely cemeteries. Over here was the Bronze and the warehouse district where she now resided, Buffy's house, the Magic Box—admirable job of rebuilding in progress there by Xander—the hospital, Xander's apartment. Fully detailed, right down to expanses of green for the parks and little bumps of pseudometal for the playgrounds. It just needed the final touch.

On one of the shelves was a tiny, ornate dish made of heavy green glass. Willow took it down and unscrewed its lid, then dipped her fingers into the glowing, powdery crystals it contained and held them over the map she'd made.

"A pinch of this will tell me true," she whispered. *"My lovely pets . . . now where are you?"*

The crystals sifted downward and spread, and pinpricks of light instantly appeared over the tabletop map.

Willow smiled as she watched. There, in glowing white, were Buffy and Giles and the others. Some might construe white to be a shade of power, but personally Willow had come to believe it meant there was something essential lacking, no *zing* in a being's soul. Case in point: There she was herself, a spot of fiery red floating over her armored loft. Sprinkled here and there around the magickal layout were dots of butter yellow and pale green, blues, purples, oranges—just about every color of the rainbow. She watched in particular for two certain dark spots—Jonathan and Andrew—but they were nowhere to be seen. They were still out of her range, but it was only a matter of time.

Scanning, she finally found a couple of things that caught her interest.

One was slightly outside the edge of town and on the far end of one of the oldest cemeteries, a roiling pinprick of reds and oranges. So nice—the shifting meant anger, a creature of fight and spice, just what she needed to pick up the mood around here. The other spot of light was very close to the same, except it was layered over with a shroud of cool blue, as if whatever anger existed inside this being had been brought to bear under an iron will. The concept intrigued her— what kind of creature could do that, control its innermost rage so that it could walk among men in daylight or dark? She might have thought it was Angel, but, like Jonathan and Andrew, he was beyond her grasp . . . unless, of course, he was paying an unannounced visit to his ex's town.

As Willow pondered this question, the other point of light suddenly changed, and her eyes widened as it, too, was overshot by another shade. How strange—the roiling black-red, the color of a mourning rose, suddenly blossomed over with white, the shade that up until now had belonged solely to Buffy and the others in her circle. Still, like the other one, its undercolor could not be completely dispersed, only masked.

Yes, Willow decided, these two beings, whoever or whatever they were, would do quite nicely to keep her company.

It took two hours for Willow to get the spells ready and the commands right, and once done, it would probably be another six before the smell of smoke and brimstone fully vanished from the loft. How sweet it was to be able to do things like this without scrounging for energy or thinking guilty thoughts—she had Giles and his jolt of seemingly endless power to thank for that— and never feel so much as a glitch in her own reserves. Protection spells, power shots and three-dimensional locator maps were all cool beans, but when it came right down to it—

Wow, she thought. *Would you take a look at my two new pets?*

"Hi, guys," Willow said cheerfully to the two confused men sprawled on the floor in front of her feet. The spell that had yanked them from where they were and whisked them over here must have done a dilly of a job on their physical bodies, not to mention giving the old psyche a good jitter. Neither one seemed able to speak, and that was just fine with Willow; she had no doubt that once they came to their senses, they were going to be a handful. But then, what fun was a dull pet? Of course, finally knowing who they were at least answered her question about the one who could control his anger. She remembered that now, and how impressed she'd been, then how disappointed when that so-called control had failed. Did he have it back? It didn't matter, because she had grand plans that would make all that self-discipline and training be, alas, for naught.

She walked across the floor and grabbed the smaller one by the back of his collar, then dragged him to the wall to the left of the fireplace and snapped a pair of steel manacles around his wrists. Still woozy, he helped a bit by automatically trying to push himself along, not realizing he was on his way to being chained. His eyes rolled when he looked at her, and she was a little hurt that there wasn't any recognition in them. No matter; it would come.

The other pet was a little heavier, but then he was in worse shape. Willow wasn't sure exactly what had happened to him right before she'd wrenched him through the ether, but he must have had a hell of a jolt.

Not only was he barely coherent, but also he looked like he'd been thoroughly beaten. Bruises crisscrossed his bare upper body, he had bite marks and gashes everywhere, one eye was black and swollen almost shut, and he had what looked like a huge burned spot that covered almost his entire upper left chest.

"Tsk tsk," Willow said as she finally wrestled his nearly limp form into place on the other side of the massive fireplace, well out of reach of his new companion. "Such a bad boy you must have been. Obviously you had no supervision. Not to worry, dear. That's all going to change. From now on, Mama will watch over you." She snapped the other set of steel manacles around his wrists, after also making sure he was safely out of reach of any sunlight. He squinted at her, then shook his head as he tried to clear his thoughts.

"Willow . . . ?"

The sound of her name made Willow beam. "Excellent!" she exclaimed. "I was starting to get concerned you'd been permanently damaged."

The pet on the other side of the room coughed at the voices, then lifted his head. Realization flowed into his face. "Willow?"

She clapped her hands, delighted, then spread her palms in a mock gesture of presentation. "Welcome to your new positions in life as my little pets." She smiled at each of them. "I think you two have already met, but since you both seem to be a bit out of sorts right now, let me make the introduction, just in case.

"Spike the vampire, meet Oz the werewolf."

• • •

"So fun," Willow murmured. She'd made herself a little sitting area in front of the fireplace, and from her comfy position she could sit with a cup of spiced tea and keep a watchful, parental-type eye on her new adoptees. They were very out of reach of each other— a necessity, since werewolves were the enemies of just about everything but themselves. And seeing as how she'd put a whammy-smackity spell on Oz to keep him in perpetual werewolf state—she thought he was much more fun this way—it was a good idea to separate the two of them. Besides, she enjoyed his growling and snarling a lot more than all the speeches about right and wrong, blah blah blah. Eventually the wolf in him had calmed down; now he waited, and watched, and occasionally let out a low, grumbling growl.

Mouth-wise, Spike had been interesting but ultimately annoying. For some ungodly reason, he was all whiny now, blathering on about guilt-this and guilt-that, while at the same time still being out of touch with what had happened. In fact, neither one of her pets seemed to know about Tara, and Willow wasn't interested in platitudes or pity—it just made her even more angry—so she wasn't going to tell. As for Spike, she'd finally had enough and put a few stitches across his lips like she had Warren's. She was growing quite fond of that method of enforcing silence, and the whole Frankenstein stitch-face thing was kind of amusing. Now there they were, lying quietly and waiting for her next whim.

Yes, it had definitely been a good idea to get some company around here.

Chapter Eight

There wasn't time to dwell on how different this job was from her old burger-slinging one. Buffy registered the changes, but only in a buzz-by-your-brain kind of way. Whereas before she'd been frying half a dozen greasy burgers and saying "You want fries with that?" now the spiel was a rapid-fire listing of their eight kinds of beer and "If you want frozen and sweet, get it at the Bronze. But hey, we got hot wings that'll knock ya right under the table!" The clientele was as opposite from the Doublemeat Palace as an honor student was from a city gangbanger. Having been used to the unflattering overlit expanse of the fast-food place, the *ding* of the cash register drawer, and the squawking of the drive-through speakers, Buffy now had to adjust to an environment where she could barely see where she had to step (and no telling *what* might be down there in the black shadows at floor level), the grease smell was heavier and mixed with loads of cheapie perfume and sweat, and the orders were punctuated by raucous laughter and frequent insults.

But the money was good, and the information had the potential to be excellent.

Buffy checked her bar slips, then shouldered her way past a couple of biker types, ignoring the risqué comment one of them muttered in her ear as she passed. Her first night here had been an ordeal of gritted teeth, and she'd lost count of the times she'd stopped herself from rearranging the really small brains of the patrons who'd had less-than-intelligent comments to make about her body, her clothes, her hair—the blonde thing was always good for some quarter-wit no-education-level joke. But she'd managed, oh yes. Her gravelly throated boss was a guy named Ash, another ex-biker who was older than the people who frequented his establishment; the passing years had given him more of a business mindset and made him think ahead to whether he wanted to spend his fifties-plus years on the back of a cranky Harley Davidson or in a nice little middle-income house. Even so, his tolerance and patience levels were about the same as when he'd been a twenty-year-old hell-raiser, so if she wanted to keep this new job, Buffy knew she was going to have to round-shoulder the jibes and the cracks, let them roll right off her like rain.

At least until the dirty one with the ZZ Top hair and beard pinched her butt as she walked past his table.

Okay, she could live with the inane jokes—"Hey,

what did the dumb blonde say when you asked her what kinda new car she bought? A blue one!"—and the ribald laughter, but fingers on her body?

Not in *this* universe.

Not in *any* universe.

Without hesitating, Buffy snagged the guy's hand and twisted it clockwise until it turned into a nice, tight wristlock. With a grunt of surprise, Mr. Grabby felt his upper body turn opposite her motion, and he found himself doubled over with his elbow bent and his hand snugged painfully against the small of his back. For a long moment he simply stood there while his friends, obviously just as surprised as he was, stared at him. From their expressions they obviously couldn't believe some little blonde girl had done this.

Then all hell broke loose.

Mr. Grabby caught Buffy off guard by dropping to his knees and rolling sideways, pulling her with him. His other two pals at the table jumped to their feet at the same time, upending the table and sending a pile of full and empty beer bottles flying. Even though she was dragged down, Buffy refused to let go of the offending fingers, preferring to give them a nice, hard twist, and the goon gave a satisfying yelp. One of the others swung at her, and she swung Mr. Grabby around to take the punch. It connected nicely with his jaw, and when he went limp in Buffy's grip, she released him and let him fall to the grubby floor. The guy who'd hit him looked dismayed, but only for a second; then he lunged for Buffy at the same time the third one did. She ducked under a punch and threw her own well-timed uppercut; it was just too bad it was too dark for anyone else to appreciate how she knocked one man into the other like a bowling ball. Fifteen seconds after the first fool had thought he could get a free touchy-feely, all three of them were at floor level. Two of those were out cold, and the third had been bonked hard enough to make him sit there and blink at her in confusion.

Buffy dusted off her hands and straightened up, then realized that the rest of the joint had gone silent as the other patrons gaped at her. She winced and retrieved her serving tray as an opening parted in the crowd and Ash lumbered through. The big ex-biker's face was flushed with anger, and Buffy thought she could see steam curling out of his ears. *Damn,* she thought, *there goes another job.*

"Buffy," he rumbled as he stared down at the pile of people, "I guess I didn't make it clear that we don't beat on the customers around here."

"Sorry," she offered. "It was a reflex. He pinched me."

One of Ash's eyebrows lifted, and then he turned to glower at the slowly recovering Mr. Grabby. "You're a dumbass, Clarkson," he said. "Told you a hundred times not to touch the help." He gave the guy a half-hearted kick in one boot-covered ankle, then shook his head and turned back to Buffy. "As for you . . . I'm sorry 'bout that, but even so, I can't have a hotheaded waitress. It's bad for business."

Buffy's face fell, but then she brightened. "Okay, so I suck as a waitress, but how about as a hotheaded bouncer? Well, really, I'm not so hotheaded, but I can handle anything that comes in here."

Ash shook his head. "Nice try, Buffy, but getting over on one set of drunken fools doesn't make a résumé." He reached to pull the tray out of her hand. "When they show up primed for belligerence and they haven't even *started* drinking, it's a whole different story."

"You think so?" She gave the tray a smart spin that made it slap his hand out of range, then tucked it neatly under her left arm.

He scowled and reached for it again. "Don't give me a hard time, girl. Just go on back to your job flippin' burgers—"

It took Buffy two seconds.

She passed his outstretched hand to her right, then grabbed his wrist and rolled his arm until the palm of his hand was facing up, all the while keeping his elbow pulled straight. Ash grunted in surprise and automatically bent at the waist to lessen the pain; when he did, Buffy stepped between his legs from the rear, hooked his right one with her foot and pulled. Off balance, he went forward and down, and all she had to do to help him along was give him a gentle little push. After all, he *was* her employer. Through it all, she never dropped her tray.

"Would you like a beer with that?" she asked sweetly. A second later she released him and stepped back.

His face thunderous, Ash turned back to face her and opened his mouth to retort. But whatever he'd been about to say faded as the corners of his eyes began to crinkle in amusement. "Maybe I *could* use someone working the door, and it sure couldn't hurt to have a knockout blonde doing it." He rubbed his elbow thoughtfully, and this time when he held his hand out for the tray, Buffy handed it over. "Tell you what, we'll try it for a week and see how it goes. You can start by cleaning out this garbage. They're all banned until next Friday night."

With that, Ash turned and stalked off. Buffy didn't wait for any more instructions—it would take an idiot not to figure that this was his first test to see how she did in her new position. It wasn't so hard—she bent and hauled the two who were down on the floor up by the backs of their collars, then pulled them toward the door. The third one's jaw dropped at the sight, and Buffy caught him in her gaze. "You don't follow me out of here right now, I'm going to turn you into something that resembles *that*." She nodded toward a reddish pile of smashed hot wings next to his left hand. "Got it?" He swallowed hard and nodded, then pushed to his feet and trailed after her.

At the door Buffy threw the first two into the alley, then gave the third one a little shove to add emphasis to the whole situation. "You heard Ash," she said. "Don't show your faces around here for a week."

Mr. Grabby stumbled to his feet, then turned and gave her a defiant stare. "Only reason you got away with that, missy, was you caught me and my boys by surprise."

Buffy grinned. "Think you can take me?"

"I *know* I could."

She shrugged. "You just keep believing that. In the meantime, whether you can or can't, it won't get you back inside until the end of day seven. So—*ack!*"

One of Mr. Grabby's buds had hung back a little, and now he'd snuck up behind her, nabbed her arms and pinned them back. "Payback time, Clarkie. Come and get it. I'll hold her down."

Clarkson shambled forward, balling up his fists. "You think this is funny, you blonde bimbo? I'll show you funny."

Buffy pressed her lips together and waited, letting him come closer. A little more, and . . .

Now.

She let the idiot holding her be her balance, and she kicked her way up the front of Clarkson's body. Her final kick was a heel to the bottom of his jaw that sent him spinning sideways. He crashed to the ground and lay there, groaning around his bleeding mouth, as Buffy twisted hard and freed herself from his friend's hold. On her final revolution she back-fisted her former captor hard enough so that his head cracked against the wall behind him; he slid down the bricks, blinked once, and passed out.

Buffy turned and smiled sweetly at the last guy. "That's two down. Care to guess who's gonna be number three?"

But number three was backing away, deciding that retreat was the better choice here, and never mind that he'd be leaving his two pals behind. Even so, his eyes were calculating, as if he couldn't wait to get something over on her, and Buffy had had just about enough of this pinch-and-punch-on-the-Slayer event. Before he could turn tail and actually run, she reached forward and yanked him off his feet.

This guy was the opposite of his ZZ Top wanna-be friend. He looked like a skinhead, an older version of one of those snaky high school creeps you just knew was masterminding some disastrous ambush that was going to leave a whole bunch of people seriously hurt. On the right man, the right kind of tattoo could be extremely hot; this lamebrain had badly lettered words like "death" and "kill" inked across his knuckles in handwriting so shaky the print looked like it'd been drawn by a four-year-old. There were a few more tats on his neck and face: small, blurred blue dots of the same type that Buffy had occasionally seen mirrored on gang members—these she recalled from visiting her dad in Los Angeles, where the gangs' crimes of the evening had been plastered on the six o'clock news. Above the collar of his dirty tank T-shirt the name "Tommy" meandered across his right collarbone in the same childish blue-black letters.

"If I were you, Tommy," Buffy said, going for the assumption that it wasn't someone else's name he'd had permanently engraved on his skin, "I'd just stay right where you are and not take the chance on irritating me any more." She tilted her head and looked at him with mock solemnity. "I can be *very* difficult to get along with if you get on my bad side. Know what I mean?"

He muttered something at her, so Buffy gave him a shake. She saw Clarkie off to the side trying to get up and gave him an offhanded side-kick that ensured he wasn't going to bother her during her upcoming conversation with his not-so-loyal friend.

"Now," she continued, "where was I? Oh yeah—I was explaining how I could be easily mollified by the passing of a little information."

Tommy squinted at her, not understanding. "What?"

Buffy pushed her face closer to his, then wished she hadn't when she caught a whiff of his breath. "In-for-MA-tion," she said loudly. "As in, I ask you questions and you give me answers. The *right* answers. Capeesh?"

A blink, a moment for the rusty head gears to catch and turn the brain wheels, and then Tommy finally nodded. "Uh . . . okay."

"Good," Buffy said, but didn't let go of his shirt. "Now, I'm looking for someone. A redhead—"

Tommy smirked. "You want a date? I can get you—"

Buffy smacked him. "Are you *trying* to bleed?"

"*Ow!* Okay, okay! A redhead what?"

"Well, maybe she used to be a redhead," Buffy amended. "She might have black hair now. Anyway, she's a woman of power. Really *serious* power, the kind that makes things happen to weasels like you and your pals."

For a man who'd been belligerent and stupidly brave only a moment or two before, Tommy suddenly had quite the trapped-like-a-rat look. "I don't know nothin' about nothin'."

Buffy shook her head sadly. "Did I mention she's not the only one with power?" She grabbed the front of his shirt with both hands, hauled him off his feet, then slammed him brutally against the wall. Tommy's teeth snapped together and his breath *whooshed* out of his chest; somewhere beneath his dirty shirt, there was a faint crack in the vicinity of his ribs, and he gave a cry of pain.

"Oh my," Buffy said. "Did I hurt you?" She sounded anything but regretful, and she didn't let go. His feet were still dangling.

"Okay!" Tommy gasped. "I've heard of her—I ain't seen her myself, but me and the boys have heard the dirt."

"Wonderful," Buffy said with a bright smile. She let him down until just the tips of his dirty shoes were touching the ground, enough to help him stand, but not enough to give him balance to kick. "I just need to know where she is so I can stop by and say hello. You know how it is with old friends."

"Sure." Tommy's head bobbed up and down. "Sure, I know. Old friends."

"And this old friend of mine would be where exactly?" Buffy asked. She gave him a mild push back against the wall for emphasis. "I could really use a physical address. It makes people much easier to locate."

Tommy gave another wheeze of discomfort. "I dunno the address *address,* but the word in the underground is that she rented her a place over in the warehouse district, one of them two-story jobbies that she's gone and gussied up all real fancy-like. I hear you can't miss it from the outside—stands out real bright." He squirmed in Buffy's grasp. "I told you what I know, blondie. C'mon—lemme go."

Buffy ignored his request. "And, of course, when I drop by, I'd want it to be a surprise." She blinked at him, looking devilishly innocent. "The thing is, can I count on you and your palsies on the ground there to keep your traps shut?"

"Oh, definitely." Tommy was nodding again, this time more vigorously. "Won't say a word, nuh-uh. We—"

"Sometimes I like to play with weapons," Buffy cut in matter-of-factly. His eyes widened, and she caught his gaze and held it. "Knives. Pointed wooden sticks—I like those in particular. You ever get poked with a wooden stick, Tommy? A really *sharp* one?"

He gulped. "Uh, n-no, I—"

"Good." She let go of his shirt and Tommy grunted as his feet dropped the rest of the way to the ground. "Let's keep it that way, shall we? I know you won't mention to anyone that I asked about this. Not even your friends when they wake up." She patted him on one shoulder hard enough to make his entire body vibrate. "Will you?"

"No!" Finally he sounded absolutely sincere. "No—not ever, not a word!"

"Excellent. You go on home. . . ." She glanced over at Clarkie and the other one, who were finally coming to. "But get this mess up and out of my alley first."

• • •

Tommy hadn't been exaggerating when he'd said Willow's new digs would be easy to spot once you knew the right area to check. Standing in the parking area by the building that *had* to be it, Buffy couldn't help but be impressed. While it might not have been Buffy's personal choice of location, Willow had clearly done a lot with what was available.

This building was just one in a mini-landscape of industrial gray block structures surrounded by concrete-covered ground and lots of black and rusting metal— signs, iron bars, disused machinery, half-crushed metal barrels that had once held who knew what kind of putrid chemicals and were now used as little more than holders for the occasional midnight fires set by transients.

But, of course, Willow's building was an island unto itself. It glistened in the light of the new moon, reflecting the stray streetlight beam and the starshine as if its surface, which was streaked with dark blue and green swirls, had been coated with mirrorlike paint. There were no windows that Buffy could see, either on the first or second floors, and the only way in was a single door in the center of the first floor. As it was, she almost missed finding that, so well did its edges fit with the walls around it. And as Buffy had expected, there was no doorknob. Willow's sociability levels had definitely gone recluse the last couple of weeks.

But who needed a doorknob, anyway?

It took Buffy about ninety seconds to find a piece of beat-up metal rod that was suitable to use as a pry bar. Still, it wasn't easy, and it took her a full ten minutes of huffing and puffing and looking over her shoulder to see if someone—maybe someone answering to Willow—was going to try and stop her. No one did, but the door itself did a damned good job on its own; at the end of that ten-minute stretch, all Buffy had managed to do was bend up one small area below the bottom hinge. No matter; that was enough to finally give the pry bar something to brace against, and Buffy shoved the metal piece under the edge of the opening and heaved with all her might.

The bottom third of the door screeched as the metal pulled outward, more and more, until there was enough of a gap that Buffy thought she could get her body through the opening. She dropped the pry bar and squeezed through, twisting not only to avoid the sharp edges, but also in case there was something along the lines of undesirable waiting for her on the other side. She felt a blast of triumph as she finally got to stand up on the other side, but that disintegrated as she gaped at her surroundings.

Plenty of light.

Plenty of mirrors.

Ten minutes to get inside—and less than one to get completely, utterly lost.

Chapter Nine

"I didn't think I was *ever* going to find my way out of there," Buffy told Giles and the others. "I felt like I was in some kind of demonic fun house maze, and I never found a way to the second story. There were hundreds of mirrors and glass windows in every direction. I went in the front door—the *only* door—and ten steps later I couldn't find it again when I tried to turn back. Even a narcissist would get overwhelmed in that place."

Giles didn't say anything for a long moment; he just sat there thinking with his chin on one hand. "Interesting," he finally allowed. "I rather think it's a symbolic structure, a representative of Willow trying to find her true self again but being too lost and confused to do so. Instead she's found yet another incarnation of herself, and this has muddied her thinking even more."

Sitting comfortably on Buffy's sofa next to Anya, Xander snorted. "Sorry, but I don't see Willow doing the metaphor right now, Giles. The only new 'self' Willow's found is Queen Vengeance."

"Really, Buffy," Anya put in. "What were you thinking would happen if you found her, anyway? Repentance? A big dose of sappy 'I'm so sorrys'? The way things have been going, if the least she did was kick your ass and throw you out on your head, you'd be able to count yourself lucky."

"No kidding," Dawn agreed. "Look at what she did to the Magic Box and Gi—" She broke off her sentence, but not before the rest of it hit home. Her pretty face went red. "I'm sorry, I didn't mean to say that."

Giles waved a hand dismissively. "Don't be absurd, Dawn. I am what I am now, and we can't all be tiptoeing about as if stating that fact will hurt my feelings." Still, there was an undercurrent of pain in his voice, a shadow of suffering across his eyes as he looked back at Buffy. "Buffy, I think Anya asked a valid question. What *were* you planning on doing if you found Willow?"

Buffy opened her mouth to answer, but nothing came out. What, exactly, *had* been the point of going over there? She had plenty of answers to that question—so many, in fact, that she couldn't fixate on one to blurt out. Because of Willow and what she had done, lives had been changed, lives had been lost—not just Warren's, but Giles's. Maybe he wasn't dead, but an entire segment of his life was gone as surely as if Willow had killed him. And while it wasn't in Buffy's job description to punish

Willow for these things, there was a big part of her that really wanted to do just that.

Yet, what would that accomplish? It wouldn't bring Warren back any more than Warren's death would bring Tara back. It wouldn't make Giles magickally walk again, and it wouldn't instantly re-create the Magic Box like those wacky little sponge pills the kids used to drop in water and *poof!* suddenly there was a dinosaur, or a skeleton, or a fill-in-the-blank toy figure.

No, none of that would happen. It wouldn't fix or change anything. She'd still be working as a bouncer at a scuzzy little hangout instead of slinging patties at the Doublemeat Palace. Funny—neither job description had shown up on the Career Day tests in high school, although she supposed the bouncer gig was probably the closest she'd ever get to fulfilling the test results that said she'd be good in law enforcement.

"Buffy!"

"Huh—what?" She jerked and realized that everyone was staring at her. Oops. "Sorry. I was just . . . thinking."

"About how to answer my question, I hope," Giles said testily.

"I guess I need to try to convince her to come back," Buffy finally said. "To us. To . . . the good side."

There was a beat of silence as the others thought about this, and then they all started talking at once.

"I hate to poop on the party," Anya said, "but she killed somebody, remember? There's no coming back from that."

"And like you haven't?" Xander demanded. "The Bible is full of stories about repentance and being saved."

"This isn't the Bible," Giles said. "It's—"

"People can repent," Buffy protested. "Depending on how they feel inside. Look at Angel."

"Oh, please. He goes back and forth like a metronome," Dawn scoffed. "This week he's good, tomorrow he's bad. It's like an every-other-Tuesday thing."

"If I can get a word in here," Giles began. "I think Willow is—"

"She's crazy, that's what she is," Anya snapped. "Crazy with grief and anger. And Buffy, if you're smart, you'll stay out of her way for about two years. Maybe by then she'll calm down enough to where she loses the urge to rearrange the anatomy of anyone who gets in her way."

"Wait?" Buffy demanded incredulously. "You're joking, right? And what about Andrew and Jonathan?"

"I say they get what they deserve," Dawn said. She punched one of the couch pillows for emphasis.

"They don't deserve to *die,*" Buffy insisted. "They might be idiots, but they didn't kill anyone or shoot anyone. In fact, they didn't even seriously *hurt* anyone— that was all Warren."

"If anyone cares to know *my* opinion," Giles cut in, "I think you should stay away from her, at least for now."

"Well, I don't agree," Buffy said.

"Buffy, her power is too great," Giles said. He

actually sounded a little desperate. "You saw what happened, what she did to the Magic Box and to *me*." He gestured sharply at his useless legs. "Do you really want to take a chance on ending up like this?"

"I have to take chances," Buffy told him. "That's what a slayer does, remember? If I don't step out on the plank, who will?" Her gaze raked each of them. "Is there anyone else here more qualified to stand up to her?" She lifted her chin at Anya. "You're the only other person who even comes close, but even being all demony, would you bet you'd win?"

Anya chewed on her lower lip before eventually answering. "No. Even with vengeance demon abilities, I don't think I would." She shrugged. "And let's be honest. I don't feel like convincing her to put her halo back on. After what she did to my Magic Box, I'd like her to be the nail and me the hammer."

"We're fixing it," Xander said.

"Sure," Anya agreed, but there was nothing particularly happy in her voice. "Nothing like going to work every day and looking at what used to be."

"In any case," Buffy continued, "I don't believe—I *won't* believe—that Willow can't be saved. I think she's on the borderline of good and evil, and that we can convince her to step back to our side."

Dawn snorted. "Good luck. You talk like she teetered around there awhile. She made a choice, remember? She could have gone either way and she specifically opted for the shadowed side. If you don't watch out, she might pull you down with her."

"I've been tempted by a lot worse," Buffy said.

"It's not even an issue." She strode over to the front closet and pulled open the door, then dug around on the floor for a bit until she found what she wanted. In another minute she was standing with a couple of sturdy nylon ropes in hand, along with a heavy aluminum hook. She gave Giles and the others a big, brave smile.

"Time to go climbing."

Back at the ground-level doorway to Willow's private warehouse, Buffy wasn't sure if finding that the door she'd damaged on her last visit still hadn't been repaired was a good sign or not. She touched the bent metal thoughtfully and wondered if Willow had even been here since then; although Buffy had forced the twisted-up edge back into place as best she could, no one paying even a fraction of attention would miss the fact that the warehouse had been broken into. Then again, with the interior so difficult to navigate, perhaps Willow didn't care. In reality, though, Buffy thought her former—was she really that?—friend would have been just anal enough to want the building to be perfect.

In any event, Buffy knew better than to try going in this way again. Instead she backed up a few feet, tested the knot she'd crafted around the looped end of the metal hook, then pitched it up and over the edge of the roof. It sailed high and over, landing with a solid-sounding thump. Buffy gave it a second or two to stop rolling around, then carefully began to pull the nylon rope toward her, firm enough to slide the hook past

anything movable, but not so fast that it would bounce
and skip past a possible solid stopping point. Ultimately it wouldn't come forward any more, and when
she tugged harder, she decided it would indeed hold
her weight.

Buffy glanced around a final time, but nothing
moved within the shadows around the buildings.
Really, she would have preferred a graveyard over this
place, which in itself was just that—a place where the
remnants of old machines, their metal pieces and parts,
went to decompose and die. Even with all the tomb-
stones, shade trees, decorative statues, hedges, and
mausoleums, a cemetery had fewer dark places to hide
than this area, and it certainly had fewer things that
could be used as a weapon. Now, as she hauled herself
higher and higher above the ground, Buffy could register all the places with ambush potential—there were at
least a dozen spots where she could have easily been
jumped and pummeled. The terrain spread out below
looked more like a war zone than any cemetery she'd
ever been in, and she definitely felt a surge of relief
when she was able to swing herself up and over the top
edge of the roof.

But the rooftop entryway Buffy had hoped to
find—maybe something for a maintenance man or air-
conditioner guy to gain access to equipment—just
didn't exist. There were vents and shafts and pipes here
and there, but no big equipment, and certainly nothing
large enough for her to squeeze into unless she could
go the Stretch Armstrong route.

Aggravated now, Buffy carried the rope over to the

opposite side of the roof and checked the area below it. Satisfied, she unwound the rope and let it drop over the side, then found a solid place to set the hook. That done, she climbed over the edge and began to rappel herself toward the sidewalk thirty feet below in small jumps, trying to make as little noise as possible.

Three hops down, she bounced softly against a part of the wall that, oddly, flexed a little beneath the soles of her shoes.

She halted her descent and hung there, frowning at the wall in front of her. It was covered in that same, slightly shining paint in which Willow had encased the entire building, a rather pretty kaleidoscope pattern of blue and green. So why had it *sounded* so different?

Another glance around—she felt terribly vulnerable, suspended there like some kind of dangling tidbit for any hungry vampire that happened to be passing below—and Buffy reached out and gave the surface in front of her an experimental tap. The result was that same hollowish thud that she'd heard before, coupled again with a slight give in the surface. It *looked* solid, but it obviously wasn't concrete, wood, or siding. So what was it?

Glass.

Of course. Willow would never live in some kind of a cave without windows—she liked light and sunshine too much. This expanse was carefully camouflaged to blend in with the rest of the building, but it was glass nonetheless, and in keeping with the whole warehouse loft construction, there was probably a line of these things across at least one, maybe two full sides of the building.

Buffy checked the area around her again.

It would be messy, and it would be loud. It might even be painful.

But glass could break. Glass *would* break.

She planted the soles of her shoes firmly against the surface and gave it a couple of light trial bounces. A final check of the ground, and then she pushed off of the surface hard enough to swing herself away from the building a good ten feet. She hit the arc of her motion, then gained momentum as she went back toward the building at full speed. At the last instant Buffy raised her legs and pulled in her toes, so that when she hit the window—at least, she *hoped* it was a window—it would be with the hard heels of her shoes. A little bit of bend at the knee to keep the impact to her body at a minimum and—

Craaaaaaack!

So much for the window.

The force of her body sent the glass shattering inward with her. She followed it through and let go of the rope as shards of glass rained down around her. She had a moment of gratefulness for her upright landing, and then she went into an instinctive crouch. Beyond the momentary ringing in her ears, she thought she heard something . . . growling? It wouldn't be good if Willow had a guard dog up here. But no, it was probably just her ears soaking up sound waves from the crashing glass.

Rising, Buffy warily scanned her surroundings.

Was this really Willow's new place? If so, as places to
live went, it was pretty darned awesome—spacious,
spotlessly clean, shining with warm wood, soft light-
ing and softer fabric, and lots of colored glass. Books,
too, and while Buffy would be the first to admit she
wasn't so high on the scholarly stuff, books *did* make
her feel secure and comfortable; after all, some of the
best knowledge about the whos, whys, and wheres of
slaying had come from Giles's sometimes rather
heavy-handed library. Obviously Willow wasn't here
or she'd have shown herself by now, and while Buffy
wanted to go over and take a look at some of the
shelves, there was still the matter of that background
noise to contend with, the sound that just wouldn't go
away.

That *growling*.

Buffy moved cautiously across the wall of windows, suddenly aware that there was more to the noise
than just its animal origin. Undercut by the soft rattling
of metal, another sound, a sort of pathetic keening, was
intertwined with it. Not loud, but almost constant and
utterly miserable, the sound of someone quietly crying
with only enough time in between to take in air for the
next sob. As pretty as the place was, it was full of shadows created by the fabric-wrapped support posts and
furniture, and the windows, with their external covering of a multicolored magickal shroud, allowed only
dim light to flow inside. The only truly well-lit area
was where Buffy had broken through at the far end.

She crept around a post, then gasped and actually
took a step backward at the scene in front of her.

Never, *ever,* had she imagined she would find something like this.

A fireplace, with a werewolf chained on the left, and Spike chained on the right.

When it saw her, the werewolf's constant, low growling changed to a flurry of snarls. It lunged at her, front legs stretched as far as it could make them, deadly claws extended. Before those claws could connect with her flesh, however, the werewolf reached the limit of its chain and the links snapped tight, jerking the creature upright so hard that its back legs flew out from under it and it landed heavily on one hip. Undaunted, it tried again, and again, with a stunned Buffy simply standing out of range and watching it, waiting to make sure the chain would hold. Finally the beast halted its charges and paced back and forth to the limit of its bonds, snapping and snarling its frustration as it watched her with malicious yellow eyes.

Convinced—at least a little— that the chain would hold, Buffy circled to the right and edged up to the chained vampire. He was curled in a ball on the right side of the fireplace, the heavy silver chains around his wrists clenched tightly in his fists. His face was buried on his crossed arms, and while Buffy couldn't see his expression, she could darned well hear him weeping nonstop, as though everything representing hope in his existence had died away.

"Spike?" she asked again. "Spike, it's okay—I'll get you out of here. I'll—"

He raised his head, and Buffy's hand flew to her mouth to stifle a cry when she saw that his mouth had been sewn shut with heavy black stitches.

He stared at her with dull eyes, and she ground her teeth to clench the anger that surged inside her. When she reached toward his face, he winced and jerked out of range—the damned things must hurt terribly. Could she cut them, or would she just make things worse if she tried? She—

"You know, most people wait for an invitation before they come to visit."

Buffy spun and saw Willow standing about twenty feet away. How had she gotten in here without Buffy hearing her? She'd shimmered, of course, something that wouldn't make a sound and of which Buffy would have no warning. At this point Willow no longer needed pesky things like doors and stairs and elevators. She went where she would, whenever she pleased.

"It's usually considered rude to just let yourself in to someone's home when they're not there." Willow strolled to the side and leaned against one of the fabric-wrapped posts. She seemed unconcerned and unafraid as she gazed at Buffy, and Buffy had to admit that the changes Willow had gone through had resulted in a sort of terrible, dark beauty. As a Wicked Witch of the West, Willow had it all over on the pointy-nosed crone of *The Wizard of Oz,* and about the only thing the two had in common was the black garb. Willow, however, was doing it up in as much style as she had her loft: lots of flowing, soft material, this time in a black that had a vague sort of star-shine to it, as though she'd pulled the pattern from the nighttime sky above Sunnydale. It seemed strange to see Willow dressed like this, but it was also right in an odd sort of way, as though her friend has passed through an invisible but very important gate, leaving her own shell behind and being reborn in this new and much more striking version.

In addition to the new wardrobe, Willow's hair was as dark as her outfit but oddly had no shine at all—it was just flat black, and it went right along with her eyes. Their formerly warm brown hue was gone, and in its place were twin orbs of depthless darkness, like bottomless pits of tar. All that was complemented by the traces of black veins running here and there on Willow's almost pearlescent skin, making her look like someone who'd stepped out of a child's dark and terrible exquisite nightmare fairy tale.

Buffy licked her lips and tried to think of something strong and profound that might get through to Willow, that might make a difference. Willow's appearance and this place—those weren't the end of her transformation. She had an . . . *aura* about her now, a sort of charged electrical field that made the hair on Buffy's neck rise and set her teeth on edge. It wasn't hard to figure it out, either—it was the sensation of danger.

"I see you've found my new pets," Willow said blandly.

Distraction, Buffy thought. *Maybe that will do it just long enough for me to at least get Spike out of here.*

Instead of bringing up the touchy subject of Warren and Tara, Buffy opted for the here and now. "Willow," she said, and gestured at Spike. "What's this? Why would you do this to him?"

Willow gave a deceptively fragile-looking shrug. "Why not? I needed some company, a familiar face without the familiar do-good mouth. Unfortunately Spike turned out to be a lot noisier than I expected. He wouldn't stop whining about his soul and blathering on about how sorry he is about all the people he's killed in his lifetime, so I stopped the sniveling for him."

Buffy's mouth dropped open. "His *soul*? Spike has a *soul* now?"

A corner of Willow's mouth turned up, but Buffy couldn't tell if it was in a smile or a smirk. "Apparently so. Although I can't for the life of me figure out what he's going to do with it. I don't think he can either."

Buffy stared back at Spike, but right now he didn't seem interested in her, or Willow, or even in getting free. She didn't have the time right now to focus on the soul part, on the hows and whys of how it happened, or what it might mean for all of them in the future. "But his mouth—Willow, how could you be so cruel?"

"Pah," Willow replied. "Don't think of it as cruel, think of it as practical." She inclined her head at the werewolf. "One noisy pet is enough. I can't deal with two."

Buffy balled her fists. "These are not *animals,* Willow! They're people—Spike, and whoever this poor guy is—"

"Oz."

Buffy's mouth worked for a moment before she could focus her jumble of thoughts into a coherent sentence. "Oz? Oh, Willow, what did you *do* to him? He had his werewolf side completely under control—"

Willow waved a hand at her, cutting off her words. "Oh, spare me the sermon, Buffy. First of all, he could only control it if he didn't get upset—you know that. Second of all . . ." She grinned. "Don't forget how he acted the last couple of times we saw him, first with Veruca, and then the way he attacked Tara. In reality I think he *is* an animal. All I did was make that part of him come out to play . . . *permanently*. Isn't he cute? Just think of him as a really cranky puppy."

"And Spike?" Buffy demanded. "Look at him— he's been beaten senseless. What's that all about?"

Willow glanced to Buffy's right, at the vampire. "He is what he wanted, or at least what his patron decided he wanted."

"Patron?"

At Buffy's confused expression, Willow continued. "I used a little magick to track him down, and I found out he went to a demon and went through a trial. You know how it is with deals with the devil, or with demons—Spikey there didn't word his request quite clearly enough. Maybe he thought he was going to get that chip hauled out of his head, or maybe he had something entirely different in mind, but daddy demon decided to give Spike a sort of celestial resurrection instead." Willow's dark eyes flashed briefly. "My timing was exquisite. I arrived right after the big event . . . just in time to take him home."

Each second that passed was making her more furious, so Buffy didn't bother to answer. Tired of arguing, instead Buffy strode over to Spike and hauled him to his feet, then grabbed one of the chains in both hands and yanked on it as hard as she could.

Nothing.

Another pull, but there wasn't even a fraction of give, not in the chain *or* the bricks to which it was attached. To make matters worse, Spike tried to pull out of her grip—it seemed that all the idiot wanted to do was go back to his private little crying jag.

Buffy twisted back to face Willow, who only stood there and smiled at her patiently. "Nice try. But even your slayer strength won't break those chains."

Buffy held on to one chain, and with her other hand she shoved Spike back toward the floor. "Magick, huh?"

"Of course."

"Let them go, Willow. Before this gets out of hand and you end up very, very sorry."

"Sorry?" Willow blinked, as if she were looking at something else. "Oh, I'm already sorry. Just not about the things you think I should be."

Buffy dropped Spike's chain. "I've had just about enough of this," she ground out. Right now she felt like she wanted to pound Willow into the floor, punish her for what she'd done to Warren, Giles, Oz, and Spike, stop her from doing anything worse, and pretend that Willow had never been her best friend and heartfelt confidant. But how would she feel tomorrow? She felt like a nine-year-old girl screeching "I don't like you anymore!" in the playground, and then making up on Friday so they could go back to playing dolls that afternoon.

But she wasn't that schoolgirl, and neither was Willow. They were adults, and each had to take responsibility for her actions. Right now it was Willow's turn.

Buffy took two steps forward, then made a leap to cover the rest of the space.

"Stop."

Willow's command was so soft Buffy barely heard it, but her body sure obeyed. It was like the great unseen hand of the universe just reached down and yanked her puppet strings straight up—one instant she was in forward motion, the next she was just standing there, facing forward. She was stopped by some kind of invisible wall, unseen but so incredibly solid that Buffy could almost feel her nose pressed against something, and for a second she thought she'd actually *bounced* back. She blinked, then rubbed her nose, but no—it hadn't actually touched anything.

Willow shook her head and looked at Buffy in disgust. "Let it go, Buffy. I'm done with the whole rock 'em, sock 'em, let's get physical thing. I've been there and done it, to both you and Giles, and I'm moving on. There's no more time in my schedule to be fist-dancing with you. From now on, if you don't like what I'm doing or the way I'm doing it—*too bad*."

Buffy scowled at her. "Willow, you let them go— and fix poor Oz while you're at it. You know he would *hate* being a werewolf all the time. You can't *do* this. It's not you, it's not how you've lived your life."

"Oh, *puh-leeze*." Willow rolled her eyes. "And what exactly do I have to show for all this time being the 'good Willow'? Excellent grades and a dead girlfriend, that's what. Hey, give me a gold star for *that* track record!"

Buffy wasn't surprised at the bitterness in Willow's voice, but hearing the words out loud made her wince. Trying to be unobtrusive, she moved one foot, testing for a barrier. Whatever had stopped her before was gone, and the toe of her shoe went forward a couple of inches without stopping. Perhaps whatever Willow had done was a one-time thing; Buffy intended to check that very shortly. "Well, you can't keep going on like this. You—"

"Like what?" Willow asked. She swept her hand in a semicircle in front of her. "This? In a private world of my own making, where I have a very short list of things I'd like to do? And also where, if you would just stop sticking your slayer nose into my business and leave me alone, I could get on my way to doing just that?"

"Things like kill Jonathan and Andrew?" Buffy demanded hotly. "Mistreat Spike and zap Oz into perpetual moon mode? That's *wrong,* Willow!"

"By whose standards?" Willow shot back. "Yours? Well, yours don't count anymore."

Buffy tensed. "Oh, yes they do. *I'm* the one who's always kept things safe in Sunnydale, and I won't have you breezing around like some kind of doom goddess who can pluck someone from his life and shake everything up!"

Once again, Buffy went for her.

Ditto on the fact that she didn't make it.

Willow's hand shot up in front of her, the fingers

curled into a gripping motion as though she'd caught a ball tossed at her. Buffy gave a strangled cry as her momentum stopped literally in midair and she hung there again. For a second her entire body quivered, and she thought Willow was going to shake her, hard, like a wolf shakes a rabbit at the end of a successful hunt.

Instead Willow just gazed at her from beneath heavy-lidded eyes. "Don't you get it yet, Buffy?" she asked softly. "I'm going to do what I want to, when I want to. You know why? Because Sunnydale isn't your town anymore. Now it belongs to *me*."

And with a sharp snap of her fingers, Willow threw Buffy across the width of the loft and out the same window she had broken getting in.

Thirty feet was a damned long way to drop, and while she was pretty banged up and bruised, Buffy supposed she ought to be grateful she hadn't actually broken anything. For that matter, she was also more than a little thankful that Willow hadn't broken *her*, because the way things were going, it was clear as crystal that she certainly had enough punch to do it. The meek little Willow of the olden days was gone, replaced by magick, speed, strength, determination, and a desire for revenge that Buffy no longer thought could be talked down.

Buffy dragged herself to her feet and looked upward, but the window she'd broken had already melted back into a smooth surface that was indistinguishable from the rest of the building. No doubt

Willow would also fix that bent door (not that Buffy could find her way upstairs anyway), and she'd probably reinforce her magickal windows to boot.

It would be an act of stupidity for Buffy to try to go back in right now anyway, without some kind of a better plan or weapons. She felt bad for Spike and Oz, although out of the two of them, Spike was definitely higher on the tormented list. The way he was, Oz was pretty oblivious to what was going on; he might be wild and vicious, but at least he wasn't in pain.

But Spike . . . Buffy shuddered, remembering the torture that Angel had endured through decade after decade of trying to come to terms with the atrocities he'd committed, how he now never stopped trying, in his own way, to atone. Spike was in the birthing stages of that, alone and ignored, when he should have had help and support from the people around him who, if they didn't exactly love him, were at least able to understand. It was so brutal of Willow to deny him that.

But there was nothing she could do tonight other than head back to the Magic Box and heal her own wounds.

Chapter Ten

Willow rubbed her hands together and walked along the inside of the circle made by the twelve women seated on the floor around her. "I'm glad you all could join me," she said.

"Like we had a choice," someone muttered in a low voice, but Willow ignored it. She couldn't tell who the speaker was, nor did she particularly care; that a few of them didn't want to be here was not her problem, it was theirs. . . . And it was also something about which they could do absolutely nothing.

"What we're going to be working on is increasing power," she continued. "Specifically, increasing *my* power. There's a little project that I'm involved in, and to see this to completion is going to require that we work together. We'll be a team, so there's going to be no arguing, no backstabbing, no plotting." She gave them all a bright smile, one that promised all sorts of unpleasant retribution should she be crossed. "I know some of you don't want to be here, but I didn't bring you all here for that kind of nit-picking. Your best and most painless avenue back to a Willow-free life is to help me as quickly as possible. You help me get this done, then I let you go and leave you alone. It doesn't get any simpler."

A young black woman to Willow's left lifted her chin. Her dark eyes were smoldering with resentment. "And if we refuse?"

Willow folded her arms and sighed as she regarded the speaker. If she remembered correctly, the woman's name was Njeri, and Willow knew she was one of the more powerful Wiccans present. Poor thing—if she resisted, her power would not be enough to protect her from Willow's anger. "Then I'll have to get ugly. Which will put me in a bad mood, which will make me get even uglier. Trust me, it's a very bad cycle and you don't want to see it."

Njeri said nothing, but Willow could see the rebellion in her eyes, and the feeling bubbled beneath the atmosphere in the room, like a pot set on simmer for so long that the contents were just about to burn. It just wouldn't do to have this one, with her feisty personality, causing dissension among the ranks, so alas, she decided a little demonstration was in order. Too bad; she really never had been one to show off, but if the occasion demanded it . . .

"For instance," she said, "if I decided that someone was getting a little, shall we say, too hot to handle? I might decide to show them how things would feel if my temperature—and my temper—*really* started to rise." She closed her eyes briefly, and when she reopened them, she could feel the flames burning beneath her eyelids, knew that the tiny flickers were dancing on the surface of her irises. Her fire-coated gaze scanned the women, then settled back on Njeri. Willow pursed her lips and blew a small, perfectly formed smoke ring toward the woman, almost like a gentle kiss. It wafted forward and wavered in front of Njeri's face, then swept itself apart in a miniature explosion.

"Party tricks," Njeri muttered, but she shifted uncomfortably in her spot on the floor.

Willow just smiled and turned back to the others. "This project of mine is very involved, and it requires a great deal of energy, admittedly more than I have by myself. With your help I can boost the reserves enough to get this done. It is *extremely* important to me."

"Why should we help you?" another woman asked. If Willow recalled correctly, this one was called Ena, the Celtic name for fire. It was a fitting name, and Ena's naturally dark nature would probably take secret pleasure in what was going to happen shortly. "To be honest, I don't think any of us are up for pitching in so that someone else—*you*—can rule the world or destroy the Great White Good or something else along those lines."

"Yeah, really," Njeri put in. Her voice sounded a little strained, and a quick glance showed that her ebony-colored skin was covered in a fine layer of moisture. More perspiration trickled down each side of her face, seeping from beneath the line of elaborately beaded braids spaced across her forehead. Without realizing it, Njeri wiped her forehead on the arm of her blouse, leaving a wet stain; the woman glanced at the two seated next to her, but they didn't seem overheated or uncomfortable at all. The two glanced at each other, and in an unspoken shared moment, each moved a little farther away from Njeri. "We know you're the new big whiz in town now, but where's it written that you can suck us dry like some kind of freaking parasite?"

Willow tilted her head. "Parasite? How very unflattering." She wandered over to where Njeri sat, then stopped in front of her. At her feet Njeri was nearly panting with heat as she swiped at the sweat now pouring off her skin. "My, my," Willow said gently. "Feeling a bit on the . . . *blistering* side?"

Njeri looked up at her sharply, but whatever she'd been about to say was lost in a moan of pain as the skin on her cheeks and the backs of her hands began to bubble and crack. Her voice rose to a shriek as a steaming, clear liquid—bodily fluids—dribbled out of the splits and spilled onto her clothes. She and several others started to clamber to their feet, but Willow's barely audible command—*"Stay."*—halted that idea before it saw fruition. All the others could do was watch in horror and listen to Njeri's screams as her flesh churned and burned. When the terrible charring moved to cover Njeri's eyelids, Willow finally slammed her palm down on the writhing woman's head.

The burning stopped.

The blistering stopped.

Njeri still spasmed in her spot, but she had no choice but to sit there and wait. Willow gave her a sympathetic look, but it changed instantly to cold anger. "I believe I mentioned that things could get quite ugly if my temper rose," she told the group. She made a point of glancing at Ena, who was sitting there taking it all in; Willow's idea that the Irish Wiccan would secretly enjoy Njeri's mini-conflagration was right on the mark—Willow could see the dark pleasure reflected in Ena's gaze. "This is just a small example. Trust me when I tell you that in a bad mood, my reaction can be much, *much* worse."

Willow gazed back at Njeri, then rubbed her thumb across the open wounds on the black woman's forehead. Njeri shuddered and whimpered, but she didn't dare protest. "But I can be forgiving," Willow said, and suddenly smiled down at Njeri. "*Once.* No more than that, though."

And with one smooth wave of a hand across Njeri's face, the blisters on the young black woman's face and hands disappeared, and the skin smoothed out to its original beauty.

Njeri sucked in air and relaxed, then sat there wordlessly and stared at Willow. Every now and then a tremble would dance across her shoulders, and Willow knew the proud young woman fought to control it. That was fine; pride could be a good thing, provided it was applied properly . . . such as to a job well done. After today's painful lesson, Willow was convinced that Njeri would do just that.

On the other side of the circle an older Wiccan named Cybele cleared her throat. "So," she asked in a calm voice, "what exactly is this important project of yours?"

If such a thing were possible, the smile that Willow directed at them was even more brilliant than the first one she'd given.

"We're going to bring my lover back to life."

The dawn was nearly breaking by the time Willow sent them all home. She fixed herself a small snack of honey graham crackers and crunchy peanut butter and sat down to go over the previous evening's happenings and the members of her new coven. Njeri, who'd endured a brutal lesson, was one of the more powerful Wiccans and was now extremely unlikely to give her any more trouble. Ena was another powerful one—of course, the two with the most pizzazz would question Willow right off—but Willow didn't think she would risk crossing her. The others varied in their degrees of light and dark, force and strength; the strongest of these was Cybele, then Sen, Kala, Ellen, Sying, Anan, Chiwa, Flo, Megan, and finally Dilek, who was the weakest. Even so, Willow was quite proud of the diversity of their nationalities and the strengths that each would bring to the spell she must ultimately devise if she were to be successful in bringing Tara back from her natural death. This was no easy task, and it would require—

"I've seen you come up with some foolish ideas before, Willow, but this is really going all out."

Willow stood up so quickly that her chair overturned. It crashed to the floor behind her, and across the room Oz scrambled to his feet and lunged in response to the noise. Even Spike stopped his rocking and muffled crying and looked in her direction, his eyes momentarily clearing a bit.

"Tara?" Willow's voice was a shocked and broken whisper. "Tara, baby . . . is that you?"

Something swirled in front of the fireplace, a shape that was first white, then gray, then shot through with a thousand different colors. Speechless, Willow could only watch and wait until the amorphous fog finally stopped twisting around itself and took on a definite, and very familiar, shape.

Willow felt behind her for the chair, then sank to the floor when she couldn't find it. It was Tara . . . yet it wasn't. The same sweet face and full mouth, the same honey-blond streaked hair. The body Willow had known so well, the hands that had held hers tightly both during their most intimate moments and just walking down the street. It was all there, it was all right, except . . . except for the brilliantly bloodstained blouse, and the fact that Willow could see the oh-so-faint outline of the fireplace bricks right through her.

"Will, what are you doing? Why can't you just let it be? Why can't you just let me rest?*"*

Tara's voice sounded reproachful and accusing, and Willow felt the surge of joy at seeing Tara again disintegrate like ashes after an explosion of fireworks. "W-what?"

Tara—no, the *ghost* of Tara—looked at her sadly.

"Why are you trying to bring me back to life? You were told it couldn't be done."

Sitting on the floor amid the crumbs of her early-morning snack, Willow found herself gripping the fabric of her long robe hard enough to deform the material. Her breath was coming in ragged gasps, and she struggled to find the right words. "W-why? You're asking me *why*? For God's sake, Tara, isn't it obvious?"

"You love me. Of course you do. But do you have to try to prove it to yourself like this?"

The Ghost of Tara—that's how Willow would come to think of her, in mental capital letters—wandered over to the left and stood in front of Oz as Willow tried to construct an answer. The werewolf crouched at her feet, the hair on his back bristling; as Willow watched in amazement, the Ghost of Tara ran her semitransparent hand along the creature's back, petting him like a dog. Could Oz see her? Sense or feel her touch? Willow didn't know for sure, but suddenly she wanted that—Tara's touch—very much.

"I don't have to prove anything," Willow managed to say as she grabbed the edge of the table and hauled herself to her feet. She started toward the fireplace. "That's not it at all."

The Ghost of Tara held up a hand. *"Stop. He'll attack you, you know. You brought out the werewolf in him, so you must have wanted him to be this way. Even you can't suppress that."*

Willow swallowed and stayed where she was. Seeing Tara like this, or what Tara had become, was mind numbing, all encompassing. "How . . . how can you be here?" Willow whispered. "How is this possible?"

The Ghost of Tara shrugged. *"All things are possible. No, scratch that—most things are possible."* She looked up from Oz, and her transparent gaze focused on Willow. *"I think you know this in your heart."*

Willow set her jaw. "I don't know any such thing," she said grimly. "I brought Buffy back from the dead—"

"That was from an unnatural death."

"Thanks for the reminder," Willow snapped, "but I got the memo. If you think back, Xander brought Buffy back too, from that same *natural* death that you and Osiris keep spouting off about."

The Ghost of Tara gave a sad shake of her head. *"It's not the same, Willow. It wasn't magick, and it was immediate, and the way Buffy died—drowning—helped make it possible. This body—"* She swept a phantom's hand down the front of her figure, then raised it back up to bring Willow's attention to the blood splatter. *"—has begun its rightful return to Mother Earth."*

But Willow only crossed her arms defiantly. "I will not accept that."

The Ghost of Tara sighed. The sound was like a small, plaintive wind, and werewolf Oz picked up his ears and tilted his furred head, as though trying to focus on it. *"You must,"* she said, *"or your heart will only be broken. The universe will give you no choice. In another month or two my physical form will be little more than bone and old air. My eyes will be no more, and there will be only ash where my heart once was—"*

"Stop it!" Willow cried. The words stung her so badly that she had to grab one of the pillars for support. The fragile fabric wrapped around it tore in her hand. "Just *stop* it! Is that why you were sent back here? To torment me?"

"No."

"Then why?" Willow was almost sobbing now. "If you're not here to support me, why even bother coming back?"

"Of course I support you. I always have." The Ghost of Tara gazed at her, and this time there was no smile, sad or otherwise, on her pretty face. *"And because I love you—I will* always *love you—I came back to be your conscience."*

Chapter Eleven

·

Exhaustion ate away at the edges of his thoughts like an insidious fever that simply would not be quelled by medication.

Giles frowned and tried to focus on what Buffy was saying just as Anya—bless her—brought him a fresh cup of tea, this one brewed twice as strong at his request. He hoped the caffeine would help, or he might have to resort to that abominable espresso that all the young people were swilling these days. On the surface it seemed ridiculous that someone such as himself—a cripple—should be so physically tired, but there was a reason for it . . . one he was not yet willing to share with the others.

He could wiggle the toes on his left foot.

Not such a huge thing for most of the people in the world, but for him . . .

The doctors at the hospital had been quite adamant about how he shouldn't get his hopes up, stressing in repetitious and quite annoying monotones that his spine had been severely damaged in the "accident" at the Magic Box. Muscles had swelled, nerves had been bruised, possibly irreparable damage had been done. Injuries like this, they repeatedly insisted, did not simply heal over time, and the miraculous recoveries routinely touted in rags like the *Weekly World News, Star* and the *Enquirer* were extremely unlikely to happen in real life, specifically in *his* real life. Of course, Giles knew that they had no idea what his real life was actually like, but the way things were going—or not going, as the case may be—with Willow, it didn't look as though any extraordinary lower back restoration was in store for him.

So he would have to handle it himself.

Until now, Giles had never realized how incredible an amount of effort it took to try to move such a small and previously taken for granted appendage such as his big toe.

But he knew now, oh God, yes. Virtually every time he had more than fifteen minutes alone, he tried. And he tried, and then he tried even harder, until sweat made his shirt stick to his back and his chest, and his hair was plastered to his scalp. He didn't want to be stranded in this damnable metal wheelchair for the rest of his days, he didn't want other people helping him bathe and dress, and he didn't want to worry about things like hidden infections and—God forbid—bedsores. Buffy and her friends might think he was old, but he wasn't . . . or at least until now, he hadn't been. So if they couldn't convince Willow to try to undo the damage, and if the doctors and nurses couldn't use all their human and medical expertise to reverse what had happened, then sooner or later, he would do it himself.

Although he had to admit that despite all his efforts, it was looking more like later.

"Giles, have you heard *anything* I've said?"

He blinked. "Uh . . . sorry. I was thinking of something else."

Sitting a few feet away, Anya frowned. "You know, I don't understand why he looks so tired all the time," she complained.

"He does look kinda 'peaked.'" Buffy sent a wan grin toward Giles.

"I try to make sure he eats right and gets plenty of rest," Anya continued. "Maybe the physical therapist the insurance company sends is working him too hard. I think I'll speak to the doctor about that."

"Hello?" Giles banged a fist on the arm of his wheelchair, then immediately regretted it when he got the mental image of himself as a crotchety old man. "Why are you two discussing me as if I'm not in the room?"

Anya flushed. "Oh. Sorry." Then she sat up straighter. "Fine—why *are* you so tired?"

"I've got a lot on my mind," he said grumpily. "And remember that just because I can't walk doesn't make me invisible. I'm still *me*."

"You know, stress is one of the nation's biggest contributors to heart disease," Anya told him. "I've been reading the medical journals. And since you can't exercise anymore, you've tripled your risk. Perhaps we should start giving you tranquilizers to keep you calm."

Giles's mouth dropped open. *"What?"*

"You mean because he's so obviously hysterical all the time," Dawn said sarcastically.

Anya sniffed. "I'm just trying to think of what's best for him. The magazines all say that anxiety can be a killer. It can also cause high blood pressure, strokes—"

Sitting next to her, Xander jabbed an elbow lightly into her ribs. "Purveyor of good news again, Anya?"

"Okay, I'll shut up now." She scowled. "Far be it from me to pass along any type of useful information to—"

"Get us back on track," Buffy said quickly.

"Right," Giles agreed. "And what was it you were telling me?"

"I was saying that the word on the street is that Willow has formed a mondo-powerful coven," Buffy said. "What isn't so clear is *why*. Some people are saying it's just to have people around her who have the same abilities, to keep herself occupied because of Tara's death and because she's now ostracized from her friends. Others are saying that's not true, that all she wants is power."

Xander ran a hand through his hair. "More power? For what? For crying out loud, she already packs enough juice to power the lights in New York City."

"I don't know," Buffy admitted.

"We can't even get close to her now," Anya complained. "Every time Buffy tries she gets thoroughly stomped." At Buffy's cranky look Anya lifted her chin. "Well, you do!"

"We also have to remember Spike," Buffy said. "And Oz. We can't just leave them there to be prisoners for the rest of their lives."

"They'll be fine," Anya said. "They're supernatural beings, after all. Besides, Spike is a vampire. It doesn't matter that he has a soul. He's still immortal."

Dawn glared at her. "Well, aren't you just so la-di-da about the whole thing. What if it were *you* chained up next to Willow's fireplace?"

Anya shrugged. "Well, it's not. And if it were, I'd know I'd be fine as long as she didn't kill me."

"Yeah, well, she's tried that lately too," Buffy said darkly.

Giles took off his glasses and fiddled with them, but they were clean. Not much dust in his life now that he couldn't get up and into the fray. He sighed and put them back on without wiping them. "At this point we've no idea whether Willow is still actually *doing* anything wrong. Jonathan and Andrew are, for now, safely out of her reach. Finding a way to free Spike and Oz is something we have to accomplish. Until we figure out exactly how to do so, we need to take steps to keep track of Willow," he said. "Very *close* track of her." He turned his head and regarded Anya.

"Why are you looking at *me*?" she demanded as she sat up straight. "I don't do *Spy Kids* stuff. I'm a shopkeeper, remember? How can you expect—" Her voice was rising now, and she started to get to her feet.

Xander put a hand on her shoulder and gave it a gentle squeeze to stop her. "Down, girl."

"Hear me out," Giles said quickly. He gestured at Buffy. "Buffy's in just about the best place she can be—she gets a pretty steady flow of information from the clientele at the bar. All I'm suggesting is that you use a little bit of your vengeance demon abilities to probe a bit deeper in the psyche of the people involved—"

"The Wiccans?" Anya asked in amazement. She glanced at the others, her eyes wide. "You're trying to get me killed! After everything I've helped with—"

"Don't be ridiculous," Giles cut in. "Of course I'm not. I'm just suggesting that perhaps you can try to get close to some of the coven members who are close to Willow." He folded his arms. "A move like this—forming a coven to generate power—isn't going to be a peaceful one. Most witches won't willingly give their power to someone else unless they're desperate—"

"Like the ones who powered you up," Dawn said. There was no missing the derision in her voice. "So you could turn around and give it all to Willow, who now has us walking on eggshells." Her gaze cut to her sister. "Or planting our butts on crushed glass. Tell me again how that was a good move?"

A muscle ticked in Giles's jaw, but he was careful to keep his voice level as he answered her. "That was a . . . miscalculation. What I'd been given was good magick. We didn't intend for Willow to take *all* of it, and certainly didn't expect her to use it against anyone."

He inhaled, then continued. "Willow may be forcing the members of her coven to cooperate. In that case they won't be happy, and sooner or later the people around them are going to know it. The fact about humanity is that we're seldom silent when someone else takes what we believe rightfully belongs to us." He raised an eyebrow. "Or even what doesn't."

"So I'm supposed to do what?" This time Anya jumped to her feet before Xander could stop her. "Dress up like a floozy and work the bars like some undercover cop on *NYPD Blue*?"

Dawn sat up. "I'll do it!" She glanced from Buffy to Giles and back to Buffy. "Can I do it?"

"No," Buffy and Giles said simultaneously.

Dawn sank back against the couch, sulking. "No one lets me do anything."

"While *I* have to do everything!" Anya said loudly.

"Oh, I wouldn't say that." Buffy's tone was surprisingly mild.

After a second Anya's scowl relaxed. "Oh, all right. It'll be good to get back into the thick of things, anyway."

Xander perked up. "Hey, don't you go doing any vengeance spells—"

"It's what I *am,* Xander." Anya regarded him patiently. "But I promise you this much: I won't change the world or kill anyone. And honestly?" She looked at the rest of them. "At this point I think that's more assurance than you'd get from dear witchy Willow."

Chapter Twelve

No no no.

Standing in the middle of her loft, Willow looked around at the women seated comfortably on the furnishings and on large, overstuffed pillows on the floor. They were researching spells, chatting amiably, and sharing a pot of the dark and spicy-smelling Persian tea that Willow had brewed a few minutes ago. There were plates of goodies—cookies, little homemade sweet cakes, walnut-studded fudge, and the like—placed here and there on the tables and floor.

This wasn't the reason these women came here day after day. They came because she forced them to, because she made them gather power on her behalf, and because if they didn't she was willing to torture or maybe even kill them.

Yet it looked like a damned sewing bee.

"I like it."

The Ghost of Tara's voice slid into her ear, and Willow had a strange moment of sudden tenseness coupled with sweet, enveloping calm. Tara's specter never left her side now, and if it hadn't been for her hope that she could restore Tara's physical body as well as her spirit, its presence would have driven her completely insane. Almost nothing she did went uncommented-on, from her solid refusal to release Oz and Spike, to the spells that she was constantly experimenting with to pull power not only from the other witches in the coven, but also from stray pulses in the ether. Power, the stuff of which Tara would someday be made, was all around her, and Willow was going to have it—*all* of it.

"This isn't the damned PTA," Willow said in a low voice.

"Just think of it as a sort of Wiccan craft show to raise money for a cause," the Ghost of Tara suggested. *"Instead of money, you're raising power. I won't say that in itself it's a good cause, or even a viable one, but you do have a lot of camaraderie going on."* Tara's spirit smiled gently. *"You have the potential for a lot of friends here, you know."*

"I don't give a bat's butt about friendship or camaraderie," Willow ground out. "You know what I want." A couple of the Wiccans nearest to her glanced up, then returned to whatever it was they were doing. Willow shifted uncomfortably, then glanced at the Ghost of Tara to reassure herself that she was still there. She found it incredible that the others could actually *see*

Tara's spirit, could even hear her words if she talked loudly enough. It also made her a little jealous. A few had actually tried to carry on a conversation, but Tara seemed to have no inclination to answer them. Alas, because they could hear the Ghost of Tara talking to Willow, there was no privacy in their conversations. At times Willow thought she would have preferred to hear the Ghost of Tara only in her mind, and if that meant she was hearing voices and looked insane to someone else, then so what? At least then she wouldn't be sharing her lover's words . . . and her recriminations . . . with the rest of the world.

"Everyone needs friends," the Ghost of Tara said. *"Don't you miss yours?"*

"No," Willow lied. She did, of course, but she missed the way they'd been before Tara's death— nonjudgmental and supportive. And Tara, the center of her life. Then she added, "I miss *you.*"

"I miss you too," the Ghost of Tara said. *"But you can't bring me back, Willow. You can't—"*

"Stop it!" Willow yelled, and she wasn't sure if she was talking to the Ghost of Tara or to the coven of witches spread around the room. Frustration churned inside her and she felt like she was ready to explode, so maybe she was screaming at both. "Just stop it right now!"

Twelve pairs of shocked eyes turned toward her, and Willow felt a little thrill of satisfaction at the fear and confusion she saw reflected there, the uncertainty about whether she was angry at them or at the Ghost of Tara. The low, companionable murmur in the room stopped abruptly, and for a moment it felt like something had sucked all the oxygen out.

Finally, Cybele was the only one who had the courage to speak. "Is there a problem?" she asked in a carefully diplomatic tone of voice. At her side Njeri's eyes were narrow and mistrustful, full of visible fear.

"'Is there a problem?'" Willow mimicked. "Of *course* there's a problem!" She waved her hand at them, and although she wasn't casting a spell, a couple of them flinched outright. "Do you think I yell just to hear myself?"

Rather than answer, they all sat frozen and speechless, afraid to move or speak as she began to stride around the loft. "So what are we making here, ladies?" she demanded. "Are we casting spells to increase power? Hell, I can do that practically by rubbing a couple of sticks together. Working on locating more sources of dark energy? Is that what we're doing? Because it doesn't look that way to me!" Willow's head whipped back and forth. "To me it looks like the lot of you might as well be putting together some kind of dairy farm *quilt*!" She was nearly screaming by the time she came to the end of her tirade.

"Willow," Cybele began. "We're not—"

Willow's pointing finger came around so fast that Cybele gasped as she realized it was only inches away from her mouth. *"Don't,"* Willow said. Her voice was low and dangerous. "Don't make me shut you up like I did that whimpering, skinny vampire in the corner."

Cybele swallowed and put her palms out in a gesture of surrender. Never taking her gaze off Willow's, she carefully backed up and sat on one of the chairs.

"I don't want to see this 'friends-for-all' crap," Willow hissed. "I want *power,* and I want a *lot* of it. I don't give a damn if you like one another, if you hate one another, or who gets squashed in the process. I don't care if you hate *me. I want power.*" Her eyes were smoldering with anger.

"We've been working on it," Ena offered. Her voice, with its rich Irish accent, dripped dark promise. "We 'aven't been as artsy-craftsy as you think."

Sying nodded, eager to appease Willow. "It's true. We've built up the power stores a good deal."

"Really." Willow folded her arms and regarded them. Were they telling her the truth? She closed her eyes for a few seconds, letting herself focus on the mental mishmash of thoughts from the women around the loft. When she opened her eyes again, she smiled widely—yes, they were being honest. Very wise of them. "Why, that's wonderful news. And I know just what to do with the might that you've collected so far. We'll use it to create an entity that will go out on its own and gather me even more!"

With darkness came the quiet, and with the quiet came the sense of anticipation.

While her location wasn't exactly the center of a booming industrial metropolis, during the day Willow's warehouse district was still fairly busy. About half of the semidecrepit buildings around her housed one kind of business or another, from parts warehousing to furniture storage to a handful of shady-looking body shops—perhaps they were really stolen car chop shops—run out of buildings that had been divided into three and four parts. Only the body shops operated at night, and, like Willow, they did it behind solidly closed doors, except their reason was to hide their activities from the prying eyes of the police cruisers that rolled through the district like silent, oversized hunting insects. They must have had several lookouts posted, because their machines would stop the grinding and whining, the lights would go out, and the doors would shut, always at least ninety seconds before a squad car would turn a corner and slink past their now-darkened building. Willow's system was much more efficient; during the day her visual cloaking spell made her building look nothing more than vacant and locked up tight.

Now, this late at night, even the chop shoppers were gone. The moon was at its peak and Oz was howling at full volume in the background. Whereas once that sound had triggered fear, Willow now savored it. Splits in the sporadic cloud cover revealed swaths of stars against the inky blackness of the sky, and the moonlight made the clouds look shadowed and angry, like the boiling stuff of a prestorm. The barometer rose along with the humidity, and Willow reveled in the buildup of pressure and promise.

For tonight's ritual Willow and the others had done away with all unnatural light—no electricity, no magickal illumination . . . at least not until later, when the spell itself was likely to create its own zingy effect or two. Some of the weaker members of the coven had a tendency to spice up their lives with color, and on any one day a handful of them would show up at the loft with richly hued scarves around their necks, long strands of pearlescent beads, and dangling crystal and stone earrings that sparkled and winked as they caught the light. Willow had put a moratorium on those things for tonight, and while they might not know it, that new law was one which she was going to put into effect permanently. The only spot of true color in the loft would always be the Ghost of Tara.

"You're corrupting them."

Willow inhaled sharply, then let her breath out. By now she'd thought she would become used to it, but the Ghost of Tara's voice still startled her, probably because the spirit had taken to staying silent for hours at a time. At first Willow had thought—*hoped*—that it would be just like before, when she and Tara had been together and shared everything. The downside, of course, would be that they could have no physical contact, but Willow had plans for rectifying *that,* so she could live with things like this for a while.

But the universe, that meant old Father of Fate, apparently wasn't through tormenting her.

The Ghost of Tara spoke only when she wanted to, and never mind that Willow might ask a question that required an answer, or relate some funny anecdote she wanted to share with the spirit of the woman who had been her closest friend and most treasured lover. As now, when the Ghost of Tara spoke, it was usually to point out some flaw or criticize, always in that sweet voice with the vaguely disappointed tone. It was that tone, the one that cut Willow to her heart, that messed her up so badly—it made her ashamed of herself and angry at the same time, constantly tugged her between the halves that her world had become.

"Every hour that they spend with you clouds the good in them more. Every nightfall sees them soaked a little more in evil."

"That's not my problem," Willow said now. She made her voice as cold as she could. "It's theirs."

"Is it?" The Ghost of Tara regarded her solemnly. She looked so beautiful in the candlelight that it made Willow ache to touch her, and the way her spirit companion always stood so close just made it all the worse. *"They did not all choose to serve you. Some did, yes; but others are bound by your threats. By fear."*

"They'll survive," Willow said grimly.

"Will they?"

Willow started to retort, then caught the inflection in the Ghost of Tara's voice, the one that she was learning to recognize signaled a period of upcoming silence. She shrugged instead and looked back at the women, who by now had formed into an incomplete circle around an oversized pentagram drawn on the floor with fine shavings of a blueish-toned metal. At the top of the circle, directly in front of the upward point of the pentagram, was the space reserved for Willow. They looked at her expectantly, and without another word she stepped into place and closed the circle.

Each of the women held a different-colored candle, with the most powerful one—Willow herself—holding the black one. The other twelve colors varied but were all rich and dark hues, such as fiery red, burnt orange, midnight blue, and the like, thus covering the spectrum of the darkest rainbow and the range of dark powers that might exist in Sunnydale. Willow had decided that whatever the power was, she wanted it— no being, from the lowliest of bug-munching beasts to the strongest of vampires, would escape the creature she was about to create.

With a slow, circular wave of her hand, the candles around the circle ignited one by one. When the last candle, to Willow's right, flared to life, they all began to chant in unison:

Come to me, come to us, come to me
We conjure you to serve our mistress
Go forth unseen and unto yourself gather
The dark powers of those who roam the night
Each end of evening when you are filled return to her
Give of yourself and start the cycle anew.

And by the time they'd completed the third cycle of chanting, their newly created beast rose from the center of the pentagram and stood before Willow, awaiting her command.

"Excellent," Willow said happily as she looked the creature up and down. "I think it's everything I wanted . . . and more."

The members of her coven, however, shifted nervously as they eyed their newly formed beast. Sleek and muscular, it towered over them, a sort of hellishly buff version of a member of that performance group whose members painted themselves bright blue. . . . Well, except of course for the three-pronged tail and the clawed, eight-fingered hands with the extra-long digits. Instead of the red that Willow might have expected, the beast's eyes were even more blue than the rest of its body, and she knew that anyone but the circle of those who had brought the entity to life would find them utterly mesmerizing. At the rear of where its skull and neck met was something that looked like an icy blue diamond—like a stone, yet it was made of bone and flesh. It pulsed with energy, sending out a sparkling little shower of light with each beat. Beneath her calculating stare, the creature first lowered its gaze, then peeked slyly from beneath half-closed lids; after a few seconds it gave her a marvelously predatory grin full of pointed, yellow-tinted teeth. To top it all off, it actually *purred* at her, something that made Willow laugh out loud.

"Look," she said to no one in particular. "A *sine kot diabl*. I have a vampire pet, a werewolf pet, and now I have a cat-beast pet."

"Be careful." Seemingly from out of nowhere, the Ghost of Tara whispered in her ear. *"Beware, my love. Cats are not as loyal as werebeasts. This one has a tendency to bite."*

Willow jumped visibly. "So much the better," Willow said, a little too sharply. Usually she was at least slightly ready for the Ghost of Tara's comments; this time, because she'd been wrapped up in her spell and the appearance of the newly born cat-beast, she'd been caught off guard.

The Ghost of Tara sighed softly, and her voice was

so low that for once the other witches in the room couldn't hear. *"Ah, but it will bite* you, *my love."*

Willow glanced at her spirit companion and frowned. "Is that a prophecy, Tara? Or just another goody-two-shoes warning?" Out of the corner of her eye she saw the cat-beast, the only being close enough to catch their words, listening intently.

"That is for you to decide."

Willow ground her teeth and turned back to the cat-beast. At first glance the creature looked hairless, but a closer look revealed very short, flat fur—this was what made it look so shiny. Unafraid, she reached up and stroked its head, noting the pointed ears, the high cheekbones, and the prominent, rounded jawline. There was something strange about the way the bottom of its face joined the top, something oddly oversized and different from anything she'd encountered before—but then, every supernatural creature should have something unique about it. She wondered if it would run on all fours, and what it would feel like to be attacked by this thing. Would it hurt? Would its victims die writhing in agony as—

Willow jerked her hand back, suddenly angry at herself for having guilty thoughts. What did she care if they did? The cat-beast would target only creatures of the night like itself, and it wasn't like all the so-called "good" little people of the world would even be bothered—the thing was literally invisible to them.

"And what about those who are good but fight against the evil within themselves?" the Ghost of Tara suddenly asked.

Willow flinched, then squared her shoulders. "Well, they ought to make up their minds one way or the other," she said coldly. "Until they do, they're fair game."

"Really." The Ghost of Tara gazed at her, then pointed toward the fireplace. *"If that's true, then how about Spike? And Oz? Perhaps they should be your cat-beast's first meal."*

Willow had to look away from the spirit's penetrating eyes. "No. They're . . . special. I told you before. They're my pets."

"Indeed."

"Stop it," Willow snapped. "Now you're sounding way too much like Giles."

"Giles isn't very talkative these days," the Ghost of Tara said softly. *"He doesn't walk anymore either."*

Willow tried to ignore her and stroked the cat-beast's head again, liking the way the creature purred beneath her touch. Giles was paralyzed? Admittedly she'd felt a pang at the Ghost of Tara's words. But no . . . she would *not* feel guilty about what had happened to Giles in their battle—the old man shouldn't have tried to stop her. How much better off would he have been had he just left her alone and let her do what she wanted? Life would have gone on as it normally did for him, and Willow would have had her revenge. Now Jonathan and Andrew still went free somewhere, and she didn't even have the memory of their deaths to comfort her.

No, at this point in her life, she'd had enough of other people steering her in the direction in which *they* wanted her to go. Now she had plans of her own that needed to be fulfilled. Abruptly she stopped her petting. "Go," she commanded the *sine kot diabl.* "Feed. Then return to me before dawn."

The cat-beast bobbed its head in agreement, then dropped gracefully into a crouch. The other women in the circle parted so that it could slink through, but then they froze as it stopped outside the circle and turned back. In barely the blink of an eye, it leaped forward and landed at Njeri's feet. She gasped when it rose back to its full height, faced her, and licked its lips.

"No!" Willow barked. "Those who are in this room are beyond your hunger—you must *not* feed here!"

There was a horribly long moment when she didn't think the cat-beast would obey her—portents of things to come, as Tara had predicted?—but then it backstepped and slid down to its haunches. When it turned its head to regard her, Willow could swear she saw resentment in its ice-blue eyes.

"Come here," she commanded. This time it didn't hesitate to slink back to crouch at her feet. She couldn't help but appreciate its terrible beauty as it swayed restlessly, like a predator impatient to be free to start its nightly hunt. Already it was looking around as if sizing up the occupants of the room; when its hungry gaze fixed on Spike shackled helplessly next to the fireplace, Willow's hand shot forward. She gripped its jaw and wrenched its face around so that it could look only at her. She pulled on its head until their noses nearly touched. She could feel its breath, as cool as the rest of its body looked, against her lips.

"Never here," she warned. "*Never.* Do you understand?"

For a long moment, the *sine kot diabl* didn't respond. Then, incredibly, while still pinned in her grip, it *growled* at her.

There's something about a cat's growl that makes the hair on a person's skin stand up, perhaps because it's so seldom heard. Snarling, hissing, yowling—those are all very common, but a feline growl is an unusual and terrible thing. There was an instant when Willow's temper made her want to destroy the *sine kot diabl* outright. She quelled the urge—barely—and instead dug her fingers viciously into its face. Only one-handed, Willow still had no trouble holding the cat-beast in place when it tried to twist away. When the creature realized it was trapped, it stopped fighting and mewled instead.

"There," Willow said. She let it go, adding a little push that made it stumble backward as it dropped to all fours and waited. She stared haughtily down at it. "Cross me again and you'll find your time on this earth extremely short." She pointed at the only open window at the far end of the huge room. "Now go, and return at dawn to give me your first evening's harvest."

This time the *sine kot diabl* didn't look at anyone in the loft on its way out.

Chapter Thirteen

"**B**uy you a drink?"

She felt a hand drop lightly onto her shoulder. Anya turned her head and saw a man standing next to her, and her first urge was to send him behind the bar and force him to put his hand in the blender. She quelled it just in time; after all, wasn't this what she had put herself out here for? To talk to people outside of Buffy's range and get information—if there was any to be had—about what was going on in Willow's now black-thinking little brain? Sure it was, and all that would be a bit hard to do if she amputated the hand of every would-be source.

Secretly gritting her teeth, she smiled as widely as she could. "I could be persuaded."

The guy grinned at her. "Now there's a statement that leaves open all sorts of possibilities."

"None of which you should explore," she shot back before she could stop herself.

Instead of mouthing off, he laughed and signaled the bartender. "I agree. And definitely not on the first drink. What'll it be? Something big, gooey, and cold, or something smaller that'll warm you right down to your toes?"

Anya's eyebrows raised. This guy was a real player, just full of innuendos. "Keep it simple," she said. "A beer, on tap, will be just fine."

"How about a shot to chase it with?" he suggested.

"No thanks."

He shrugged, and she waited while he ordered and the bartender pulled down the two beers. After surveying her choices, Giles and she had decided that really the only place to go was the Bronze, where Buffy and the rest of the gang didn't hang out much anymore. With all the fighting against evil—blah blah blah— then Giles's injury, Anya couldn't recall the last time any of them had gone out for a night of just plain fun. And that was just too bad—humans had such short and pitiful life spans. If they really *had* to be stuck on this earth, it was a shame they didn't get to have more fun while they were here. Besides, sometimes the Bronze could yield up the skinny.

"My name is Ross," he said as he offered her the beer. "I know it's going to sound like a cliché, but do you come here often?"

Anya couldn't help rolling her eyes. "Honestly, is that the best you can do?"

"Come on," he protested. "It's a valid question. I

do—come here often, I mean. At least for the last couple of months. And I don't recall seeing you around. What's your name?"

"Anya." She took a sip of her beer and looked at him speculatively. "So, you've been trolling, huh?"

He looked offended. "That's a pretty hard judgment."

Now it was Anya's turn to shrug. "Life's a beach, and sometimes the truth is just a sandy little piece of it."

"What—if you don't like it, don't wear sandals?"

She grinned in approval. At least he wasn't so dense he missed the metaphor. "Something like that."

Ross laughed. "So, back to my question."

Anya settled herself on the chair a little more comfortably. "I used to hang out here a lot. I've been . . . busy lately."

Ross raised his beer at her. "Too bad. Maybe you and I could have hooked up a lot sooner."

Anya ignored that, asking instead, "So, if you spend so much time here at the Bronze, you must be really up on what's shaking around town."

He lifted one eyebrow, and she noted that he had very nice eyes. They were a sort of sea foam green, very unusual. Maybe he was a demon in disguise. The thought pleased her—human men were usually so boring. Well, except for Xander, of course. He was an exception to almost everything, at least in her mind.

"I keep my eyes and ears open," he said. "I like to be informed."

"So, what incredibly interesting things did I miss

while I was gone?" Anya sipped her beer and waited.

"Depends on where your interests lie," Ross answered. He leaned forward. "Maybe we could find that out by going somewhere else and having dinner."

Anya had to laugh. "You certainly believe in moving fast, don't you?"

He grinned widely. "Forward is the only way to go."

She studied him. "There's something odd about you, but I can't put my finger on it. I don't think you're—"

"Human?"

She blinked. "Well . . . yes."

"I'm not. But then, neither are you." Before she could respond, he sniffed the air. "But you do hang out a lot with them, right? Just not here."

Her eyes narrowed. "Okay, I'll bite—"

"I'll bet you would."

"—if you're not human, what *are* you?"

Ross spread his hands. "Nothing majorly malicious, I swear. Just a lower-level demon trying to score with a beautiful woman."

She felt a grin tug at the corner of her mouth. Even in his confession, this yodel was still trying to make that date with her. "Really. What kind of demon? What do you do?"

For a moment he actually looked shy. "I don't really have a solid job description. I just . . ." He looked away, and his eyes brightened as he scanned the room. "I just cause a little aggravation now and then. Sort of like a poltergeist, except I get bored really easily so I don't stick to only one person."

Anya shook her head in mock dismay. "How typical—a flighty man." She tilted her head. "So what are you called? I mean, your actual demon *type*?"

Ross shifted, obviously embarrassed. He said something under his breath, then sipped his beer.

Anya leaned forward. "What's that? You're mumbling."

He took a deep breath. "I said if you really have to know, I'm a *kwaad schepsel*. A mischief creature." He paused, then added, "We're very rare."

Anya studied him. Green eyes, stylishly cut black hair, and a nearly perfect *GQ* face made him definitely fall into the eye candy category. "You're very attractive, too," she said bluntly. "I don't know why you're so embarrassed."

He picked at the table's edge. "Well, I'm not so powerful, you know? Where I grew up, I was kind of in the lower range of the pecking order. And I got pecked at a lot. I mean, look at what I do." He turned his head until his gaze stopped on a couple of guys over at the pool table; a single blink and the shot one had been making screwed up royally and sent the pool cue scraping across the fabric in a long, loud rip. Amid the cussing and the laughter that followed, he turned back to Anya. "Compared to what someone like you, a vengeance demon, can accomplish, I'm like cheese doodles next to smoked lobster." He gave her a knowing glance. "I can always spot a beautiful vengeance demon, you know. You ladies just shine to someone like me. Still, we're a total dimension apart."

"True," Anya agreed. "But that doesn't mean

you're not an okay guy." She squinted at him suddenly. "Unless you go around breaking women's hearts as part of your duties. You don't, do you?"

"Nah," he said. "That takes too much time and involvement. I'll tell you right now that I don't stick around one person, man *or* woman, for more than an evening or two. Hard to get involved really deeply in that span of time."

"Unless you're a stalker," Anya said. "I've seen a few of those in my time."

"I'll bet."

"So," Anya said, "back to my question." When he looked at her blankly, she added, "What's going on around the Bronze these days?"

"Oh, that." Ross looked thoughtful. "Not much. I mean, I can tell you're looking for event-specific info, but I'm not sure exactly what. Can you give me a hint? Even go warm or cool?"

Anya laughed. "Maybe one of those shots you were talking about will loosen up those memory cells of yours." She raised her arm and waved at the bartender. "This round's on me."

He brightened. "Excellent! I'm always up for that."

"Let's go something more yummy than straight booze," Anya suggested. "I think they have something called a 'bloody brains.'"

"That sounds absolutely disgusting," Ross said solemnly. "Let's have two."

Anya and Ross came out of the Bronze arm in arm a couple of hours later, laughing and perhaps staggering a bit. Anya couldn't remember when she'd had this much fun. For heaven's sake, most of her life and everyone in it seemed to be "kill this and smash that and run from this and research that before something ends the world right now, kaput." While on some level she realized that was who and what she was, on another level—the one from when she was human and desirous of humanly things like love, marriage, and children—still lingered. Where was it written that she didn't have the right to go out with a handsome male friend now and then? To sit and have dinner, drink expensive wine, and have a nice filet mignon with the "cool red center" that all the posh restaurants labeled as rare? None of that meant getting intimate, or serious, or even making out. She loved Xander, but let's face it—he thought a night high on the hog was pizza and a six-pack of beer. And although he loved her back, Xander had certainly made it clear—to *everyone*—that he wasn't going to marry her.

Giggling, she and Ross made their way down the sidewalk. Anya licked her lips and tried to count how many bloody brains she'd had on top of that first beer. Five, she decided. It had to be five, because no way could she have had six. That was just way too many.

Abruptly Ross stopped, or at least tried to. It was more like a sloppy skid, but eventually he stood in one spot. "Hey," he said. His words were just a tad on the slurred side. "You wanted to get the slow down, er, lowdown on Bronze info. And since you were such great company, lemme tell you about something I heard before I forget." He shook his head a little, trying to clear it. "It was . . . yeah, this table full of women. They were talking about it right before you came in." He grinned at her tipsily. "I would have mentioned it, but your beauty dazzled my thoughts into other directions."

"Oh, please." Anya laughed and gave his shoulder a companionable push that almost knocked him over. "Oops—sorry."

Ross righted himself and waved away her apology. "No biggie. Anyway, you should have seen these gals, all done up in black right down to the eye makeup." He frowned. "Never did like that stuff. I think it makes women look like raccoons." He made circles around his eyes with his fingers.

"Or Zorro," Anya put in with a giggle.

"Right. So there they were all knee-deep in eye kohl, and they're all whispering and stuff. Being a demon has its advantages, as you well know." He reached out an arm, found the wall, and used it as a handy steadying tool. "First of all, I can sense power, and mood—that's a big thing—and this bunch was not to be messed with tonight."

Anya gave a little shake of her head, trying to clear away enough of the booze so she could focus more on what Ross was saying. "What else?"

"And hearing," he said proudly. "I've got *great* hearing. Demons like me, we can actually hear grass growing."

Anya squinted at him, wondering just how scintillating it was to listen to grass. She decided not to ask.

"So," Ross continued, "I don't remember that much about their conversation now, but I think they were talking about some big creature they created earlier tonight."

Anya stood up straighter . . . or at least tried to. "They made something? You think it was something badass?"

Ross nodded vigorously, then scrubbed at his eyes when the movement made him dizzy. "Oh yeah. From the sound of it, I'd say it was right up there on the major dreadful scale."

"Yeah?" Anya peered at him. "What did they say about it?"

Ross leaned back against the wall. "Well, I only caught part of it. Even with my hearing—*especially* with my hearing—you get a lot of interference. Other conversations, bar noises, the music. To be honest, I wasn't interested enough to follow along."

Anya scowled at him and he held up a hand. "But hey, anything to please a lovely lady. I remember they were talking about how they thought it was way too dangerous, and that it wasn't going to obey her—"

"Her?"

Ross pressed his lips together, trying to concentrate. "I dunno—she had a name like a bush or something, a plant. A tree?"

"Willow?"

He brightened. "Yeah! Willow—that was it. Anyway, they didn't think it was going to, uh, come back each night or something, that it would keep all the power it gathered for itself and not turn it in." He shook his head. "Freaky stuff. I try to stay away from people like that."

Anya put her hands on her hips. "I thought you said you like to stay informed."

"Oh, I do." He gestured at himself in an almost flamboyant manner. The movement kind of reminded Anya of an actor she'd once seen in a pirate movie. "But I like to do it from afar. It's much safer that way."

"I see." She snickered. "So you're just a basic save-your-own-ass kind of guy, right?"

"Hey, I never made any big claims," he protested. "I'm up front and forthright and all that kind of garbage."

"Right." She turned to go. "Garbage."

"Hey, wait." Ross shoved away from the wall. "I admit, I'm flawed. But we've had a great time here— don't go away all mad over one minor personality detail. I'm a great . . ."

"Look," she said, turning back when he didn't finish. "I'm not interested in getting involved with any— *gah!*"

His head was gone.

Well, not *gone* gone, but it *was* completely inside the mouth of some kind of only partially visible blue creature.

Anya froze. A part of her lightly inebriated brain whispered to her to simply stand there and be still, that this horrid beast wouldn't see her if she just stayed put, like a fawn hiding in bright daylight by lying in a sun-dappled patch of grass and leaves. She wanted to believe that, she really did, but there was the whole . . .

sucking thing going on only a few yards away from her, and it was all happening around Ross's head . . . or where Ross's head used to be, under the thing's mouth. The creature faded in and out of her view, but when she *could* see it, it looked kind of like a cat. But was it, really? The way its jaw had apparently opened, then completely closed over Ross's entire skull, was more like a snake, one of those mutantly oversized anacondas that by all rights belonged only on the Discovery Channel. Was it actually going to swallow him whole? When she could focus on the thing, she saw it was standing upright and flexing a three-pronged tail tipped with sharp-looking barbs. And poor Ross—he was hanging from its grip and jittering as though someone had fastened a hundred electrodes to his limbs.

Just don't move, her mind whispered. *It hasn't noticed you. Maybe it'll be full when it's done.*

On the heels of that: *I can't just stand here. I have to try to help him.*

Ross's shuddering abruptly stopped and Anya knew, *knew,* her evening's companion was dead and any assistance she could have given would have been too late. The cat-creature made a sound that was half purr and half disgusting burp, then pulled its mouth off Ross's head with a noise that was so much like a *pop* that Anya knew she'd never again make that sound with her finger and her cheek. It looked at Ross and tilted its head, as though it couldn't understand why its meal was so small and all used up; then it tossed him aside.

And turned its inquisitive gaze on her.

Just stay still—

"Screw you!" Anya screamed, and instantly changed her form. When she did, the cat-beast suddenly became fully and completely visible, and she wasn't sure if her curse was aimed at the voice in her head or the creature staring at her.

She ran for her life.

There was only one way she was going to have any chance of getting away from this thing, and that was to stay in her stronger vengeance demon shape. But the transition was surprisingly difficult—she was half drunk and it was hard to concentrate when she had something that was a cross between the alien of her worst nightmares and a hungry lion panting down the back of her neck. Finally Anya managed to make the transformation hold steady; her speed picked up threefold, and she put everything she had into her legs and sprinted ahead.

It wasn't enough.

It caught her as she turned the corner out of the alley that led to a residential stretch of houses. The sad fact was that she just didn't have the traction to take her around the turn like the creature chasing her did—she stumbled while the cat-beast *flowed*. The thing brought her down with a claw-tipped, long-legged leap much like that of a cheetah's when it stretches out and grabs the flanks of a fleeing gazelle. Anya howled in pain as she hit the pavement, but by then she'd already twisted and was fighting back for everything she was worth.

She kicked, she flailed, and at one point she even bit the thing that had hold of her. There was a lot of pain, but Anya felt it only as a sort of background sensation—funny how a person can push pain to the back of one's mind when survival is at the front. Everything she had was concentrated on one thing: *not* ending up like she had seen Ross—shuddering in this thing's mouth until everything he was had been sucked out and all that remained was a dead and empty shell. She thought she was even getting the upper hand, until the thing's triple-digit tail whipped forward, wrapped itself first around one ankle and then the other, and dragged them together. With her kicking out of the way, it was simple for the stronger being to pin down each of her wrists and position itself over her.

Still Anya fought and thrashed and screamed, whipping her head back and forth right up to the point when the beast unhinged its lower jaw and pushed its slime-coated mouth over her head. There were teeth in there, and the worst of the agony hit when they pierced the skin at the nape of her neck and under her jaw, locking into place so she couldn't pull free. There was a roaring in her ears that drowned out everything, and fighting only made the teeth sink in deeper and the pain increase. Dimly, Anya finally understood why Ross had simply hung there.

The roaring increased to hurricane level, and Anya let go of her hold on her vengeance demon form. She'd spent so much of the last few years as Anya rather than Anyanka that now, drowning in fear and pain, it felt completely natural to meet death as the more fragile human woman. Within the mouth of the demon she surrendered and felt her flesh melt and reform, relax into the smooth-skinned Anya's—

—and the cat-beast jerked its mouth off her skull and flung her away.

Gasping for air, Anya hit the fender of a parked car, rolled, and ended up sprawled across its hood. An instant later the car's alarm went off, sending a piercing *whoo! whoo! whoo!* through the quiet street. Three yards away the cat-creature shook its head, then spit a gooey, scarlet-tinged mass onto the sidewalk; Anya felt moisture trickle down in a ring around her neck and realized the red in the beast's saliva was her blood. Why had it let her go?

As if it could sense her confusion, the blue creature swivelled its head and glared at her, then spat again. Too terrified to take her gaze away, Anya blinked. It was the strangest thing—it seemed to be fading in and out of her vision again, like it had right before she'd changed into her vengeance demon form. It was as though it had the power of invisibility but couldn't decide whether it should or shouldn't be seen. Still staring at it—or trying to, at least—Anya slid off the hood and ended up sitting on her butt against the front tire, too exhausted and in too much pain to flee.

Of course, she was never too tired to make her opinion known, and who cared if she couldn't quite see what she was yelling at?

She balled her fist and shook it at the empty air in front of her. "That's right, you ugly thing! I'm too good for you to eat! That'll teach you!"

For a few seconds the cat-beast winked back into sight. It snarled and took a tentative step toward her, and she found a reserve of strength that let her scramble backward as she tried to put the car between her and it. The car alarm still blared *waaaah! waaaah! waaah!,* but it had changed its tone, obviously programmed to draw as much attention as possible. And it was working—lights were snapping on in windows along the darkened street.

A quarter of a block down, someone opened a door and shouted, "Hey, get away from that car or I'll call the cops!" Farther down the street a window opened and a woman cried, "Hey, that's *my* car alarm!"

The cat-beast swiped an arm across its mouth and glanced toward the voices. Then it looked back at Anya with an almost perplexed expression, as if it couldn't altogether decide if it should try again—maybe she wouldn't taste so bad the second time around.

"Get *away* from me!" Anya yelled at it. She struggled to her feet, preparing for another sprint. "Go munch on a mouse, you overgrown feline!"

There were footsteps now, running toward them from the tree-lined shadows farther down the street. With a final, bewildered look, the cat-creature turned away from her and melted into the darkness. Straining to watch it leave, Anya couldn't decide whether it had run . . . or simply disappeared.

Chapter Fourteen

Eleven minutes before the sun came up, the cat-beast came back home to mama.

Willow sat on one of her overstuffed chairs and waited for it, watched as it slunk quietly through the window. She loved to watch the creature—the way it moved in particular, like water flowing in all directions. As the last of its triple tail cleared the windowsill, the opening automatically sealed itself, just as it had opened in response to the creature's approach. It looked larger than it had upon its creation, fatter—obviously it had fed well on its excursion through Sunnydale's lovely nightlife.

"Come," Willow commanded.

It obeyed, slinking down and lying across her feet like a warm, living rug. Enjoying the feel of something alive in the room, she let it stay there for a few minutes.

Even if it wasn't human, even if it was no better than the werewolf that Oz had permanently become or the mental mess of Spike, at least it was civilized. At least she could talk to it and get some response.

"You can talk to me. You can always *talk to me."*

The cat-beast lifted its head and stared at the Ghost of Tara as Willow sighed. She didn't want to look at the spirit, but she couldn't help herself; as always, the sight of the blood-splattered blouse deepened the tears in her heart and made her secretly want to cry.

"Perhaps if you did, you would feel better."

"Stop reading my mind!" Willow snapped. "You have no right to do that!"

The Ghost of Tara shrugged. *"I can't help it. I am in . . . everything you are."*

Willow clenched her jaw against the urge to tell the specter to just go away, too afraid that if she uttered the words it would actually happen . . . *forever.* She'd become convinced that the universe had it in for her like that. For years she had been the boyfriendless bookworm, the one who did the research and watched as other people went to parties and fell in love, including Xander. That bookworm tendency had caused her to inadvertently loose a demon, which she then mistakenly trusted, and which took on a mechanical form— Moloch—that killed a number of people and nearly added her to its tally before Buffy destroyed it.

Then she'd met Oz and all that changed, but didn't it just figure that Oz's cousin would bite him and turn him into a werewolf? Yet they still made a go of it, until she made a mistake with Xander and nearly lost him. But again she had turned things around . . . and then the one thing he couldn't change came between them. Well, it did more than come between them—it nearly got her *killed*—and Oz left her to go find a way to control his nature.

The pain of losing him had nearly been unbearable. On the outside she'd been the same old Willow, but on the inside she was shattered.

Then Tara had come into her life, not like a blinding ray of light, but like soft, dappled sunshine through the clouds after the storm of the century.

And now all that was left of Tara was a blood-speckled ghost.

At her feet the cat-beast purred as she reached down and absently stroked its sleek, blue fur. If only she could touch Tara like this! How often had she taken for granted that her lover would be there, even after their breakup over Willow's over-indulgence and subsequent addiction to magicks? If only she had known the danger that Warren presented, she would have eliminated him—in secret, if necessary—long before.

But she would bring Tara back. She *would*.

She stopped her petting and slid her hand down to the blue-white flesh stone embedded in the base of the cat-beast's skull where it met its heavily muscled neck. She covered it with her palm, then pressed down hard. "Give me what you've collected tonight," she ordered.

The creature turned its head and looked sideways up at her, and for a moment she didn't think it was going to comply. Then it lowered its head and hunched its shoulders in a vaguely pushing motion as the air in the room grew thick with a buildup of static electricity. Willow dug her fingers into its fur and concentrated, hard, and after a two-second lag she felt the hair beneath her palm rise, and power flowed through her palm and up her arm.

She was gorged, for now, and the beast was hungry again.

It wouldn't take long for the new power within her to settle and make room for more. In the meantime the cat-beast prowled the room like a ravenous panther painted in shades of Warhol blue. Willow had to keep an eye on it constantly—she simply didn't trust it to stay away from Oz and Spike if she turned her back. She had no urge to leave the loft right now, but if she did, she'd have to find a way to contain it. That wasn't an easy task—when she created something, she did it *right*. The beast was strong and shrewd, and it even had a smidgen of the thought processes of a human. The cat of today might not have opposable thumbs, but this one did, and it wasn't a far-fetched idea that it would figure out how to turn the lock on a human cage. No, she'd have to come up with a magickal container, and right now, well, she was simply too lazy, too full of the power she'd pulled from the cat-beast's excursions of the previous evening.

"You mustn't sleep."

"Huh—what?" Willow jerked and sat up. She'd been lying on top of her bed, enjoying the cool feel of the silky comforter against her cheek.

"Look at your creature, Willow."

Rubbing her eyes crankily, Willow scanned the loft and saw the cat-beast sitting calmly not three feet away from where Spike crouched next to the fireplace.

"*Damn* it!"

She slid off the edge of the bed and strode over to where the creature was, then stepped between it and Spike. It regarded her impassively, with no trace of apprehension or regret for its disobedience. In fact, it actually yawned, showing a darker blue tongue that quickly traced the edges of its own teeth before the mouth closed with a snap.

"Get away from here," Willow ordered. "I *told* you there would be no feeding on anyone or anything in this loft." She pointed to the other end of the room. "Now *go!*"

It simply sat there.

Willow scowled. She knew it understood her . . . didn't it? Was this disobedience or simple ignorance? Or even just stubbornness?

Willow jumped when the Ghost of Tara spoke right next to her. *"The creature is hungry. It will not obey you. Be careful, Willow. Your creature is not to be trusted, and it will turn on you the first chance it gets."*

Suddenly the cat-beast growled, not at Willow but at the Ghost of Tara. Willow stared at it, fascinated, then felt her temper burgeoning. If the damned thing understood the Ghost of Tara's words, then it must also understand hers—it was simply ignoring her!

She slapped her hands together to get its attention, and her seething anger made sparks jump from between her palms. "You will do what I command or I will destroy you," she ground out.

Staring up at her from a sitting position, the creature gazed from beneath half-closed lids, looking downright dangerous. Willow tensed herself for a fight, but then the cat-beast suddenly turned and crept away in the direction she'd indicated, giving her a single resentful glance as it settled into place at the far end of the loft.

"I'm not sleepy anyway," Willow said to no one in particular. Instead of going back to her bed, she sank onto one of the chairs in front of the fireplace and glared at the low flames, watching them dance and flicker, occasionally snapping her fingers at them and causing a minor flare-up. Even as obnoxious as it was, as threatening, her newly born creature was serving the purpose for which it had been created. She could feel the increased power within her bleeding into her essence and establishing itself as a permanent source. If she could keep it under control for just a couple of weeks, Willow would have enough power to do what she needed, she was sure of it. While it was bound as part of its existence to return to her each night, the thing was like a willful child; if she came down on it too hard, it might rebel completely and refuse to hunt for her.

Worse, it might waste its energy by beginning to attack normal people who could give it no power at all, drawing attention to itself and to her, and throwing away all the effort she'd put into creating it. If so, Willow would have to kill it, and it would certainly serve no purpose if it were dead.

In the meantime she could get her rest in the hours of the night when she sent the cat-beast out to prey.

"So who is controlling your destiny here now?" asked the Ghost of Tara. *"You? Or this demonic thing you've created?"*

Willow whipped her head around to stare at the Ghost of Tara. "I thought that was obvious," she said bitterly. *"You* are."

Chapter Fifteen

Xander banged on Anya's door, and when there was no answer, he banged that much harder. Damn it, he'd bang right through it if he had to, because he knew she was in there—he'd seen the light in the bathroom turn off from the outside—and he wasn't going away until she answered. He hated this whole separate apartment thing anyway, although he sure couldn't do anything about it. It would be amazing if Anya ever totally trusted him again, and who could blame her?

"Anya, open this door! Come on—it's me! And I am *not* going away!"

Finally, *finally,* he heard the lock turning, but when the door did creak open, it was only a few inches and the only view he got was darkness.

"What do you want?"

"Anya, where have you been? You were supposed

to go out and dig up some info, then report back, remember? You didn't even check in—"

"You know, I never applied for the *I Spy* job slot!"

Even though it was coming from only a small opening in the doorway, Anya's voice was shrill and furious enough that Xander took an involuntary step back. "Whoa, wait—what brought this on? Did something bad happen to you?"

"Oh, *now* you ask! Men—you're all just *jerks*!"

She started to slam the door, but this time Xander was ready and he got the steel-encased toe of his work boot into the opening just in time. "What's wrong?" he demanded. "Are you all right?" When all she did was keep pushing on the door, Xander put his shoulder to it and forced her back until he could open the door all the way. She couldn't hold it, and a secondary part of his brain wondered at this—a demon without the strength to hold a door shut?—but didn't have time to dwell on it.

Inside her apartment now, Xander saw her spin and storm away, leaving him to close the door without being told. He followed her down a hallway he thought was way too long, fumbling in the dark, and unfamiliar with her new place. Up ahead her silhouette turned to the left into an area that at least had a little bit of light. He hurried to catch up.

"Anya, come on—talk to me. What's wrong?"

He found her sitting on the couch in her new living room, leaning forward and covering her face with her hands. Since Anya was dressed in nothing but a robe and her hair was wet, Xander thought she'd probably just come out of the shower. He sat down next to her and tried to take one of her hands. "Anya?"

She slapped his fingers away. "I *told* you guys I didn't want to go out, that I wasn't cut out for this kind of thing!" Her hand zipped back up to cover her face again and she inadvertently slapped herself. The impact made her moan, and suddenly the hair on the nape of Xander's neck stood up and he felt sick. Something was wrong here, dreadfully wrong.

"Anya, let me see."

"No." Her voice was muffled from behind her hands. "Please—just go away and leave me alone."

Xander didn't ask again. He reached forward and pulled both her hands away.

Anya cried out, then hung her head. For a long, shocked moment Xander couldn't say or do anything but stare at her.

Then he pulled her into his arms and held her close for a long, long time.

At the Magic Box, Giles frowned, then leaned closer to peer at Anya's face and jawline. She flinched when he reached out to touch her skin, then squared her shoulders and motioned at him. "Go ahead. It doesn't hurt." She looked away. "Much, anyway."

"Hmmmm." He pushed delicately at her skin, staying away from the places where there were open lesions. It flaked beneath his fingertips, sending a powdery white residue into the air. Beneath her jawline was a line of puncture wounds that reminded him of the injuries on shark-bite victims, and Anya had lifted the back of her hair to reveal a matching set. The creature that had attacked her had literally ringed her head with its teeth. It gave him an awful mental image, and even though he'd been through some horrendous experiences in his own life, Giles found it difficult to imagine the kind of terror Anya must have endured.

"What do you think is causing that white stuff?" Xander asked anxiously. "Will it go away?"

Giles pulled a handkerchief from his pocket, wiping his fingers free of the skin dust while he thought it over. He was reluctant to offer his opinion on this, but they were all watching him and waiting—there just wasn't any way around it. Besides, given enough time, they'd probably come up with the answer on their own.

"I think it's the result of digestive fluid," he finally admitted. "And yes, I think Anya's skin will eventually heal itself. Her demon properties will go a long way toward making that happen."

"But it's not going to be fast," Anya said crankily. "I can tell that kind of thing, you know. And there's still a good part of me that's human-like. I don't heal instantly."

Xander patted her arm. "I know."

Giles took off his glasses, polishing them carefully. "So, how did this happen, Anya? Xander said on the telephone that you'd tangled with a demon of some sort. Is that correct?"

Anya looked decidedly ticked off. "Isn't that obvious? For crying out loud, I was nearly killed, and for what? To get *you* guys some information." She crossed her arms in a jerky movement, and beneath the ashy patches and bruises, her cheeks flushed with anger.

"Why don't you just tattoo the word 'fodder' across my forehead and be done with it?"

Dawn stared at her. "I thought as a demon, you would be extra tough and all that."

Anya whirled on her. "Fine! You go out and see what it feels like to have your head completely in some blue cat-demon thing's mouth! See how *you* like feeling its teeth lock in under your jaw!"

Dawn's face went pale, and she was at a loss for words. Finally she managed, "I'm sorry—I didn't realize it was that bad. I—"

"No, you didn't!" Anya said loudly. She glared at all of them. "But it was. It *was* that bad!"

When Giles couldn't think of anything to say, Buffy stepped forward and put a hand on Anya's arm. "Anya, honestly—we *are* sorry. If I could make it unhappen, I would. But I can't, so how about if we at least try to make sure it doesn't happen to someone else? Or even to you again, or one of us?"

"Fine," Anya said again, but a lot of the grumpiness had gone out of her voice. She sank back onto her chair. "Just . . . fine."

"What did it look like?" Giles asked. "You said it was . . . blue?" He tried not to allow too much disbelief in his voice. "And it just attacked you, without provocation?"

Anya nodded, reluctantly focusing on the memory. "Oh, it sure did. I mean, there we were, just coming out of the Bronze after having a few drinks, minding our own business—"

"Wait," Xander said. "We? Who's we?"

"Ross and me," Anya said. "And so we'd had a few drinks and we were in the alley—"

"You were in the alley with someone named Ross?" Xander blinked. "Just who is this Ross guy, anyway?"

"Dead, that's who," Anya said. "And not a guy—a mischief demon. So we were talking about what we were going to do next, and then I turned around and—"

"You were going to do something next?" Xander glared at her. "Like what?"

"Xander," Buffy said sternly. "Quit interrupting and let her finish her story."

"But—"

"Shut *up,*" Anya said. "After all these lectures to me about manners, you ought to preach what you practice."

"That's 'practice what you preach,'" Dawn said helpfully.

"That, too," Anya said. "Anyway, I turned around and there's this . . . this . . . *creature,* and it's got Ross's entire head in its mouth. And he's j-just *hanging* there, like a human-size rag doll, and he's shaking and everything, and I knew that it was too late to save him, or even t-try."

Even the clearly jealous Xander was silenced by this image. "Then what happened?" Buffy finally asked.

Anya swallowed. "It spit him out," she said. "I guess it was all done with him, like he was some kind of candy stick that it'd sucked dry or something." Giles was about to ask again about its appearance, but Anya beat him to it. "It looked like a cross between an overgrown cat and a man," she told him. "Except it had way too many fingers and a tail that was split into three parts. Lots of teeth, too." She shuddered. "Way too many teeth."

"So then it came after you?" Giles prodded.

Anya nodded. "It turned around and looked at me, and I figured the only way I was going to have even a remote chance at outrunning it would be in demon form, so I shifted." She frowned. "It's strange, but that almost seems to be what made it chase me."

Giles considered this. "So it wasn't going to until then?"

Anya shook her head. "I don't know. I'm not sure, but it didn't seem like it. Anyway, I ran, and it came after me. It—it caught me really q-quickly." Remembering her terror put a stutter into her words every now and then. "It was awful. I tried to fight it, but it got me down. Then the thing just opened its mouth and . . . and . . . *swallowed* my head."

They all shifted uncomfortably as they considered this, until Buffy broke the silence by asking, "How did you get free?"

Anya blinked as she moved to the end of her bad memory. "I'm not sure. There was a lot of pain and this . . . noise, like I was in a wind tunnel." She hung her head. "I knew I was going to die, and I was so scared. I lost my demon form and went back to human. And suddenly it let me go."

Giles sat forward, his eyes suddenly sharp. "It released you then? Precisely at that moment?"

Anya nodded. "Actually, it kind of *threw* me. And then it spit out my blood." She scowled. "Like I didn't taste good or something. What was that all about?"

Giles rubbed his jaw. "Maybe it—"

"Oh!" Anya's hand flew to her mouth. "Wait—I forgot to tell you one thing. It was sort of invisible, but not all the time. Just sometimes."

Buffy watched her carefully. "Sometimes?"

"Yeah." Anya looked to Giles, as if he could explain everything. "It kind of went in and out, like it couldn't decide whether I should see it or not."

"Really." Giles steered his wheelchair over to one of the newer bookcases that Xander had built, a lower one designed specifically so Giles could reach it. "And?"

Anya made a motion that was half shudder and half shrug. "And then I yelled at it and it ran away. It had thrown me against a car, and an alarm went off, so there was all kinds of noise and people were starting to open doors and stuff. It didn't come after me."

"Interesting," Giles murmured. "Very interesting."

Anya tossed her head. "I almost die, and you call it interesting? Thank you for your concern!"

Giles's eyes widened. "Sorry—I didn't mean it like that. I just find it quite fascinating that the creature seemed to attack you while you were in demon form, yet released you when you went back to human."

"I'm just glad you're all right," Buffy said.

"Yeah," Dawn said. "And I'm sure your face will heal in no time."

Anya didn't say anything, just rubbed self-consciously at her cheeks.

Giles pulled first one book then another from the

bookcase. "I believe I've heard of this creature," he said. "It's extremely rare—I've never seen one in person."

"Darned good thing," Anya said bitingly. "If you had, you'd have probably been an appetizer."

Giles shook his head as he glanced quickly through one book then set it aside in favor of the other. "I don't think so. Here, look." He found the page he was looking for and offered it to her. "Take a look at the *sine kot diabl*. Is this your attack-beast?"

Anya bent over to look at the page and visibly cringed. "Oh, yeah," she said, pulling back. "I never want to see that thing in the flesh again. I'm telling you, it *eats* people."

"Actually, no," Giles said. "It doesn't. . . . Well, not in that specific sense of the word. First of all, it focuses specifically on demons, or those infused with darker powers, and it consumes their power." He raised an eyebrow at her. "Such. as you when you were in vengeance demon form. That's why it let you go when you shifted back to human."

Buffy tilted her head, trying to work this out. "So what you're saying is that if Anya had stayed in human form when she first saw it, it wouldn't have gone after her?"

"Likely not." Giles picked up the book and began to read from it. "The *sine kot diabl* is a creature conjured specifically to find those with the powers of darkness, extract their power, and give it to its creator. It will not attack a human being in its natural form, because a human being generally has no power on which it can feed."

"But I'm not a human being," Anya protested huffily. "I'm a vengeance demon. Just ask my friends."

"Uh, we *are* your friends here, remember?" Dawn put in. "I don't know about the others, but *I* always think of you as a human being, whether you do or not."

"This beast is invisible to the human eye," Giles continued. "It is visible only to those whom it targets as power sources. This is so that it can move freely and seek out its victims without having to hide from the lighter presences of the earth."

"But that's not right," Anya said. "It kept fading in and out of my sight, like it couldn't make up its mind."

"I think that's more an indication of what *you* are than what *it* is," Giles told her. "You may think of yourself as a vengeance demon, but the fact is you've been more human than demon over the past several years. This may have played a part in providing you with a sort of camouflage. It may also explain why it released you—you slipped into human form, and it thought it was feeding on something it shouldn't . . . or *couldn't.*"

"Well, I'm just glad you got away," Xander said. "And you're not going out by yourself again. Not until this thing is caught and killed."

"Definitely," Buffy agreed. "And I'd say now's as good a time as any to go hunting."

"You're going to have quite the difficult time doing that," Giles said mildly.

Already on her way to the front door, Buffy stopped and looked back at him. "Why is that?"

"Might I remind you that you can't see it?"

Buffy blinked. "Oh. Oops."

"The devil is in the details," said Dawn.

Buffy's mouth turned down. "Can't we . . . I don't know, spray it with paint or something?"

"Have to find it first," Anya said. "I might be able to—"

"Oh, no," Giles said. "That's much too dangerous. It might have some kind of mark on you, a scent or connection. We know very little about this type of demon. Now that it's had one-on-one contact with you, it might be able to do something to force you into vengeance demon form and hold you there, make you unable to escape while it feeds on you."

The idea made Anya's face go pale. "I believe I'll bow out of this specific demon hunt."

"Good idea," Xander said.

"There is one thing we haven't mentioned," Giles said.

Buffy came back to the table and sat down. "What's that?"

"I think it's very likely that the *sine kot diabl* was created by none other than our very own Willow," the former watcher told them. "Specifically to gather power." His gaze swept the rest of the gang. "We all know there isn't anyone or anything else in Sunnydale that has the kind of Wiccan skill that could bring a creature to life like this."

Buffy tapped her fingers on the table. "But why does she need more power? I thought you said she pretty much got it all from you in the big battle."

Giles inhaled, secretly surprised at the distress the recollection of that brought him. "Well, she took everything that I had to give—quite a lot, knowing my original sources. But that doesn't mean she doesn't want more, although I can't imagine for what purpose."

Dawn glanced at Giles's useless legs, then looked away. "I wish it was for something . . . good," she said softly.

Giles said nothing for a moment, then cleared his throat. "Well, at this point the Willow we all knew and loved is fundamentally different. Unfortunately we have to assume that it's not for the greater benefit of the good people of Sunnydale."

Buffy stood. "Well, I guess I'll just have to go back and see if I can find out. Once I'm there, maybe I can figure out a way to get rid of this nasty cat thing." She hesitated, then looked to Anya. "Uh . . . you did say it was blue, right?"

Anya nodded. "But remember, according to Giles you won't be able to see it anyway."

Buffy shrugged and gave them all a game smile. "True, but what the heck. A slayer has to try."

"So, back to Ross," Xander said suddenly. "He was what, some guy who tried to pick you up in the bar? And you were going somewhere with him?"

Anya gave an exaggerated sigh. "We were drunk, Xander. And I don't know where we were going, actually—we just figured it was time to leave the Bronze."

Xander's mouth twisted. "So you were leaving the Bronze with this guy you met—"

"Actually, demon."

"Okay, with this *demon* you met." Xander stared at her. "And you were going to do what, exactly?"

Anya shrugged. "Beats me. Walk off the bloody brains, I guess. Maybe get something to eat."

Dawn's eyes grew wide. "You were eating brains?"

A smile touched at the corner of Anya's mouth, lightening her mood a bit. "No. We were drinking them."

"Color me grossed," Dawn said and flounced back on her chair.

"It's a drink," Anya told them. "Made with peach schnapps, Irish cream, and grenadine. When you make it just right, it looks like this marvelously bloody little piece of flesh floating around in the shot glass. It's excellent."

Dawn scrunched up her face. "Ewwww."

"So back to Ross," Xander began. "You and he were—"

"Doing nothing but having a good conversation," Anya finished for him. She turned back to Giles. "And you know, I think you're right about Willow being where that cat-creature came from. Poor Ross was actually a pretty good info source before he got turned into the night's main meal. He overheard a bunch of witchlike women talking about something like the beast that ultimately did him in."

Xander cracked his knuckles absently. "And you're just now telling us this?"

Anya hugged herself. "Giles asked me how it happened, and I told you. It's all about Willow anyway— what's the difference if I say she created a cat demon and it tried to eat me, or a cat demon tried to eat me and Willow created it?"

Giles nodded and flipped through first one book, then the other. "Well, I can't find anything about it in here, but I'm sure I recall reading that the creature we're dealing with can be eliminated by destroying a talisman, a sort of sister object that's created with it."

Buffy brightened. "Now, that's the kind of good news I like to hear. So what does it look like? I am *so* all about destroying talismen."

Giles smiled slightly but didn't bother correcting her. "In all honesty, I have no idea. Again, I can't find it in the reference materials we have here." He cocked his head. "Still, since the object is always created with the cat-demon, I'd venture that it can't be very far away from it. It's likely to be a requirement that they be in close proximity."

"Here we go again," Anya muttered. "Going after something and we don't have the faintest idea what it is."

"True," Giles agreed. "But find that talisman and destroy it, and we've destroyed the creature that almost killed you."

"All in favor say 'aye,'" Xander said.

Anya nodded vigorously. "Oh, double aye-aye."

"This is all great and dandy," Dawn said. Something in her voice made them turn around to look at her.

"But what are we going to do about *Willow*?"

Chapter Sixteen

Willow sent her cat-creature out for two more nights, and at the start of the third night she knew there was going to be a problem.

Okay, more than just a problem.

"You need to destroy it."

"Absolutely not," Willow said grimly. She refused to turn and look at the Ghost of Tara. "I want the power it gathers each evening. I can control it."

"You are a fool. You think you control it, but that is only an illusion."

"Like you?" Willow said, whirling around. "And how can you call me a fool?" she demanded. "Everything I'm doing is for you—to bring you back to me. How can you be so ungrateful?"

As she always was, the Ghost of Tara had been practically right on her heels, so when Willow turned around, for a disorienting moment she felt like she was running into her. But of course she wasn't—and she never would be if she didn't get the things done that she needed to.

"How can I be grateful for something that can never be?" The Ghost of Tara looked at her sadly. *"My presence torments you, yet to watch you on this futile path breaks my heart."*

"It is *not* futile," Willow said grimly. "I will *not* be denied. You just wait."

"Well, obviously I won't be doing much else."

"I can do without the sarcasm," Willow snapped. "Is that a new trait?"

The Ghost of Tara tilted her head. *"What you're taking as sarcasm isn't that at all. It's simple honesty . . . and you don't want to hear the truth."*

"Gee," Willow said. "Do you really think so?"

"Yes."

Willow sighed. "That was a rhetorical question. You didn't have to answer."

"Yes, I did. That is as much the truth as your knowing you should eradicate your demon."

"I won't," Willow said simply. "Don't bother asking again." She turned away from the Ghost of Tara and studied the cat-beast a few feet away. Yes, at the end of each evening it was still bringing her a glut of power, wonderfully overstuffing her stores of energy . . . but each session was a more serious fight to get the creature to release it to her. Willow had done her research on the thing, and she'd known full well what she was creating, but nowhere in the textbooks she'd studied had it mentioned just how greedy and self-centered the *sine kot diabl* really was. The thing had no desire or inclination to please her. It did so only because it *had* to . . . at least so far. She emptied it of power each night, but it was also stronger with the setting of every sun—obviously its body naturally took in as food part of the energy it harvested. What would the creature be like in another three weeks? Or another three *days*?

"*Destroy it,*" the Ghost of Tara whispered. "*Before it gets stronger and turns on you . . . and feeds upon those it shouldn't.*"

Willow blinked and glanced over at Oz and Spike. They were fine, and the cat-beast was nowhere within their range. In fact, it was clear across the loft, having learned its lesson well from the last time she had disciplined it. But still . . . there was no mistaking the hungry look in its ice-shard blue eyes as it watched the werewolf and the vampire from beneath sleep-heavy, half-closed eyelids.

"One more night," Willow finally agreed in a voice too low for the cat-creature to hear her. She had no idea if it truly understood human words, but she wasn't taking any chances. "Just one more night. I'll cancel the creation spell that made it when it returns in the morning."

"*But—*"

"That's the absolute *best* I'm going to do," Willow said loudly. The escalated volume of her voice made the cat-beast lift its head and regard her with interest, while Oz gave another of his frustrated snarls and Spike only winced and kept rocking in his private, apparently mostly mad world. Seeing its attention on her, Willow snapped her fingers at the cat-beast, then pointed toward the window. "Go," she commanded. "Hunt as is your purpose and return to me."

Her cat-creature inclined its head in subservience before slipping out the window and into the night, but Willow could swear the look in its eyes was nothing short of calculating. Could she really call it *her* creature, any more than any cat owners could really say their cat was theirs? Cats were such independent things, and she had made one with more size and strength, more intelligence and diabolical purpose, than any normal person would ever contemplate.

Time would tell.

Meanwhile her research into the more important issue of resurrecting Tara was ongoing. There was no more trinket-making, no more of the ridiculous little spelling-bee PTA atmosphere. Her coven members gathered at the loft each night and helped Willow, in whatever way possible, to further her research. At any given moment there might be at least two translation spells going on, and at another there might be a locator ritual to help find a missing tome or recreate the holographic image of a section of text that had been obliterated long ago. The loft was a dark and busy place these days, and while she waited for the cat-beast's late-night, final return . . .

Willow loved every moment of it.

The sun was still only a hint of the coming dawn when the five of them gathered outside the Magic Box for a final check before heading for Willow's loft.

"I'm still not sure this is a good idea," Giles complained. Stranded in his wheelchair, he looked vaguely angry and helpless, and Buffy wasn't sure she could even comprehend the kind of frustration he was enduring on a daily basis. "I found more references to an artifact, but we still have no idea what it looks like."

"No matter," Xander said. He sounded like he was desperately trying to be brave and cheerful; unfortunately, he ended up coming off only as slightly lame. "Artifacts are generally easy to recognize. We'll know it when we see it. Bang and smash, and voilà—no more invisible creature stalking Anya."

"This can only be a good thing," Anya agreed.

"I think you're all full of rocks, Xander," Dawn said. "Mostly in your head. I can't think of a single artifact right now."

"And she says *I* have a head full of rocks," Xander commented to no one in particular.

Dawn glared at him. "Okay, so I'm a little nervous. I mean, think about it—Anya was nearly human sushi and we're hunting the creature with the Ginsu-sharp teeth? We must be insane."

"It tried to eat me only because I'm part vengeance demon," Anya pointed out. "You probably don't even taste good to it."

"I taste as good as the next person!" Dawn said defiantly.

Buffy looked from her sister to Anya. "Uh, can we just not go there?"

"Anyway," Xander said emphatically, "Giles could

be on to something here. I mean, this is Willow's realm now. We've never encountered her like this—she has an entirely new personality. We don't know what's going on in her head, or what's—"

"Oh, we know," Anya interrupted. "Murder and mayhem." When the others simply stared at her, she shrugged. "I think I heard that phrase on a mystery documentary."

"Well . . . sure," Xander said. "Murder and mayhem. I guess that applies."

"She's certainly murdered," Anya said ominously.

Dawn lifted her chin. "I don't care what you think. I'd call it retribution."

"And yet you're still one scared little teenybopper around her," Anya said pointedly.

Dawn cringed. "What have you been watching? Movies from the fifties?"

"Sometimes," Anya answered defensively. "They can be a great source of information on social standards—"

"Turning back to the topic at hand," Giles said hastily, "we have absolutely no idea what we're getting into here."

"Oh, I think we do," Buffy said. "Been there, got the butt-kicking, remember? But hey," she gave them a halfhearted grin, "I'm game to try again. If at first you don't succeed, fall on your backside again."

Dawn sniggered. "I don't think that's how that old saying goes."

"Then it's time to update," Buffy said with exaggerated blandness. She glanced at Giles, who only looked even more frustrated. "Okay, back to beeswax. We go to Willow's loft, and somehow I get her to come outside. Xander, Anya, and Dawn then go in and do the spell-thingy that Giles came up with, the one that's supposed to break up that coven that Willow's got going. Once all the evil witch-types are kaput, you search for the cat-artifact thing and destroy it, which gets rid of our feline overpopulation problem." She spread her hands. "What's so hard about that?"

"Let me count the ways." Anya leaned against the doorway and began ticking off points on her fingers. "First, you don't know if you can get Willow to come out of her loft, or if we can find a way inside it assuming you do. Second, I'm really interested in seeing if and how this grouping of, what, twelve other death-minded Wiccans is going to sit around and wait while we read off the spell for their destruction."

"I think it's a fair guess that one of you will have to read it while the other two fight to keep that person safe," Giles said.

"Third," Anya continued, "assuming we don't all get turned into wart-covered toads, we have no clue what exactly it is we're looking for in reference to that stupid, overgrown cat. And fourth, even if we do blow the coven to the four corners of the earth, what's to stop Willow from doing the same to us after she's through pounding Buffy into the ground?"

Buffy raised an eyebrow. "Hey, thanks for the vote of confidence."

"Fill me in again on exactly why we have to be *in* where Willow lives to do this?" Dawn asked. "And why we can't just look at her window and do the collective read-aloud?"

"You can't see the window," Buffy said. "You have to break through it to find it."

Xander's mouth tightened into a thin line. "Oh, great. So we're supposed to just bounce off the outside of the building until we get lucky?"

"Oh, no," Anya said. "*You're* going to do that. There's no sense in all three of us getting banged up when one person will do just fine."

"Thank you so much." Xander rolled his eyes. "Your kindness is overwhelming."

"Actually, it's more fundamental than that," Giles offered. "To have a spell like this perform properly, one must go to the center of the power source. The farther away from the center you are, the less effective the spell becomes—we could end up sending away only one or two of the twelve Wiccans, and then you'd find yourself in one ugly situation. Even with Willow otherwise occupied with Buffy, that center is still where she, as the leader of the coven, lives and works most of her spells. It *has* to be in there to work."

"Great," muttered Dawn. "Can you say 'negotiate'?"

"Oh, they won't," Anya said. "I'm certain they'd rather just kill us." She looked at Giles. "Daylight would be better, don't you think? The dead of night has always tended to bring out the worst in people. And, of course, in demons. Perhaps we should wait a couple of hours, until the sun comes up."

Giles looked like he was about to say something,

but Buffy held up her hand. "Enough of this. It isn't getting us anywhere. We can stand here and argue all night, or we can go on and get this over with."

"But I like the talk idea," Anya said with a nod. "There's nothing wrong with healthy discussion and preplanning. In fact, we could even—"

"No, we can't," Buffy said brusquely. She turned and headed down the sidewalk. "Let's go. It's time for a little Wiccan deconstruction."

Chapter Seventeen

"*Your cat-creature has finally returned.*"

Willow looked up from where she'd been double-checking a long and complicated list of ingredients for a spell, then nodded at the Ghost of Tara. "I knew he would. You have no faith in me."

"*I have faith in the old you,*" replied the spirit. "*The new you . . . disturbs me.*"

"People are always ill at ease around things with which they aren't familiar," Willow replied. "They like things to be predictable and comforting."

"*Other people like these things. We have never had that kind of existence.*"

"No," Willow agreed as she watched the *sine kot diabl* slink through the mirrored facade that gave camouflage to the window. Instead of coming over to her, it stretched and then took on a sort of hunting wait-and-see pose. The darned thing just wasn't going to come to her, no matter how many times she told it to. Thankfully the other Wiccans were at the farthest end of the loft, poring over a bunch of Celtic spell books Ena had located the evening before. For now they were out of harm's way. "Predictable isn't exactly an overused word in our vocabulary, is it?"

"There are some things a person should be able to count on," the Ghost of Tara said softly. *"Special things that should never change."*

"There are a lot of things that should never change," Willow retorted. She could hear the bitterness in her voice, but she was unable to stop it.

"True," the Ghost of Tara said agreeably. *"But while you can't control some things, you have the power to keep others from turning upside down."*

"Don't you have something better to do than criticize me constantly?" Willow snapped. She regretted her words instantly, wished she could take them back and examine them before they hung there. Life, she thought, ought to have an ongoing time delay—ten seconds for you to consider what you'd just said or done so you could change it before it became permanent.

"I'm not criticizing, my love. Only remembering."

Willow turned to stare at the spirit. "Remembering? Remember what?"

"How it was when we were together, when you were at your happiest. Times when we talked for hours into the night, mornings when we held hands and walked in the sunshine. Often you were the calm, the voice of reason and my source of strength when things

were going wrong." The spirit's expression saddened. *"Now it's like, the more misery you cause, the happier you are. It breaks my heart to see that, to see the woman you've turned into."*

"I told you," Willow said. The Ghost of Tara's words hurt to her core, but she'd be damned if she'd show it. "People and things change. Things around me did, so I changed with them."

"You have a choice most of the time," the Ghost of Tara told her. *"You're the one who steers your destiny."*

"If that's true, then tell me why you had to die," Willow demanded. "No one gave *you* a choice in that. The universe didn't *ask*."

"I can't answer that question," the Ghost of Tara said. *"For life and death there are much bigger designs, and yeah, most of the time we have no say in it. But on this plane"*—the Ghost of Tara spread her hands—*"discretion can be our best ally."*

"Speaking of discretion . . . ," Willow said. She turned her gaze back to the *sine kot diabl*. The beast had apparently thought her attention was sufficiently diverted elsewhere and had crept toward Spike. The half-mad vampire was huddled next to the fireplace, but chained up and with his mouth still sealed, he could do little to get away from the cat-creature but roll his eyes and make a strained-sounding moan. Willow scowled as she saw her demonic creature crouch and prepare to leap.

"Stop!" she commanded.

The beast glanced back at her, and she could have sworn it actually shrugged, as if it really didn't give a damn what she'd said. Then it turned back, opened its mouth wide, and leaped toward Spike.

Willow's hand shot forward and she grabbed at the air. Across the room the *sine kot diabl's* midair vault jerked to a stop and it hung there, hissing and spitting in fury as it rotated slowly to face her.

"Bad kitty," Willow said with false gentleness. She jerked her hand back to her side, and the creature's body tumbled down and skidded forward until it stopped at her feet. "Gonna make mama angry," she told it. She was vaguely surprised at the strength of the cat-demon, and the amount of power it took to hold it—it must have fed well this evening. "Give me your power," she commanded it.

For a long moment the cat-creature stared at her, its frosted-blue eyes glittering in the loft's candlelight. Then—*"Willow,"* the Ghost of Tara said suddenly.

Startled by the unusual urgency in the spirit's voice, Willow frowned and glanced at her. "What?"

"Beware!"

The *sine kot diabl* turned on her.

"Alrighty then." Xander peered up at the swirly colored surface of Willow's building. "Refresh me on how exactly we're supposed to get in there?"

"You're going to crash through a window," Anya told him.

"I was afraid of that," he said unhappily.

"That means we climb onto the roof, and you just kind of bounce off the sides of the building until you find a window to break," she continued.

"Sounds painful," he said.

"I did it," Buffy offered. "It's really not so bad."

"For a slayer." Xander's gaze ran along the surface of the building. "Personally I'd prefer to use the door."

"I tried that," Buffy said. "It's steel, which is bad enough, but I think Willow reinforced it with a protection spell."

"Of course she did," Giles put in. "Any self-respecting Wiccan would take steps to protect her abode from interlopers."

"Interloper or not, remember I told you I got inside," Buffy said. "And that's where the really big whizbangs are. The little fun house that isn't. Trust me, up the outside is the way to go inside."

"Well, pardon me if I don't like the idea of being used as a human wrecking ball," Xander complained. "I'm breakable, you know. And I don't—"

One of the windows above them exploded outward.

As Anya, Dawn, and Xander cried out and ran for cover, Buffy shoved Giles's wheelchair out from under the jagged shards of glass raining down on the sidewalk. She'd barely gotten him out of the way when she saw Willow come tumbling out of the sharp-rimmed opening. Her former friend was screeching at the top of her lungs, cursing and flailing, as far as Buffy could tell, at nothing at all.

There wasn't enough time to leap forward and try to catch her, but Buffy needn't have worried—Willow did that just fine on her own, braking sharply and turning upright about four feet before she hit the ground.

There wasn't much time to dwell on it, but Buffy had an instant to think that Willow had never looked more beautiful in her life. In fact, it seemed that each time Buffy saw her, she looked even more so—now her hair and eyes were raven black and shining, and her skin, except for the trails of black veins, was porcelain white above an ink-colored cape covered in glitter. Willow had seen them—Buffy was sure of that—but paid no attention; instead she spun and waved her hand at the same time she spat out a mouthful of guttural-sounding words. Instantly something . . . *nothing* . . . crashed against the side of the building.

Buffy whirled and gestured at the others. "Get up there, quick! I don't know what she's doing, but you won't get a better chance than this. Giles, Xander— you've got the walkie-talkies?"

"Yes, of course," Giles answered. He peered at Xander. "Don't forget—one of you has to look for the artifact while another performs the spell. Without that object we won't be able to destroy Willow's cat-beast."

"Check that," Xander said. He patted his pocket. "And check on the walkie-talkie, too."

"Then *go,* now, while you're in the clear!"

Xander cast a wary glance at Willow, but she was busy with something else, although none of them had any idea what. The cat-beast? Maybe, but he didn't have time to think about it. After another second of hesitation, he yanked free the rope and hook he'd tied at his waist and tossed it up toward the edge of the roof. It missed, of course, thunking back to the ground and nearly braining him in the process.

"Damn it," he muttered. He grabbed for it, but Buffy beat him to it, hefting rope and hook high into the air and over the roof's edge in one smooth swing. There was the hoped-for faraway thud, and then she hauled the rope toward her until it caught on something and held.

"Nothing like experience," she told him. "Now go, already!"

Xander didn't need to be told a third time. They had pre-tied knots at intervals along the rope to make the climb faster, although as he hauled himself toward the roof, he didn't think it was going to help in the easier department for Anya and Dawn. It took less than a minute for him to get up there, although it felt like hours. "Come on!" he shouted down at the women when he was over the edge and looking down.

Below him Anya cast a glance back toward Willow, then took a deep breath and grabbed the rope. She wanted to slide into demon mode—it would be so much simpler to just morph onto the roof than deal with this idiotic piece of hemp—but there was this pesky feeling of terror in her stomach that told her she didn't dare. The *sine kot diabl* was clearly Willow's creation, and there was the Wiccan herself acting all whacked-out just a few feet away. Was the cat-creature there? In human form Anya couldn't see it, but could it see her? If so, it would also see her demonness, which apparently in its brain translated to dinner.

No thanks.

Hand over hand, she pulled herself upward with both Xander and Dawn shouting encouragement, unable to decide if she liked it or just wished they'd shut up. Even so, it wasn't too long until she was up and crawling, breathless, over the edge to hunker down next to Xander and wait for Dawn to join them.

Buffy made sure Giles was pushed as far out of danger as possible, and kept an eye on her three friends as they made their way up to the roof. When she saw Dawn finally drag herself over the edge and tumble out of sight, she squared her shoulders and went to face off with Willow. She'd taken three steps forward when she realized she was looking at something she'd never, *ever,* imagined she would see again.

Tara.

Chapter Eighteen

"*I warned you.*"

Willow ground her teeth and turned, following the *sine kot diabl* as it circled around her and searched for the best angle from which to attack her again. The creature had grown so much stronger—*too* strong, in fact—that the same motions and quick minispells she'd used previously to bring it back in line no longer affected it. In fact, almost nothing she'd thrown at it so far had done anything beyond postpone what was obviously going to be a major battle.

And now she had to listen to this.

"Tara," she snapped, never letting the cat-beast out of her sight, "I love you, I really do. But I so do *not* need the 'I told you so' spiel right now." The *sine kot diabl* snarled at the sound of her voice and started to advance, then retreated a few feet when she raised both hands threateningly. "You are *mine*," Willow told it in a harsh voice. "*Mine!* I can destroy you in an instant!"

"*It knows you can't do that so easily,*" the Ghost of Tara said. "*It knows that if you could, you would have already.*" She paused. "*It's testing you.*"

"I can and I will," Willow retorted. "If I have to!" She started to say something else, then saw a movement out of the corner of her eye. What was that? Someone climbing up the side of her building, and going over the edge! "Oh no," she said grimly. "We can't have *that* kind of nonsense!" No big deal, nothing that a small whirlwind spell wouldn't handle. By God, she'd sweep them right off the wall and into the next county. She'd—

"Tara?"

At the sound of the familiar voice, Willow jerked and spun, momentarily forgetting the cat-beast *and* the people on the roof. Buffy stood only a few feet away, looking utterly shocked—no doubt seeing the Ghost of Tara for the first time had thrown her for as big a loop as it had Willow. "Oh, for crying out loud," Willow said, exasperated. "What the hell else is going to happen here?"

Suddenly there was a roaring next to her head, and the ground, dirty and full of industrial grit, came up hard to meet her.

"We have to hurry," Xander said urgently. "She saw us."

"Baloney," said Dawn, but the tone of her voice sounded less than convinced. "She would've whammied us if she had."

"No." Anya pointed. "Xander's right. But look—she's fighting something, and Buffy's in on it too. But as soon as she recovers, you can bet we'll be her prime target. Let's get inside while we have the chance."

"All right." Xander looked at each of them in turn. "The window's on the other side of where Willow is down there. We've got one chance, and that's to go through all at once—"

"Wait," Dawn cut in. "All at once? As in all three of us on that one itty-bitty rope?"

"That's right."

"This scrawny thing right here?"

"Yep."

"They always break in the movies."

"This isn't the silver screen, or TV." Xander had already forced the metal hook free from where Buffy's throw had lodged it; he headed across the roof and Dawn and Anya followed. "Unless you want to call it the Wiccan World Reality Show."

"I'd rather not be a contestant," Anya said.

Dawn swallowed. "Ditto."

"Then let's get to it, do Giles's dissolution spell, and get out," Xander suggested. "Preferably *before* Willow figures out we're doing the unannounced drop-in and shows up to rearrange our body parts." He didn't wait for further argument; instead he looped the rope with the hook around a pipe on the roof, made sure it was secure, and wrapped it around his waist. "Come on, ladies," he said. "Time to go for a ride."

"Are you sure this rope is going to hold our weight?" Anya asked. She looked anything but pleased as he twined the rope around first her waist, then Dawn's. Finally he wound the remainder of it around all three of them one last time.

"I feel like a piece of macramé," Dawn complained.

"Or some badly executed Boy Scout project," Anya added.

Xander tightened the rope until they were all a little on the breathless side. "Let's avoid using words like 'execute,' shall we?" He gave them a bright, falsely courageous smile as he crab-walked them to the edge of the roof. "Hey, can anyone do the Tarzan yell?"

Xander jumped, taking them with him.

The trio swung free for one long, wild moment (during which only Xander's desire that Willow *not* turn her attention toward them kept him from trying a Tarzan yodel), and then they went through the already-busted window like a human wrecking ball.

Xander released the rope, and the three of them plunged to the floor in a mass of wood splinters and the rest of the glass that had been rimming the window. They scrambled up after struggling free of the rope, then instinctively formed a circle with their backs together so that no one could sneak up on any of them.

But the circle didn't hold. Dawn had no choice but to yell, "Look out!" when she saw that one of Willow's dark coven had recovered from her shock and was storming toward them from the far end of the loft. The woman was tall and Asian-looking, her hip-length black hair streamed out behind her, and her black eyes glowed red with anger. She had the unsettling appearance of flowing rather than running, and Dawn knew they were going to have to split up rather than offer themselves as a central bull's-eye.

Dawn dropped and rolled at the same time Xander and Anya did. A good thing, too—the bolt of red-tinged energy that shot out of the furious witch's palms zigzagged over their heads and missed by barely an inch. Where it hit the wall, it left a scorched circle more than a foot around. More of the Wiccans were regaining their wits and pairing off. Some of them were yelling now, and others remained confused and were doing little more than turning one way or the other as they tried to figure out what to do.

Someone tried to grab her, and Dawn punched automatically, connecting with a dark-skinned woman's jaw. "The spell!" she stage-whispered at Anya. "Do it—quick!"

But Anya was already on the money. She'd backed up into a corner created by the wall and a tall, earthy-looking armoire, and was fumbling with the small packet that Giles had made for her. A few feet in front of her Xander had picked up a chair and was swinging it like a scythe, trying to keep the Wiccans away from Anya while at the same time hoping he wasn't too much of a stationary target.

Dawn had been convinced, wrongly, that she would be prepared for the sight of Spike and the werewolf-Oz chained up like animals . . . but she wasn't. It was utterly shocking to see them, and while Spike wasn't doing much except pacing against the wall and watching everyone from swollen, shadow-rimmed eyes, all the noise and movement, the screams in particular, were driving Oz into a frenzy. Was that really Oz under there, a young man who had supposedly once loved Willow and helped the Scooby Gang stake vampires? It was inconceivable. Snarling, the hairy beast lunged at whatever got too close, be it human, Wiccan, or inanimate object—at one point he attacked a glass jar that rolled within his reach, biting into it and spraying blood in every direction when it shattered in his teeth. Dawn could only hope Willow's magickal chain held, because if it didn't, she had a feeling that more than one person was going to be dead—or wake up a were-wolf—tomorrow.

Dawn jumped as Xander's chair broke into a dozen pieces, destroyed by an energy bolt thrown by a tall black woman who looked a lot like Queen Latifah. She raised her hand again, and Dawn leaped the five feet separating them and tackled her, going down on top of her before the woman could make Xander into today's dark-haired potato crisp. She pounded on the woman but took a couple of painful hits herself. Somewhere in the background she heard Xander screaming into the walkie-talkie: "Giles! Giles! A little help here wouldn't huuuurrrrt!"

The former librarian must have heard Xander, because suddenly the air between Xander and the rest of the loft shimmered and thickened. Dawn thought it looked a lot like those force fields that she saw on all the old science fiction programs, all liquid-like and glistening. It was obviously a great thing, because as Dawn backed away, the three Wiccan women who'd been heading for Xander hit the wall of shining light and bounced off it like rubber balls against bricks. Ticked off, they picked themselves up and tried again, then tried a couple of other things. None of it—small fireballs, energy bolts of varying colors, heavy objects hurled at it just out of spite—worked. It all would have been a great and grand event, except for the fact that when the three of them, and the Wiccans, turned and looked at Dawn—she was on the wrong side of the force field.

Willow rolled with the cat-creature's attack, getting dust in her eyes and mouth and feeling the beast's claws rake her back and part skin through the fabric of her clothes. Darn it, she *liked* this outfit, and now this stupid demonic feline had ruined it. She got a hand under its chin and pushed its teeth-filled mouth away from her face—did it really think she'd let it bite her?—then punched it as hard as she could, putting a good deal of extra oomph behind the swing. The *sine kot diabl* squalled with pain and surprise and flew backward, crashing into a pile of mostly empty steel barrels. It struggled back to its feet and crouched, growling viciously; clearly it wasn't done trying.

"Your choice," Willow told it harshly. "Obey me and give up your power as you were meant to, or die."

"Okay, call me crazy, but who are you talking to? And how did you end up with Tara's spirit here?"

"Go away," Willow told Buffy without turning to look at her. She knew better than to take her eyes off the *sine kot diabl* again. "I don't have time to deal with your patheticness right now."

"You don't have a choice," Buffy replied, and tried to grab her.

Willow whirled just as Buffy's hand brushed the back of her shoulder. She slapped it aside, then walloped Buffy a good one on the side of her head. Buffy toppled backward, rolled in one of those slayer-type movements that had always made Willow a little jealous, and was back on her feet almost instantly. Meanwhile Willow still had that stupid cat-demon to deal with, but it saw its opportunity and seized it. Amazingly, Willow found herself in the middle—Buffy advancing on her right side, and the *sine kot diabl* leaping at her from the left.

Willow gave a mental shrug and stepped back out of the line of attack.

"The spell!" Dawn screamed. The time for stage whispers and trying not to be noticed was over—she was seriously outnumbered here. She didn't know which was louder, her heartbeat or her hollering. *"Anya, do the spell!"* She thought Anya might already be doing it—was that her voice she heard through all the screaming and crashing of furniture? Dawn thought she heard words—*"With the end of this scattering spell, break apart this group of hell . . ."*—but she wasn't certain. The Queen Latifah woman she'd tackled was majorly irate, and while a big clot of the other Wiccans were still busily trying to break through Giles's force field, tall, dark, and ticked off had decided to focus all her attention on Dawn.

"Say," Dawn said as the other woman scowled at her and began to get up from the ground, "I think we got off to a bad start here." She tried to sound companionable and friendly—ridiculous given the circumstances, but what the heck. She'd always been told it was hard to be angry at someone who was smiling at you, so she plastered a big-and-bright all the way across her face. "My name's Dawn. What's yours?" In the background she could hear Anya continuing her chant—*"Like the wind takes of the seed, stop them from their own dark deeds, in every direction, no two together . . ."*—and since Giles had made it clear he wasn't sure how long his shield would hold against the amount of power concentrated up here, she needed to keep ol' Queenie's attention somewhere—*any*where— other than on Anya and Xander. There was something about this woman that gave Dawn the distinct impression that she was one of the more powerful members of the coven Willow had put together. It didn't help that the area around Anya was starting to emit a sort of bluish-white glow, like a small, growing star, making it a certainty that she'd be noticed at any moment.

"My *name*?" The dark-skinned woman didn't so much stand as *rise* into the air in front of Dawn. Her expression was thunderous and incredulous at the same time. "For you, my name is *death*!"

"Oh, hey," Dawn said and gave the woman her best this-is-all-just-a-big-misunderstanding expression, "why don't we just let bygones be bygones?" Dawn knew the words to Anya's chant and could tell she was almost there, if only she'd just *hurry*. Really, there was only so much circling around that Dawn could do without running into one or more of the other witches, and right now she was happy to let them batter away at the protective shield separating them from Xander and Anya. Still, the shield itself was starting to show wear, breaking down a little at the edges and forming cracks that were crawling toward the center like safety glass in a windshield that had taken a big hit from a rock. It didn't look like it was going to hold much longer.

The smile Dawn got in return was wide on the Wiccan woman's dark face, and also filled with big, bright teeth. "Bygones," she said, almost pleasantly. "That's a good word. For what you're going to be! Oh, and just so you know before you die? My name is Njeri."

The Wiccan swept her hand toward Dawn, but the teenager was already ducking, thanks to some heretofore dormant sixth sense that told her to get the hell out of the way, right *now*. Something like lightning, only a whole lot redder, blasted across the space where Dawn's head had been only a second before. Then she smelled something familiar and not at all welcome.

"Hey!" she protested. "You singed my hair!" Besides that, her knees were throbbing where they'd clunked against the floor.

Njeri's fire-studded gaze flicked toward Anya and Xander, and Dawn knew her two friends were in trouble. The witch looked like she'd suddenly forgotten about Dawn in favor of focusing on the other two.

Not good—this one had mucho power, so much that Dawn could feel it practically leaking out of her. She was probably second in command under Willow; if anyone could put a wedge into the cracks of their Giles-generated protective wall, it was she. In fact, the area behind where Dawn had been was now a smoking, blackened ruin, and she didn't want to think about what her head would have looked like had she not done the drop and roll.

"Hey!" Dawn yelled as loudly as she could. "I'm *talking* to you!" Njeri paid her no mind, which added aggravation to Dawn's anxiety—why were the adults in her world always ignoring her? Njeri looked like she was working up to the bigger bang, and Dawn glanced frantically around for something, *anything* to break or throw. Off to her left on the floor was a bottle with a stopper in it, a pretty little thing with a long, slender neck and a bubble-shaped bottom. It had some kind of bright yellow liquid in it, but Dawn didn't have time to worry about the how and why details. She snatched it up and tugged on the stopper—no use—so she wound up like a baseball player and threw the bottle at the floor in front of Njeri's feet.

There was a nasty flash, and then acrid yellow smoke exploded upward, blocking the space between Njeri and the protective wall and blinding out just about everything. She ducked her head to the clearer air at floor level, and through the smoke Dawn could hear Njeri first coughing, then gagging as the yellow substance filled her lungs. Above it all Anya's clear voice rose in the final lines of Giles's spell: *"And no*

*ability to then re-gather, send them off to hither and
yon, away with them, be far and gone!"*

Buffy was fighting for her life.

Against . . . *Nothing.*

Well, nothing she could *see,* anyway, at least not as
more than a vague, sometimes shadow that wobbled in
and out of her vision as though it couldn't make up its
mind about its own tangibility. She *could* hear it, and in
a this-isn't-really-happening-to-me sort of way, she
realized the noise in her ears was purring, like she was
being nuzzled by a great, overly affectionate cat.

Except the damned thing was mostly invisible.

Buffy yelped as lines of pain streaked across the
front of her shoulder, and when she instinctively
looked at the area, she saw a pattern of evenly spaced
bloody stripes materialize seemingly out of thin air—
only claw marks could have made those wounds. She
took a wild swing at the air and felt her fist connect
with flesh—maybe—but the blow must have been
ineffectual, because in another second she was on the
ground and staring up at the sky in amazement. How
could she be anything but incredulous when she could
feel the weight of something huge and heavy sitting
across her stomach and hips but not see it?

She bucked, hoping her invisible attacker would
instinctively throw its arms forward for balance—if it
actually *had* arms—so she could wrap them and roll it
off her. No luck; instead those claws she couldn't
see—but oh, could she *feel* them!—dug deeply into the
outside of each of her thighs as the unseen beast held

on with its back feet. Ultimately it seemed all she was going to be able to do was flail wildly at the air in front of her face and hope to God she'd connect with something.

She tried a blow, missed, tried another, and missed again. The weight was on her chest now and it was *huge*. Buffy felt like a mouse on one of those life-or-death animal shows, the ones where they explain in excruciating detail exactly how a boa constrictor *really* kills its prey. Still she kept struggling—as far as people went, her lung power fell on the side of pretty extraordinary. The weight abruptly increased, as if the thing were leaning forward; before she could give it a good, hard wallop, she felt something wet and sharp slip down and over her head. The sensation around her neck was way too much like a big ring of teeth, and her mind rebelled at the thought. She wanted to open her mouth and scream, but she couldn't hear anything over the sudden roaring in her ears, a sound she could only compare to that of a hurricane-tossed ocean. She also wanted to fight, but nothing in her body would work anymore, she couldn't feel anything.

Then everything in front of Buffy's eyes went black, and the world was smothered away.

Chapter Nineteen

Willow jerked as a sudden blue-white light streamed out of the broken window overhead. *My coven!* Her eyes blazed as she realized what was happening, and her fists curled at her sides. Gaze tight on the window, she stepped forward and began to concentrate.

"*Willow.*"

Something in the Ghost of Tara's voice was strong enough to cut through her consciousness and break the fragile thread of her focus. So much for an easy teleportation. "Not now, Tara! I have to get up to the coven before they destroy it and ruin every—"

"*Buffy is dying.*"

Willow hesitated, her thought process now completely derailed. "What?"

"*Your creature—it's feeding on her. She has*

maybe two more minutes—if she's very, very lucky—to live."

A movement out of the corner of her eye drew her attention for a bare second—Giles, of all people, trying desperately to wheel that chair of his over to help Buffy. It would be useless since he couldn't actually see the *sine kot diabl,* but Willow gave a careless snap of her fingers anyway. One of his wheels jammed, sending him turning in frustrated circles as he cussed at his metal mode of transportation.

"Willow, you must focus on what I'm telling you. Don't let yourself be distracted."

Willow shot a longing look at the window overhead, then sighed and scowled at the Ghost of Tara. "Don't be absurd, Tara. The *sine kot diabl* feeds only on sources of dark power. Buffy is good—she's like some kind of freaking white fairy or superheroine or something. Lara Croft, only shorter. Come on—everybody knows that."

The Ghost of Tara gave a delicate shrug, and when Willow's gaze would have turned once more toward the busted window, the spirit moved around to stand between the building and Willow. That old saying— "You make a better door than a window"—did not apply here, and it made Willow's insides twist when she realized she could see the wall of the building through Tara's semitransparent figure. And always that nasty scarlet stain to remind her of the unfairness of life and death.

"There are people, including Buffy herself, who've questioned the source of her power," the Ghost of Tara

reminded Willow. *"Her own dreams suggest that it may partly be born of a demon or darker being. You know this, Willow, and she was once your best friend. Can you really let her be murdered at the hands of a creature you created because you were hungry for power?"*

Indecision razored through Willow, making her take a step toward the building, then stumble back. "Stop it, Tara!" she finally yelled. "I can't be there for Buffy anymore! I'm not that person now!"

But the Ghost of Tara would not accept that. *"Of course you are. Inside, you are the same old Willow."*

"I am *not*!" Willow's scream was so loud and piercing that the cat-creature a few feet away actually mewled. Willow whirled toward the sound, then couldn't help gasping at what she saw. She'd turned herself off at the notion of what would happen to Buffy at the mercy of the *sine kot diabl,* but actually seeing it tripped that mental switch to a big fat *on.* While the light spilling from the window thirty feet above her built to an eye-blistering brightness, Buffy's slender form hung from the cat-beast's grasp like a lifeless human rag doll. It was horrifying, almost indescribable, and for a too-long second Willow lost every bit of her air.

Was that how Buffy was feeling now?

As always, the Ghost of Tara was right there, inescapably close. *"How many times has Buffy saved your life, Willow?"* she whispered in Willow's ear. *"How many times has she put your safety, your life, before everything else? Do you remember when Faith held you prisoner? Do you remember the sacrifices that Buffy made to gain your freedom? Your life?"* The specter paused, then her next words were even more ominous. *"It's eating her alive."*

Willow screamed then, louder than before, almost louder than she ever had—only Tara's death had made her more frustrated, more furious. She put her hands to her head and gripped her night-black hair and pulled, then screamed again, her voice stretching on and on and on until it sounded more like a tortured wail than anything else. With a last, agonized look at the rays of light leaking from the broken window overhead, Willow spun and leaped onto the back of the *sine kot diabl*. Her hands, so full of rage and power—more than ever before in her life—splayed into claws and dug into each side of the cat-creature's head, really dug *into* it, in and in and in, through hair and blood and bone and brain matter until there was nothing in between her fingers but her own skin and the shrill and seemingly never-ending death scream of the *sine kot diabl* itself as she yanked its mouth off the Slayer's skull.

And then it was over.

Willow stood there for a long moment, blinking and wincing in disgust at the blood and bluish goop dripping from her hands. Buffy lay on the ground at her feet, still as a corpse . . . no, not quite. There, right *there,* Willow saw a slight rise of her chest, the barest flutter of an eyelid. Buffy, her former friend, her current enemy, a nemesis like no other would ever exist for Willow, had survived. And for this Willow had only had to sacrifice—*My coven!*

Gnashing her teeth like the beast she'd just destroyed, Willow spun toward the window, then vaulted upward. When she rolled through the window, she felt like she'd opened her eyes in the middle of a lightning storm. There was a huge hole in the air in the center of the loft, a whirling white and silver vortex that was sucking nearly everything in the room into it, like the black holes scientists claimed existed in space. Anything lightweight and loose was already history—the smaller pieces of furniture, the knickknacks and precious spell books, the potions and lotions and jars of things most useful. Willow couldn't tell how many of her coven had already fallen victim, but the air was filled with the screams of her remaining witches as they tried to hold on and avoid a similar fate. Her bellow of rage only added to the chaos, and to make it worse, for the first few seconds she was back inside, Willow lost her balance and was nearly sucked into it herself.

"No—stop!" At first Willow's voice could barely be heard, and she hated herself for her weakness. Then fed by her anger and fear, Willow's lungs found power.

"CONSISTĔRE ET FINEN IMPONĔRE!" Her voice was like a huge and living thing, hammering through the nearly hurricane-force squalls. For an eternal moment she thought nothing was going to happen, so she bellowed again.

"CONSISTĔRE ET FINEN IMPONĔRE STATIM!"
And then—

Silence.

But the quiet didn't last long. Willow made damned sure of that.

The vortex, that howling, swirling hole that led to parts unknown around the world and which was to have been their saving grace, was gone.

Still reflexively squinting, Anya finally uncovered her eyes. "Wait . . . where'd it go?"

Xander started to reply, then choked off his words. All he finally uttered was, "Uh-oh."

The two of them still bug-snuggly behind their somewhat battered safety shield, it was a less than comforting sight to see Willow standing amid a pile of smashed glass below one of her former windows. Her expression went beyond anger or rage; it was positively black with fury. Here and there around her, the remaining members of her coven were groaning with pain and exhaustion, some crawling across the floor until they could find something to help pull themselves upright while others had fallen unconscious. A number were missing entirely—now Willow's carefully chosen coven was down by five. Dawn slumped in the corner, one arm still wrapped around a heavy carved post on one side of an antique buffet.

So far, Willow had eyes only for Xander and Anya, and Xander hoped he could keep it that way until Dawn could escape. Afraid to turn his attention away from Willow, Xander thumbed the button on the walkie-talkie. "The spell stopped," he said urgently into the microphone. "Giles, the spell stopped, it's gone, kaput. Was she supposed to do that, to be able to stop it? Was she?" He was babbling, but he seemed unable to stop himself—fear had taken control of his tongue. "Giles, are you there? How did she—oh, man, we are *so* in trouble here!" The walkie-talkie dropped from his grip, and he clutched Anya by the arm and backed up; only Anya's gasp and last-second push turned them toward Spike and kept them out of range of Oz's reaching claws.

And speaking of claws . . .

Through the faintly shimmering curtain of power in front of them, Xander and Anya watched helplessly as Willow raised her right hand, then bent the fingers into hooks and raked them across the air in front of her. Like the marks of some huge supernatural grizzly bear, four slashes appeared in their protective shield, gaping wounds that instantly began to spread outward, eating away at the reinforcement until the gouges met at the edges and their protection disintegrated right in front of their eyes. Five seconds, no more, and it was gone entirely.

"Well," Anya said with false cheerfulness. "So much for that. And it was such a brilliant idea too. Very science fictionish."

"That's not true." Willow's voice was hollow and frigid, like the wind on a black and freezing winter night. "I'd say it's easily the most moronic thing you two have ever done."

"Actually I was talking about the shield," Anya said.

"Willow, wait." Xander's voice was thick with

anxiety, like someone had tucked a tennis ball in his throat and he was trying to talk around it. "Think about what you're doing."

She tilted her head. "Hmmmm. Interesting thought. The world is full of choices—I think one of you, or maybe it was Buffy, told me that once. No . . . it was probably Tara. I really can't recall, but no matter. It just means I have decisions to make." She gave them a smile that was so wide and dark it was painful to look at. "Shall I flay you alive before I cook you, like I did Warren? Or shall I just skip to the good part and go instant barbecue?"

"Oh, hey," Xander said. He wasn't feeling very brave, but he stepped in front of Anya anyway. "Getting a little testy, aren't we? I mean, it's not like we killed them or anything. We just, you know, sent them, uh . . . away."

Willow stared at him, never blinking, never looking elsewhere. "Are they here?"

Xander frowned. "Well, no. I just said—"

"Then you two shouldn't be either."

Xander and Anya barely had time to cringe as Willow turned her palms up—

And Dawn rolled into Willow's legs like a human bowling ball.

"*Bitch!*" Willow screamed, but for all her power and experience, she still took several surprisingly hard punches from Buffy's little sister. "Get off me!"

"You leave them alone!" Dawn yelled as loudly as she could. "You just back off right now and let them go!"

Another hard punch, and suddenly Dawn was raining blows into empty air. Actually, Dawn was *in* the air, rising and rotating in a pose that was uncomfortably close to a corpse hanging from a hook.

"Stupid girl," Willow hissed. Dawn jerked and yelped as an unseen hand smacked her hard across the jaw. "You are just one more gnat I'm going to have to swat. Or maybe I should say, toss onto the bug zapper." There was a three-second sensation of electricity building in the room, hot and savage, as Willow pulled her hand back and readied herself for the throw of power that would finally rid herself of most of the Scooby Gang.

"*Stop.*"

Willow gasped and lost her concentration. The buildup of energy and its abrupt and unplanned letdown left her sickeningly dizzy, and she stumbled and went down on one knee, feeling the wooden floor *thunk* painfully against her kneecap. Ten feet away Dawn suddenly dropped out of the air and crashed to the floor. The teenager pushed herself up on one elbow, wobbled a bit, then sank back down and lay still.

"Tara?" Having been cowering next to Spike and Xander, Anya now rose and stepped forward, her astounded gaze focused on the Ghost of Tara's semitransparent form. "My God—is it really you?" Incredibly, she seemed to forget where she was, and their dire situation, as she turned her eyes toward Willow. "I can't believe you would do something like this!"

"What are you talking about?" Willow snapped.

She turned on one hip and rubbed angrily at her knee. "Do something like what?"

"Trap her spirit here!" Anya said hotly. "And out of what? Your own neediness? I've been known to be incredibly selfish, but even *I've* never gone that far!"

"Oh, don't be ridiculous." Willow struggled to get her footing amid the suddenly too-generous folds that made up her robes. "I did no such thing. I don't know where she came from. Now where was I? Oh yeah—I was about to end your miserably earthly lives so I can get on with mine."

"Willow, you mustn't."

"Tara, will you stop berating me already?" Willow cried. "I can't do what I need to with these idiots getting all into my stuff!"

"You can't kill them, Willow. They're your friends."

"They are *not*! They're just old . . . phantoms, that's all. Leftovers from a life that doesn't exist anymore, a life I don't want!"

The Ghost of Tara looked at her with an anguished expression. *"Isn't that exactly what I am, Willow? A phantom? Someone who doesn't exist anymore?"*

"No!" Willow balled her fists at her sides. "You're more than that—so much more. God, don't you realize that? The way you are, you should be seeing it all, Tara. How much I love you. How much I need you." Her head jerked sideways and she jabbed a finger in the direction of Anya and Xander, making them flinch automatically. "Those two, and Buffy, and Giles, and even Dawn—they're all keeping me from getting you back. They're the stones I keep tripping over!"

The Ghost of Tara shook her head sadly. *"No, they aren't. The only thing holding you back is your own refusal to see the truth."*

"I don't want to hear this," Willow said. Despite her words, her expression was getting bleaker by the second. "I just want to do what I have to do. I know what you're saying—I'm not so dense I don't understand, Tara. But I don't believe it. I *won't.*"

"Oh, Willow . . . sometimes no matter how much you want it, you can't always get your way." The Ghost of Tara stretched out a hand toward Willow's face as if she were going to stroke it. For a long, breathless moment, Willow imagined she would feel Tara's touch, her gentle fingers slipping along one cheek, the warmth of her skin . . .

But no.

At least, not *yet.*

Willow set her jaw and turned once again to face Anya and Xander, pulling energy from her reserves in preparation. No matter what the Ghost of Tara said, these two—or rather, three when she included the still-unconscious Dawn—had to go. She'd let Buffy live, but that was enough mercy for tonight. If nothing else, the deaths of Anya, Xander, and Dawn would thin the ranks by sixty percent, and really, the crippled Giles wasn't worthy of claiming half of the remaining forty that was him and Buffy. She pulled back, then—*"If you kill them, I'll leave you."*—froze.

Had her heart stopped?

No.

Yes.

Or maybe just somewhere in between.

"You . . . you would do that?" Willow's voice was a fractured whisper that was still, somehow, audible to everyone in the loft. Even Xander and Anya, as terrified as they were, drew in breath and stopped, as did the remaining members of the coven who were dragging themselves upright and trying to recover from Giles's devastating spell.

"I won't have a choice, Willow."

"But *why*?" For all her strength and power, all her deadliness, now Willow was near tears. "I've done everything you've asked of me, even when I know it would have been better not to, that it would have helped me accomplish my goals. Even when I didn't *want* to do it! And in spite of all that, you would choose *their* lives over me, when all I'm trying to do is bring you back?"

"There are lines in the universe that must not be crossed. If I can't stop you from stepping over them, I can't stay with you."

"Stop me?" Willow stared at the Ghost of Tara. "What the hell does *that* mean? Who made you my keeper?"

"Hell has nothing to do with it," Tara's spirit replied in a voice that was so whispery, so faint, that for an awful second Willow thought the Ghost of Tara really *was* leaving.

Willow said nothing. The silence was uncomfortably thick and dangerous in the spaces between her and the Scoobies, as though it were their own life forces hanging in the balance rather than Tara's departure. In reality it was both, and no one dared to move. The time for trying to escape or fight was long since past.

Abruptly Willow whirled and marched over to where Dawn lay. The teenager was finally awake, groggy but just cognizant enough to shy away when Willow reached for her. A futile thing—Willow's physical strength had grown proportionately with the potency of her magickal skills. She grabbed Dawn by one arm and pulled her savagely to her feet.

"It looks like you'll live to see your next birthday after all," Willow snarled. She jerked Dawn around and faced her toward the fireplace, then shoved her at Xander and Anya so hard that Dawn's feet left the floor as she tumbled forward. Willow was so angry, and it took so much effort to contain her fury, that all she could do was stand there and tremble as she glared at them. "You've failed in what you tried to do," she said in a low voice that sounded more like an inhuman growl than anything else. "Don't come back here and try again. Tonight you get to keep breathing, but only"— She cast a glance at the Ghost of Tara—"for Tara's sake. Screw me over again and I'll have a whole new attitude about it."

"Listen, Will," Xander began as he helped Dawn get up. "Don't you think we can talk about—"

"*Don't push me!*" Willow's scream came into their faces borne on a blast of wind filled with enough heat to singe the finer hairs on their skin.

Anya pushed in front of Xander. "Thank you so

much, Willow," she said. Her back was ramrod straight, her manners impeccable. She sounded like a bright, automatic robot. "You have a nice evening, and I believe we'll be leaving now."

"Oh, yes," Willow said with a disturbingly evil pleasantness. "I definitely think you will be." She brought her wrists up in an *X,* then yanked them apart at the same time she snapped her fingers.

Suddenly the three of them were spinning in the air, faster and faster and faster, as if they were caught in the Hellmouth's version of the hurricane from *The Wizard of Oz.* All of them screamed in surprise, and then their cries merged into something like *"Whooooooooooooaaaaaaaaaa!"* as the intensity went to crazed roller-coaster ride. Willow jerked her chin toward one of the open windows and the mini-twister containing Xander, Anya, and Dawn shot through it, whirling in the air over the parking lot. In a fifteen-second span her tiny tornado had cleared away every bit of debris, wanted or unwanted, within a one-block range; finally it bounced down to the concrete lot and belched out the three of them like something foul it had eaten for breakfast.

In the troublesome quiet that followed, Willow sealed her windows back up and set to work assessing the damage that a wretchedly crippled, onetime watcher had somehow succeeded in bringing into her formerly neat and orderly existence.

Chapter Twenty

At the second-floor level of Willow's loft, the lights suddenly increased tenfold, pulsing and dancing wildly. Then Xander, Anya, and Dawn literally fell out of the air and landed in a hard and painful heap in front of where Giles was kneeling next to Buffy's unconscious form.

Yelping and grunting, it only took a few cusswords for each to struggle away from the others and stumble over to Giles and Buffy; in addition to looking bruised and disheveled, all looked decidedly disappointed, and that was, perhaps, the biggest indicator that the Scooby Gang's grand anti-Wiccan plan had done a great big belly flop.

"All right, I assume the spell didn't work." Giles was so tense he looked like he might vibrate right out of his wheelchair. "So what happened? Where did it go wrong?"

"Willow, that's where," Anya said sullenly. "Honestly, Giles. She's got more power than anyone I've *ever* seen."

Dawn knelt painfully and peered at her sister. "Buffy? Buffy, can you hear me?" She looked anxiously at Giles, but the expression he sent her—*She'll be okay when she wakes up*—let her relax enough not to interrupt.

Giles turned his attention back to Anya, and for a moment he looked utterly speechless. "Wait." He looked from Anya to Xander, then back again. "Are you saying she just *stopped* it?"

"What part of 'yes' don't you understand?" Xander rubbed at a painful spot on one arm. "And if I've got this whole chain of command thing correct, you were the one who gave her that Wiccan starter power pack." He gave himself a mock slap on the forehead, then winced. "Gee, who would've thunk she'd turn around and use that zappability *against* us?"

"Sarcasm isn't going to accomplish anything," Giles said. His voice was decidedly bristly. "We need to gather ourselves—"

"I think you mean ice-pack our wounds," Dawn cut in. The teenager's clothes were ripped and dirty, and one eye had definitely gone swollen and psychedelic.

"—and see where we need to go from here," Giles finished, stubbornly ignoring her comment.

"Well," Anya said. "On the bright side, at least we don't have to worry about cat thing anymore." She glanced off to the side, where *sine kot diabl* lay in a crumpled blue ball a dozen feet away.

"I think we should go," Dawn said. "Willow's level of aggravation up there was on the upper end of volcanic, and personally, I don't want to be around for the eruption." She leaned over and shook Buffy's shoulder gently. "Come on, Buff—you've had harder knocks on the head. Time to wake up."

Buffy opened her eyes and looked into nothingness.

Wait—no, not quite. There were pinpricks of light in front of her eyes . . . stars, the real kind, not the twinkly spread that was the precursor to unconsciousness. She'd certainly seen enough of those, so at least she could tell the difference. She blinked but didn't yet try to move; parts of her body had no sensation at all, as if she'd been injected with a dentist's huge dose of Novocain—"Would you please supersize that, Dr. Bright-and-Smiley?"—and it was just now beginning to wear off at the edges and drop into that half-tingling, half-pinprick sensation on her skin. Other parts, particularly the area under her jawline and around to the back of her neck, felt like raw meat, bleeding and freshly tenderized with one of those spiky-ended hammers her mom had once bought because all the chefs on the Food Network used them.

"Buffy? Buffy, can you hear me?"

Buffy blinked at the sound of Giles's voice and opened her eyes once more, only now realizing she'd

closed them again. Had she dozed off? Surely not . . .
well, maybe. She was so *tired,* more tired than she
could ever remember being in her life. Where was she
again? Oh, right—the sidewalk below Willow's loft,
lying on the ground. . . . and why exactly was she
doing that, anyway?

"Buffy, do you think you can sit up? I can help pull
you up if I can just turn this wretched wheelchair
around and get a fair amount of leverage."

"I can get her up," Xander said.

Buffy nodded . . . or at least wanted to. Xander's
voice sounded far away and kind of cool, like he was
joking around and talking through one of those tubes
that you got when you ran out of wrapping paper.
Whether you used them as improvised telephones or
cardboard swords was always a toss-up.

Something picked up her left arm and tugged at it.
She wanted to ignore the annoying pulling, but her
body reacted differently—it wanted to get up, that old
slayer instinct overriding her tired mind. Her right arm
pushed out automatically, and she managed to wobble
upright to at least a sitting position; she swayed there,
back and forth and back and forth, while her brain
fought to clear out the cobwebs, and, almost regret-
tably, the eerie sense of anesthesia began to wear off.

"There we go." Giles sounded both smug and anxious, as though he were trying to put on a big act for
her sake. Buffy steadied herself with one hand against
the concrete and scrubbed at her eyes with the other.
The motion made her face hurt, particularly beneath
her chin—and then it all came rushing back at her.

Buffy jerked involuntarily and her breath rushed out through her teeth, making a ragged, fear-filled hissing noise. Somewhere she found the strength to stagger to her feet. She tottered there, turning and squinting at the darkness, but there was nothing there, no blue cat-creature, invisible or otherwise, to make her slayer abilities seem like no more than paltry girly punches. There was only Giles, and the industrialized landscape around them, and Willow's loft with its broken windows overhead.

"Are you looking for this?" Giles asked quietly.

Buffy turned her head and saw him steer his wheelchair back a few feet. So there it was, finally visible—the creature that had bested her and nearly killed her, lying dead on the ground.

Buffy started to speak, then had to cough before she could get her lungs to push air around her bruised vocal cords. "W-what happened to it?"

"Willow killed it," Giles told her. "Before it could kill you." He didn't elaborate.

Buffy's mouth stretched in a smile. "Willow did this? See, I told you she wasn't all bad. I told you—"

"I wouldn't be so hasty to forgive our Wiccan friend," Giles interrupted. "The kudos for this one go to Tara's ghost, not Willow. I'm afraid your old best friend would have indeed left you to perish had not Tara intervened on your behalf."

Buffy and the others turned to stare at it again as they considered this. Then, whether Willow was responsible or it was the creature's natural way of decomposition wasn't clear, but the creature was dissolving, melting into itself as a quickly constricting puddle of blue ooze. As they stared the puddle got smaller and smaller, until it was no bigger than a pancake that suddenly burst into a hot, blue flame and fizzled away. All that remained on the ground was an ugly and unpleasantly fragrant brown spot that looked like a pile of overcaramelized onions.

"Yuck," Dawn said. "That's disgusting."

"And to think it had once had my head in its mouth," Anya added.

Buffy's expression fell. "Oh." She gave herself five seconds, no more, to let it sink in that Willow would have let her die, then steeled herself and asked, "Were you guys able to—"

Xander swallowed and looked crestfallen. "No, I don't think so."

Buffy's eyes widened. "Giles—you said it would work!"

Giles held up a hand. "I'm not sure how Willow managed to stop it," he told her. "They asked for help and I did the best I could—I put a protective shield around them that should have held long enough to complete the spell."

Buffy stared at the blasted-out windows above them, then at Giles. "But it didn't."

Giles hesitated. "No," he said finally. "I'm afraid not. Willow went back through the window after she killed the *sine kot diabl.*"

"Then I've got to go back in there," Buffy said. She managed to stand, but her knees still didn't have full strength.

"Oh, no!" Giles reached out and snagged her wrist. "Not this time. We got . . . *most* of what we wanted. The coven's whittled down, the creature's dead. It's enough for now. And Dawn's right—we need to *go*, before Willow decides to come after us."

Buffy started to protest, then looked helplessly at Dawn, Xander, and Anya instead. Her body was screaming, full of aches and pains—okay, they were more like stabs and strains—and she definitely needed recovery time. If what Giles said was true, then maybe they *had* done enough for tonight. Perhaps for tonight it was best to leave it as it was and be thankful that everyone was safe and the fur-faced demon was dead.

"But I still don't understand what happened," Giles commented. Nevertheless, he struggled and finally managed to turn his wheelchair in the general direction of the Magic Box. "You three escaped and Willow stopped my spell. How could she have done that?"

"Well, it was the cat-demon thingy that obviously helped boost her power," Anya said confidently. She watched Giles for a moment, then moved behind him and began pushing; really, he was a fine librarian and watcher, but he couldn't steer worth a darn. "But everyone knows cats are selfish creatures, and it was only a matter of time before the beast went all grand mutiny."

"Even so," Giles said, trying to twist so that he could look back at her. He finally gave up and resigned himself to staring straight ahead when everyone else seemed to be trailing behind him. He felt a little like

Saint Patrick, except that instead of leading the poisonous snakes out of Ireland, he was dragging behind him a raggedly little pack of beaten-up pet garter snakes. "That doesn't explain why Willow let the three of you escape. I mean, I'm assuming that if she had the power to stop the disbursement spell, it would have taken her hardly any effort at all to stop you from going anywhere."

"She didn't *let* us do anything." Xander's voice, coming from behind Giles on his right side, was low and exhausted. "She threw us out, Giles."

"But *why*?" he demanded.

"Because of Tara," Anya said. "Or rather, Tara's ghost. She—it . . . uh, whatever, threatened to leave Willow if she hurt us. She basically made Willow choose between her and killing us. And Willow chose her."

Giles was silent for a long time as the group moved slowly and painfully down the sidewalk. "Interesting," he finally said. "We'll definitely have to file that away for future reference. To begin with, while it's quite bizarre that Willow is essentially being haunted by Tara's spirit, it's not altogether unheard of. But to have the spirit talk to her and control her as if they were both living beings . . . extraordinary."

"Yeah," Buffy said. "There's a lot that's extraordinary. Like how badly we got our collective asses kicked." She'd moved up to walk parallel to his wheelchair, and she sounded half sarcastic and half agonized. When Giles glanced over at her, he realized with a start just how badly injured she was. Even for a quick-healing slayer, it was likely that the ugly, blue-black bruises that ringed her neck, each bearing a deep and bloody, perfectly centered puncture wound, would take days to close and fade.

"This isn't finished," Buffy said, almost as though she could feel the vibrations of Giles's sympathy. She didn't say anything for a moment, then added, more to herself than to the others, "I can't help but wonder if Willow and I will ever be friends again." It was a question that kept coming back in her mind, and she wondered if she would ever know the answer.

Whether Buffy expected a response or not, Anya decided to put in her nickel's worth. "The way she is now? I doubt it. If the spell had completely worked and we'd separated her from her devilish dozen . . . maybe. I just know that our charm needed to work a *lot* faster than it did." She frowned at the back of Giles's head, even though he couldn't see her. "I mean, come on—I thought it would be an instant poof and disappear, not an Auntie Em tornado re-enactment."

"I think at least ten of them were blitzed," Xander offered.

Anya laughed, but there was no real humor in the sound. "In your dreams, carpenter boy. I counted at least seven left, excluding Willow herself. It won't take her long to rebuild, and you can bet that every time we try and fail she'll take even more steps to make sure our chances of succeeding are squeezed down to zilch."

"At least Buffy beat the *sine kot diabl*," Dawn pointed out. "That's something, anyway."

Buffy pressed her lips together until her mouth

looked like a gash across her pale skin. "No, I didn't."

"What?" Dawn stared at her.

"I said, I *didn't*." Without knowing she was doing it, Buffy's left hand reached up and massaged her battered throat. "It beat me. I fought it, but I couldn't stop it. All of a sudden the damned thing had me in its mouth. The next thing I knew, I was lying on the ground and looking up at the sky."

"Giles?" Dawn asked in a small voice.

The former watcher cleared his throat. "Willow again," he told them. "I couldn't get close enough to hear what was going on, but there's no doubt I saw Tara, or her spiritual manifestation. Obviously that had something to do with it."

"Well, *great,*" Anya sneered. "Let's just holler for Tara's ghost every time we need a helping hand with Willow. I'm sure she'll be glad to lend some otherworldly relief." If she hadn't been pushing Giles's wheelchair, she would've thrown up her hands in surrender. "Aren't we just batting ten thousand in this ball game!"

Rather than argue the point and put Anya on the defensive—and frankly, she was right on most counts—Giles chose another avenue. "I think we need some downtime," he said. "I still believe we had a decent plan, but perhaps we didn't smooth out the details of its execution." He squinted back at Willow's loft, but Anya and the others had been moving more swiftly than he'd realized and it was nearly out of sight. "In any case, I'm certain we got to at least part of the coven."

"Sure," Xander said. "Sent them off on a celestial vacation, courtesy of a universe-size vacuum. No bags required."

"We need to be better in the future," Buffy said quietly.

"And stronger," Anya added. "We so much need to be stronger."

"You got that right," Buffy said. "A *lot* stronger." She glanced at each of them in turn, her normally clear eyes hooded and bloodshot. "If we're not, the next time we cross Willow's path and she doesn't want us there? We may find ourselves at the end of Willow's permanent vacuum hose."

Chapter Twenty-One

The darkest part of the night is the quietest and sometimes most deadly part. And yet it was anything but—Buffy's mind would not be stilled, her thoughts would not be muffled. Mentally she felt as though someone had put a computer virus inside her skull, something so tiny it was invisible but which could loop itself around and around until it drove her insane.

Willow.

Tara's spirit.

Spike, tormented.

And Oz, trapped.

And again . . . Willow.

Did this new path of Willow's truly mean the end of their friendship? Again Buffy felt the unseen presence of that imagined bug inside her brain, twisting her around like a helpless mouse dangling by its tail above the mouth of a cat. The unintentional analogy made her shudder, so close was it to what had actually happened a few hours earlier.

Yes, Willow had done the unforgivable and killed a human being. Even so, Buffy found herself unable to condemn her for that one horrid act. Although she couldn't condone it, she couldn't help but acknowledge that Willow's reason for doing so had been, perhaps, ultimately the only great equalizer in such matters. There was so much that was unexplainable in her world; who was Buffy to say that somewhere in the universe there wasn't a great, golden scale for each and every person, and that Willow's own golden scale had gone haywire from Tara's death, then re-balanced by Warren's?

But there were, of course, darker avenues to consider.

Goody-goody thoughts aside, maybe Willow was just flat doomed. She wouldn't be the first good soul to lose her way on her personal path, whether it was righteous or not—Buffy had seen scores of those since being called as a slayer. And sometimes the smallest, most intangible thing—such as a soul—could make all the difference in the world. The most obvious instances were the vampires, her first and foremost enemies. They were, for the most part, unredeemable, but Willow . . . she could be saved, damn it. Buffy was sure of it. But *how*?

Sitting downstairs in the empty living room, staring out the darkened window and waiting for a sunrise that felt like it was a million miles away, all Buffy could do was wish for things to be like they'd been just a few short weeks ago. If someone walked up to her and told her she had one chance to go back, Buffy knew exactly the place and time she'd pick: the sun-dappled day in the backyard when she'd been talking to Xander, mending the rift that had opened up between them because of Spike. Still, there was always that one, pointed question, wasn't there?

Would she have been able to make things come out any differently?

Sure, if she'd seen Warren just five seconds sooner. She could've jumped him and beaten him into a grass-flecked mush, then dragged him and his ugly weapon right down to the Sunnydale Police Department. Voilà—no gunshot to her heart, no stray shot to go whizzing up through the bedroom window and into the unsuspecting Tara's back.

No one dead . . . including Warren himself.

But the world was full of hindsight and if-onlys, and as God and all her friends knew, Buffy had a whole bunch besides the one she was contemplating tonight.

Dawn could almost hear Buffy thinking downstairs.

Well, not really, but she knew her sister was down there instead of in bed where she belonged, knew she was thinking about her failure tonight and the times before that, when Willow had either beaten her nearly senseless or just gone on about her Willow business and not given a damn about what Buffy or anyone else thought anymore.

Such a strange and terrifying thing this was, the

notion that her sister might really not be able to win the battle this time. Yet that was certainly the way things seemed to be heading, and each new attempt turned out to be nothing but a repeat performance of the flop before it. She'd seen Buffy lose fights before, sure, but never over and over again, never *permanently,* without somehow, some way, being able to ultimately redeem herself and triumph over the evil in the end.

Maybe that was the deal here—maybe the entire problem was that Willow wasn't really evil, and that was why Buffy couldn't get the upper hand. Dawn could listen to Giles and Buffy and Anya and Xander, or anyone else who cared to expound on the matter, but she would never believe that what Willow had done to Warren wasn't justified. Okay, so maybe she could have been a little less gory about it—a quick and simple broken neck would have worked just fine—but the end result was the same. An eye for an eye and all that.

The problem, as Dawn saw it, was that Willow wasn't stopping with the you-punched-me-so-I-punch-you game. Maybe Jonathan and Andrew deserved the same as Warren and maybe they didn't—Dawn was actually a little divided on that—but *everyone* around Willow was getting punched, and all because of Warren's big and dirty deed. Bad enough that Buffy was regularly getting her clock reset, but where was it written that because Willow wanted revenge, Giles should spend the rest of his life in a rolling metal prison? Or that Spike should be chained up like he was in Willow's loft, with his mouth sealed up like some twisted version of a Raggedy Andy doll? Tormented by the rediscovery of his own guilty feelings and with no one to help him through it, the vampire's existence now was probably worse than the version of hell everyone believed awaited him.

Added to the whole situation was the Oz thing, and while Dawn didn't know the man all that well, she wanted to know the wolf version of him even less. A creature that snarled and snapped and howled all the time just couldn't be expressing inner visions of ecstasy, especially when everything she'd heard about him said Oz had wanted nothing more in the world than to subdue that beastly part of himself. And what the heck were they going to do if he ever got loose?

No, very little of what was going on in Sunnydale was right, and her sister could sit down there and think on it until the sun turned blue. . . .

But this time Dawn just didn't think Buffy was going to be able to fix things.

They walked to Xander's apartment together, but they didn't touch. Not yet.

Moving beside Xander, Anya was acutely aware of the differences between them. Tonight more than other nights, perhaps because of the events of the last several days—her near-death in the mouth of the *sine kot diabl* and again in Willow's loft, and Buffy's repeat defeat by Willow. Things were changing in Sunnydale, and the changes weren't for the better. In past years the evil they fought had, most times anyway, come with a recognizable face. With the exception of Angel and Faith, the Scooby Gang had usually been able to trust one another, but what would happen now that one of their own had turned into one of the big bad *them*?

Xander didn't say anything, but after a block or so he reached out and took her hand, holding it tightly. Anya sort of wanted to pull away, but she didn't, because a big part of her didn't want to do that, either. His touch both thrilled and infuriated her—she didn't know *what* she wanted where Xander was concerned. As long as she'd known him and even after what he'd done to her, her heartbeat increased and her blood raced at the slightest feel of his fingers. . . . Yet what right did he have to do that after the way he'd abandoned her at the altar and smashed her then-human heart to smithereens? It was true that she had a vengeance demon's heart now, but the scars that Xander had etched upon it in its human form would never fade. But if that were so, why couldn't she simply cut him out of her life?

Perhaps for the same elusive reasons that Willow could not let go of Tara.

Xander was, Anya supposed, a part of her on some elemental level that had no name. A true love, even broken, never lost its fundamental essence, that thing between two people that had happened in the beginning and had carried them through the years to whatever end, good or bad. Ten years from now or a thousand—it didn't matter. In the millennia to come, long after he was beyond even dust, Anya knew that she would still pull the memory of this man from the cobwebbed recesses of her mind, and, God help her, a part of her would always love him.

Did he feel the same way about her? If she died tomorrow, or chose to leave Sunnydale and never return, would he even miss her? He did and he would, she was sure of it. This was why he kept coming back, even though he swore that he'd gotten past the false visions he'd endured on what was supposed to have been their wedding day. Well, "gotten past" wasn't quite accurate, was it? Because if Xander had indeed put them behind him, they wouldn't be in this relationship predicament. They'd be married, she'd still be human, and maybe they'd have a baby on the way by now. Instead they played their never-ending game of I-can't-stand-you-but-I-can't-leave-you, and all because Xander was afraid of what *might* happen. Too bad they didn't have a crystal ball that would let them see it all. Of course, if they had, Tara might still be alive, Giles would still be whole, Angel might still be with Buffy . . . and so forth and so on.

At the door to Xander's building she hesitated instead of going right inside with him. She should go home to her own apartment, get some rest in preparation for what would surely be more challenges to come with the darker side of Willow. When she paused, Xander turned back to her questioningly, then wrapped his muscular arms around her and held her close. Nothing more, just that. Anya could feel his heartbeat against her chest. It sounded so . . . human—fragile and oddly strong at the same time. They had such courage, these flesh and blood and bone creatures, such endurance for beings who could be so quickly and easily killed. It made them seem silly and laughable, and, to her, irresistibly enticing.

Anya lifted her face to Xander's and met his gaze. For once he was silent—no offhand remarks, no sarcasm. Their lips touched briefly, and then Anya took the initiative and led him inside.

No crystal ball for any of them, but then where was the fun in fixing anything if you always knew the right thing to do?

I will do this, Giles thought. *Damn it all, I* will *do this. But not tonight.*

He slumped against the backrest of his wheelchair and sat there without moving for a long time, feeling the sweat roll slowly down his temples, tickling the side of his face as it went. His shirt was damp all the way down the back until it met the waistband of his slacks. There, all sensation stopped. No wetness, no pain. Nothing.

But it picked up again at his toes. Giles had been sitting here for at least a half hour, working on them. There wasn't much progress. . . . Well, actually, there wasn't any progress at all, not since the last time he'd put some effort into this. But then he hadn't lost any ground either. He could still wiggle them, ever so slightly. And if he could do that, it meant things inside his body were slowly repairing themselves, nerves were reconnecting, muscles were, at least in some tiny way, responding to commands from his brain.

It was a start, and while he might have a million miles to go, a half inch of forward movement was better than none at all.

Too tired to struggle with it anymore, Giles wheeled himself to the dresser on the other side of the room, taking care to go slowly to minimize the noise. Carpeting was a fine thing, but it didn't stop rafters from squeaking, and while he appreciated everyone's concern, he really wasn't in the mood for company tonight. There was too much frustration boiling inside him, too much of a sense of failure. No one, including Buffy, had questioned why he hadn't gone to her aid when she'd been in the grip of the *sine kot diabl*. Giles should have been relieved, because even with his justified answer of Willow's circling spell, he still felt guilty about it. But had anyone even remembered he'd been there? It seemed not.

He reached for the decanter of scotch on the dresser, then hesitated. Too strong—if he started indulging in that stuff in his present mood, he'd end up in a downright black depression before finally passing out. Bad show, that. His hand wavered among the choices for a moment, and then finally Giles plucked a smaller bottle of Drambuie from the selection, a home-made batch that he'd made some time ago from the best scotch and a good dose of rock candy. Good stuff and let's face it, it had built-in consumption control: Two small glasses of the strong, nearly sickly sweet liqueur would give him enough of a drowsy headache to send him to bed long before he could get unpleasantly hammered.

Unfortunately the sweet drink did little to sweeten Giles's mood. How could it? Sitting in the semidarkness, with only a faint glow from the low-wattage bulb at his bedside, Giles couldn't help but study the room. A thought, blacker and more morbid than anything he could have imagined so far tonight, suddenly blossomed in his mind. This spacious room, with its de-frillified comforter and curtains and the decidedly masculine things carefully arranged around what few personal belongings he'd brought, had first belonged to Joyce Summers. Joyce had been dead for several years; Willow had since taken residence here, and she'd moved Tara in with her. And now Tara, too, was dead.

Perhaps he was next.

"Don't be ridiculous," he said out loud. "Rooms don't get cursed."

Still, once voiced, it was impossible to shake the notion, like telling someone, "Don't you dare think of white polar bears!" It hovered there, prodding and nibbling at his brain, making him drink more than his self-allotment of two glasses, sending his mind spiraling ever downward toward a pool of waiting self-pity that he wanted at all costs to avoid.

No, Giles thought suddenly, and he barely stopped himself from hurling his fourth drink against the nearest wall. *I will not go there.* He set his glass down and pushed it away, then rolled his chair around the bed and into the bathroom. There he brushed the liqueur taste from his teeth and splashed warm water on his face before finally going back to the bedroom and struggling into his pajamas. By himself it was more like a wrestling match, with him twisting and turning his upper body and holding with grim determination on to the rails that Xander had fixed to the wall by the bed.

But he would *not* be defeated.

Not tonight. Not *ever*.

"I can do this," he said to the empty room. His words were a little slurred, but he was still quite coherent—it could have been the drink, or it simply could have been exhaustion. It didn't matter. Right now he wasn't talking about himself or his legs. He was talking about something much, much bigger. "*We* can do this," he said more firmly. "All of us."

At last Giles was on the bed, panting from exertion and wanting nothing more than to sink into oblivion . . . but only for one night. As he leaned back and let his eyelids close, Giles felt at peace with himself and the world, even if just for a little while. He had done the best he could with the circumstances handed to him—he had *always* done that, always given his all. Whether the bloody Council knew it or acknowledged it, he had been the best damned watcher that had ever existed. Maybe he didn't always watch by the rules, *their* rules, but he was good at it, damn it. And if he got beaten in a fight, he always came back for the duration; when he did, he brought more force, more power, more determination.

And so would they.

He, Buffy, Xander, Anya, and Dawn—they would all face Willow again, of that he was certain. And whether he ever walked again or not, they *would* defeat her, keep her from killing Andrew and Jonathan, and free Oz and Spike.

No, they wouldn't simply defeat her. They would do better than that.

They would *save* her.

Epilogue

What were they doing tonight, that small group of people who had once been her friends and, in addition to Tara, the center of her small, personal universe?

Willow stared out at the night, balancing herself on the windowsill but not feeling the shards of glass that still peppered the frame. Occasionally she might detect a prickle as one bit through fabric and into the flesh along the backs of her thighs, but she paid it no mind—she had more complex things to think about.

Shortly after sending Xander, Anya, and Dawn spiraling out of the window, Willow had stepped up to this same vantage point just in time to see the *sine kot diabl*'s body go up in smoke . . . pretty much like her plans for its existence. Too bad; while she felt no true loss at the creature's death, bringing him into being had certainly turned out to be a significant waste of time. Sure, he'd given her a night or two of power, but the Ghost of Tara had been right on all accounts about the cat-beast—Willow had known it would turn on her almost from the beginning, but she just hadn't been willing to admit it.

And now, with what was she left?

Dregs, and that was about it. Like with the leaf-filled leftovers at the bottom of a cup of home-brewed tea, all she wanted to do was spit them out and cleanse her mouth, brush away the taste of defeat.

"Why do you think you were defeated?"

Willow turned to regard the Ghost of Tara, then shrugged. "Because I was. It doesn't get any simpler than that."

"Victory is a customized point of view," the Ghost of Tara said. *"I think Buffy and the others view the outcome quite differently."*

"Their point of view doesn't matter," Willow said. Her tone was sharper than she'd intended, and she made a conscious effort to soften it. "*They* don't matter. My opinion is the only one that counts." The instant the words left her mouth, Willow realized how ridiculous they sounded. Nothing on this earth would make Willow admit the truth to anyone else, but it was really the Ghost of Tara who was calling the shots here, not her. Manipulation through love, whether for good or evil—mankind had been doing it for eons.

The Ghost of Tara said nothing, and for once Willow was grateful. It wasn't that she didn't want to listen to the spirit—the truth was, she'd listen to *any-thing* the Ghost of Tara had to say, whether it was support or criticism. Sometimes, in fact, the periods of silence from Tara's spirit drove her crazy. But tonight . . . tonight she was *tired*. Buffy and her friends might think she was the victorious one, but they had no idea how much of a power drain tonight's battle had been, how substantially weaker she was now, in the aftermath. And who was there to soothe her wounds, both mental and physical? Not Tara, but a facsimile of her, a poor substitute. All the spirit but none of the substance.

Outside, the world—at least as much of it as she could see from her perch—was silent and still. Somewhere people laughed and loved and slept, all the things that had been taken from her. Willow seldom slept anymore, thanks to the huge infusion of power, then the repeated recharging by the *sine kot diabl*. It was as though her body had become a huge electrical conduit and she could feel the currents zinging through her bones, veins, and nerves. Even now, as exhausted as she felt, there was still a deep, internal humming, the antithesis of white noise. Only the Ghost of Tara's voice seemed to be able to drown it out, to make Willow forget that she was no longer a normal human woman. That she would never be normal again.

Warren, Jonathan, and Andrew had done this to her. She might fight against Buffy and Giles and all the others, but it still really boiled down to those three. Warren more than the other two, but still, they all needed to pay for what they had done, what they had caused. There was one way, and one way only, that she would allow them to go free. And, of course, if she happened to find them in the meantime, well . . . those were the breaks.

Amazingly, Willow dozed for a while, sitting there balanced on the windowsill like a black-shrouded sentinel. The deeper sleep still eluded her, but she went under enough to find at least the fragments of dreams—she saw flashes of herself and Tara back in their days at college, the times they'd studied together, the first time they'd held hands. But the dreams, like now, were incomplete and unsatisfying: Willow could see Tara's nearness and imagine her warmth, watch as her fingers reached out . . . but she couldn't touch, she couldn't *feel*. Forever denied, in the dream and in reality, she was left with nothing inside her but the want.

And the anger.

Willow opened her eyes and realized she'd been crying in her sleep.

"Willow."

From behind her right shoulder, the Ghost of Tara's voice as she tried to be comforting was like a sad, bittersweet sigh, a reminder to Willow that while she sat up here in her loft, accompanied by her two pets and the ghost of her dead lover, she was nothing but *alone*. Tara's spirit was both balm and thorn, a constant reminder that she and Tara were separated. The Ghost of Tara touched her mentally but not physically, offering her spiritual comfort but no real-world company or affection.

In a small house elsewhere in Sunnydale, Buffy and her gang slept and dreamed the dreams of the beaten but not defeated. Buffy had friends around her and people who loved her, even a love interest, because even if she did not return the emotions, only a fool would deny the feelings shining from Spike's eyes when he looked at the Slayer. Willow had once had all these things, and she should still have them tonight. And tomorrow, and the day and months and years after that.

And she would have them again.

Would things ever be the same as they had been before? Willow couldn't answer that. She was a changed woman, a ruthless killer who would stop at nearly nothing to get what she wanted. She knew that, and so did everyone else. And what she wanted was Tara, back from the dead and whole again, like Buffy. Things had gone back to normal for the Slayer, or so close to it as to make little difference. Why couldn't the same be done for her beloved Tara?

"Because it's not the same," whispered the Ghost of Tara in her ear. *"The circumstances are different. My* death *was different."*

"It doesn't matter," Willow responded, then wondered if her reply had been the truth or merely an automatic denial.

"Yes, it does. And you know that."

Willow turned her head away from the spirit's semitransparent face. "I don't know any such thing." She paused for a moment, then continued. "I will find a way to bring you back. I swear it."

"Do I need to remind you?"

Willow scowled at the darkness outside the window, but refused to look back at the Ghost of Tara. "No."

"I think I do."

And before Willow could protest, before she could

even *blink,* her agony and her loss were all there, all over again and again and again, as if she were reliving it in this current and oh-so-painful moment. Even more unfairly, she was seeing things she hadn't known about at the time, experiencing perspectives that she had no right to know about—

The sun is a bright ball in the sky, sweet and warm. Through Buffy's senses Willow can smell the freshly mown grass from where the neighbors to her right have worked on their lawn early in the morning, can see the noticeable difference in the now neatly trimmed line of bushes that separates their yard from hers. A light breeze ruffles the greenery overhead and carries a bit of bird song to her ears as she pokes aimlessly at the ground with her stick and listens. Xander's words fill her with warmth as she realizes they are mending their differences, at least trying to go back to the way things were before she and Spike got so heavy into it.

"I don't know what I'd do," he says. "Without you and Will."

"Let's not find out," Buffy answers. She drops her stick and hugs him. "I love you. You know that, right?"

But Xander doesn't respond the way she expects. Instead he goes stiff in her arms, and when he speaks, his voice is full of shock and fear. "Buffy—"

Willow knows it is only a vision, yet still she wants to shout a warning as Buffy turns out of Xander's arms and sees Warren, his face twisted by hatred and the beating she'd given him the night before. Warren says something but Buffy doesn't catch it because there is a weird sensation in her chest. Willow feels it on Buffy's behalf, a vague sort of thumping, and while it doesn't actually hurt, it kind of . . . takes everything away from her. Feeling, awareness, air, most of her heartbeat. What's left is an erratic attempt by the muscle in her chest to keep going around a sudden, new orifice, one that pumps out as much blood as the rest of her body tries to push through it.

Buffy doesn't feel the ground against her back, doesn't hear Xander as he calls her name, doesn't know Xander's hands are inexpertly trying to stop the flow of her lifeblood through the bullet wound she doesn't realize she's received. Willow watches Buffy as Buffy stares past the sky and the sun and knows in a quickly dimming part of her mind that eternity is finally coming for her.

Willow jerked herself out of the walking dream state and pushed herself off the windowsill. "Stop it," she growled. "I have enough pain."

"Do you?" Even in her nearly translucent form, the Ghost of Tara's eyes sparkled. *"You've sunk so deeply into your own suffering that you have forgotten about the pain that the people around you are also feeling."*

Willow's frown deepened, and for the first time since Tara's spirit had appeared, she actually backed away from her. "No, I haven't—"

Willow feels Xander's heart as it races and hears his wish, somewhere in the garbled, panicky thoughts in his head, that his pulse could be Buffy's, because surely he has enough adrenaline and fear to power a whole football field of people right now. The paramedics are moving around Buffy like busy little army ants working on a helpless, dying beetle; they look determined and knowledgeable, and the fact that despite a thousand television shows Xander doesn't understand a single thing about how or what or why they are doing makes him want to scream to get their attention. Willow knows he doesn't dare; he thinks it might surprise them, they might make a mistake, something critical. The best he can think to say—"What does that mean? Is she going to—"—gets him only an order to get out of the way. He blinks and watches helplessly, not sure whether he was going to ask if Buffy was going to be all right or if she was going to die, horribly afraid it was the latter.

He turns, and Willow sees herself from behind Xander's eyes, walking toward him like a living zombie, her shirt covered with the splattered, brilliant scarlet evidence of Tara's death. She feels his shock double as he thinks that she, too, has been shot—"Willow, God—are you okay?"—feels his divided attention refocus on Buffy when he realizes Willow's all right. Her question, that all-important starter, and then his answer, the password to all things that were to come in their small slice of existence: "Warren. He had a gun."

Willow sees through his eyes as she walks away, then shares the emotion as the paramedic calls him to get in the ambulance.

And then he's gone.

And while he had seen the blood, he'd never asked where it came from, whether it was Willow's.

Or Buffy's.

Or Tara's.

Willow came out of the spirit-induced vision more enraged than she'd been in days. She spun in the center of the loft and spotted the Ghost of Tara at the far end, not cowering but certainly avoiding her. Every time Willow strode to where the Ghost of Tara stood, she would disappear momentarily, then show up on the complete opposite end of the room.

Willow wasn't surprised. After all, what could the spirit say to her right now, what words could she use to undo the last few minutes? It was far too late for that, because the spirit Tara had made a grievous miscalculation, one so typical of the sweet-natured personality that she'd had in her too-short life. But in death . . . well, death was the key to it all, wasn't it? And it was Tara's death that had changed everything, had changed *Willow*. Why couldn't Tara have lived, like Buffy? Why couldn't they have been sitting on the bed instead of standing? Why, *why, WHY?*

Oh, no. While the Ghost of Tara had thought to guilt Willow into forgiving Buffy's resistance to Willow's new powers, or into giving up on her search for that elusive resurrection spell, what Willow had seen and experienced in the two visions only made her all the more determined.

She would forgive no one, and no matter what the universe, or Osiris, or anyone else said, Willow *would* find a way to put things back to normal . . . or at least as close to it as she could pull off. She *would* bring Tara back.

Or everyone around her would pay the price for her failure.

ABOUT THE AUTHOR

Yvonne Navarro spent her youth (which is ongoing) making up stuff. When she "grew up" she started writing more and more, and now she's had nearly a hundred stories and over a dozen books published. She's even managed to get a few cool awards (most recently the Bram Stoker award for *Buffy the Vampire Slayer: The Willow Files, Vol. 2*). She has no spare time, that stuff having been stolen away by various evil entities in her life, such as husband Weston (acquired in 2002) and a deaf Great Dane (another creature with an ongoing youth) called Chili Lily Beast. She finally moved to southern Arizona in 2002 and is now secretly trying to figure out how to raise the temperature of the high desert surrounding her home by about fifteen degrees. Yvonne maintains a big old Web site at www.yvonnenavarro.com with all kinds of fun stuff on it. She's also the owner of a little online bookstore called Dusty Stacks (www.dustystacks.com). Come visit!

As many as 1 in 3 Americans
who have HIV... don't know it.

TAKE CONTROL.
KNOW YOUR STATUS.
GET TESTED.

To learn more about HIV testing,
or get a free guide to HIV and
other sexually transmitted diseases:

www.knowhivaids.org
1-866-344-KNOW